Blood Mask

ALSO BY LAUREN KELLY

Take Me, Take Me with You
The Stolen Heart

Blood
Mask

A Novel of Suspense

LAUREN KELLY

for Gail Godwin

BLOOD MASK. Copyright © 2006 by The Ontario Review, Inc. All rights reserved. Printed in the United States of America. No part of this book may be used or reproduced in any manner whatsoever without written permission except in the case of brief quotations embodied in critical articles and reviews. For information, address HarperCollins Publishers, 10 East 53rd Street, New York, NY 10022.

HarperCollins books may be purchased for educational, business, or sales promotional use. For information, please write: Special Markets Department, HarperCollins Publishers, 10 East 53rd Street, New York, NY 10022.

On page 147, the quoted remark is taken from *Andy Warhol* by Wayne Koestenbaum (Viking Penguin, 2001), p. 161.

FIRST EDITION

Designed by Joseph Rutt

Library of Congress Cataloging-in-Publication Data

Kelly, Lauren.
    Blood mask : a novel of suspense / by Lauren Kelly.—1st ed.
        p. cm.
    ISBN-13: 978-0-06-111903-3 (alk. paper)
    ISBN-10: 0-06-111903-2 (alk. paper)
    1. Women art collectors—Fiction. 2. Artists—Fiction. 3. Missing persons—Fiction.
4. New York (State)—Fiction. I. Title.

PS3565.A8B495 2006
813'.6—dc22

2005049509

06 07 08 09 10 BVG/RRD 10 9 8 7 6 5 4 3 2 1

Prologue

Blood Mask I, it was. There were to be others.

It was an entire head, a man's head. It was frozen, kept under re-frigeration, in a locked display case on an altar-like platform. My aunt brandished the magic key: "You can touch it, Marta! Like this."

You could not see this, but the head, the bust, had been sculpted out of clay, and covered in a masking of blood. The entire head cov-ered in a quarter-inch mask of congealed and frozen blood. It was a man's head but it looked like something mineral, primeval, raw tis-sue that has become fossilized, skin peeled away so that you can see what is beneath the skin. Clearly this was not a living thing, yet you could not help expecting the shuttered eyes to open, the fleshy mouth to stir. I had never seen anything so ugly, I stood staring. The adults were laughing at me.

Bio-art it was called. *Bio-anatomical-art* it was explained. An ex-perimental and highly controversial European art movement begun in the 1990s. The sculptor had made a model of his own head in clay and "masked" it with his blood, which was then frozen. He'd used several liters, he said, in an embalming process called plastination.

My aunt urged me to touch the mask, its texture was "uncanny."

"It's frozen solid, don't be afraid. You can't damage it."

It will damage me! If I touch.

The sculptor stood close by, observing. The display case was bathed in incandescent light. My aunt had a key to the case, for my aunt owned the gallery in which *Blood Mask I* was being exhibited.

She was becoming impatient with me, reaching for my hand. As if impulsively.

My aunt's sudden unplanned gestures. You were made to think they were unplanned.

"It's the most profound art, I think. 'Bio-art.' To make of ourselves, such blood masks, to outlive us."

My fingers were made to brush the stiff-quilled top of the head that was layered in frozen blood, the forehead with its ridges and creases, so lifelike. My fingers were made to caress the thick-jowled cheeks. The blood mask was kept so cold, almost my fingertips mistook it for extreme heat.

"Marta, don't be so squeamish. You're not a child. Frozen blood is altogether different from liquid blood."

No! It will bleed onto my fingers.

I could smell the blood mask, I think. Frozen and solid it wasn't supposed to have any odor. A work of art is not supposed to have any odor.

Blood Mask I was the decapitated head of a man of about forty with a fiercely ugly face, lined cheeks and fleshy lips set in a disdainful expression. The eyes were shut, not in relaxation but in strain. The lower jaw was angular, defiant. You would think that the blood mask was a death mask but the living sculptor loomed beside us smiling with pride in his achievement. It was something of a shock to see the living man beside the monumental head: a paunchy sallow-skinned man with undistinguished features, faint acne scars and thinning hair. He had not shaved for two or three days, his jaws covered in glittery stubble.

"And one day, Marta, we may arrange for Xenia to do *you*."

Xenia was the sculptor's name. He was "Scots"—as he called himself—from Edinburgh. He'd repudiated his "Scots" name as he had repudiated his national identity, in the service of art.

I must have flinched, the adults laughed at me again. I wanted to think that their laughter was a fond sort of teasing and not something else.

Aunt Drewe was locking up the display case. The ordeal was ending. She and the Scots sculptor Xenia would go on to dinner somewhere in TriBeCa, with others. It was speculated that they were lovers. It was known that my aunt had commissioned Xenia to draw her blood and "mask" it on a model of her head: *Blood Mask II.*

I remember: watching my aunt's fingers with their blunt tips, the playful gleam of her rings. She was a rich woman. She was a rich desirable woman. She was my father's older sister much envied and disliked in the family. She spoke in a voice throaty and seductive yet oddly wistful, like a girl's: "The blood masks will never decay, as we will. So long as they're kept refrigerated at, or below, thirty-two degrees Fahrenheit."

Another time the adults laughed, it must have been a joke.

This was sometime in mid-November 2002. For days afterward I would wash, wash, wash my hands that were already chapped and reddened but the blood-odor would remain.

I

Something Wounded

. . . calling to report an emergency situation here, something wounded in the underbrush, maybe an animal but maybe a person . . .

The call comes in to the Shale River Mountain State Park Emergency Service at 10:20 A.M., April 2, 2003. In a hiking area of white pine and serrated shale outcroppings above the Shale River, at the western edge of the park, hikers report having seen something crawling in the dense underbrush on the riverbank, approximately twenty feet below the hiking trail. The creature had seemed to panic at their approach, crawling frantically into the underbrush to escape. They'd called to it, "Hello? Do you need help? We won't hurt you . . ."—wanting to think it was an injured deer, or a coyote or stray dog, though it more resembled a human being, possibly a child.

Crawling into the underbrush on all fours.

At this time of year the Shale River Park, as it's commonly called, is mostly deserted. Upstate New York thirty miles northwest of the Hudson River at Newburgh, it has the feel of late winter and not early spring. Most of the snow has melted except at the highest elevations but fresh snow has fallen during the night and is slow to melt in the morning. Ice crusts form on small ponds and puddles. The light is razor-sharp, hurting the human eye.

One of the hikers descends into the underbrush, slipping and sliding, thorns tearing at his jeans. "Hey! D'you need help?" There are outcroppings of shale underfoot, weirdly shaped like steps, treacherously sharp-edged. There are patches of marshy soil that suck at the hiker's boots. Below the trail the river isn't visible but the sound of its rushing and plunging, swollen with mud-colored water, is deafening.

Whatever is fleeing the hiker is crazed with fear, forcing itself through such dense underbrush. The hiker gives up the search. Seeing on thorns at ground level, bright blood glistening like glass beads.

No way to tell if it's animal blood, or human.

Something wounded isn't found until 12:05 P.M.

The hikers have moved on. Several park rangers have been searching the underbrush without luck. There's a blood trail, but it's confused and doubles back upon itself and leads into a thicket impossible for an adult male to penetrate without equipment. Then, one of the rangers thinks to investigate a park services cabin about fifty feet away, a shuttered little building resting on cinder blocks. When the ranger squats to look below it, into a shadowy space no more than six inches in height, he sees what appears to be a human figure.

Calling, "Hey: who's there?"

The figure is lying very still. But the ranger can hear him, or her, breathing.

It isn't an adult male but possibly a boy, or a small-bodied woman, or a girl, lying on her side, knees against her chest, face hidden. A swath of what looks like hair. A very pale, bare foot.

The ranger identifies himself. "I'm not going to hurt you, I'm trying to help you. D'you hear me?"

The breathing has become quick terrified panting.

"Let me help you, O.K.? Here—"

The ranger stretches an arm beneath the cabin, to his shoulder. Grunting with the effort, blindly groping.

"Hey! Damn."

A muffled cry. The girl has kicked at him.

The ranger calls to the others, who come to investigate. After twenty minutes of effort, they manage to pull out from beneath the building a struggling, seemingly deranged adolescent girl: *Caucasian female approximately fifteen-to-eighteen, weight one hundred five, probable assault victim, needing medical attention, raving & delusional, schizophrenic/meth overdose.* There is no I.D. on her person, she doesn't respond to questions, has to be considered dangerous. Her blood pressure is abnormally low but her heartbeat is rapid and erratic so emergency medics can't give her a sedative until it has been determined at the hospital what drug or drugs might already be in her bloodstream.

The girl is strapped to a stretcher. It's presumed that she has been raped, beaten. Dumped and left to die in the Shale River Park.

"Jesus! Watch out she don't bite you."

Abducted

Straube, Annemarie.
19, resident Chateauguay County.
abduction/assault victim hospitalized Newburgh General 4/2/03.
found Shale River Mt. State Park perpetrators unidentified.
address: R.D. 7, River Road, Chateauguay Springs.

taped interviews, Newburgh General Hosp., 4/4/03, 4/5/03, 4/6/03, Chateauguay Co. Sheriff's Department Detectives Lindemann, Armsted, O'Striker, Gervais.

. . . said they would kill me, come back   and kill me   heard their voices   said they had killed my aunt   laughing I heard them
   I think I heard them   dumped and left to die   crawling in the underbrush   something is wrong with my head   can't see, only things moving   so afraid   they will come back   stomp me to death like a broken-winged bird something wrong with my head
   in my brain   something seeped into my brain   hurting, so white terrible white like laundry detergent   burning my mouth

*   *   *

my jaws had been forced apart, I was forced to swallow   burning
my mouth   he held my head   tried to spit out the poison he
cursed me   said he would kill me   my aunt they wanted   my
aunt they wanted to kill   I was gagging, choking   started to
vomit   something was slung over me, to blind me   I heard my
aunt scream   I was being carried somewhere   later I was dumped
dumped and left to die   this terrible thirst I was lapping water
from puddles   on fire with thirst   couldn't see where I was, so
hungry   eating rotted leaves, dried grasses   tearing with my teeth
there was water somewhere nearby   could hear water   smell water
thought it was near home the river near home Hudson River where
we lived   my aunt took me in   my aunt made a home for me
Aunt Drewe saying *This is your home now Annemarie, I will protect you
from harm and shame*

turned off the paved road onto gravel   I could feel the tires crunch-
ing   in the country somewhere   believed that they would kill me
now   he had his feet on me   on my back, on the floor of the van
there was something clanking like metal on metal   sounded like a
flagpole, no flag and   something clanking against the pole   they
dragged me from the van   threw me from the back   my head hit
the ground, I couldn't move   heard them drive away   must have
fainted, when I wakened it was another time   it was dawn   I think
it was dawn   the covering over my head was gone   my head, my
shoulders   they'd blinded me   I was afraid they would come back
I began to crawl   *Am I dead* I thought *is this what it is*   my bones
felt broken   my head   my eyes, there was something wrong
couldn't see

like fire, flames   my eyes   I was dragging myself   I was calling for Aunt Drewe   there was like a mist   by the river   so cold

thought I heard her voice   Marta help me, don't leave me   but
there was nothing

upstairs at the house   in my room   heard voices somewhere in the
house   my aunt had visitors   most nights my aunt had visitors

there's a loft studio my aunt has in the older part of the house
there's the barn   used to be a barn now it's a gallery   exhibits

my aunt has guests who stay overnight   there are artists in residence   I help my aunt, I'm on the staff   I am not an artist I am on
the staff   I was helping in the barn, in the exhibit   went to bed
late   I wasn't undressed I fell asleep dressed   the lights were on
wakened by voices about 2 a.m.   downstairs somewhere   I think I
saw   Aunt Drewe where she'd fallen   bleeding from her face   her
forehead   I tried to scream, I was on the stairs   she tried to shield
her face   they were stooped over her to lift her   their hands on her
I screamed at them   one of them ran at me, yanked me down the
steps to my knees   my face was struck   my head was gripped in
the crook of a man's arm   it was like my head was gripped in a vise,
the vise was tightening   I thought he would break my neck   he
would squeeze my skull out of shape   my jaws were pried open
one of the men held me, another tore open a plasic bag   a gritty
white powder like detergent was forced into my mouth   I was terrified, I thought it might be lye   I thought they would burn out
my mouth   I tried to spit the powder out, my jaws were clamped
shut   I couldn't breathe   I was struck on the head   a man's fists
striking me   I think I saw a tarpaulin being wrapped around my

aunt   her body wrapped in it   her head was covered, blood was
soaking through the tarpaulin   my aunt was struggling clawing
my aunt is a strong woman   she would not die easily

didn't hear, didn't see   their faces I didn't see   something over my
head suffocating   couldn't breathe, I was being dragged   carried
from the house lifted into the back of a van   too frightened to beg
for my life   could hear them, their voices but not their words
couldn't think not even *I am being taken somewhere to be killed*   in the
morning they were gone   there was no one
    so cold! I was freezing   mud in my mouth, my hair   I could
not see clearly but I was alive, I could crawl   birds by the river, I
could hear birds   sharp cries like nails   nails in my skull   but
    I was alive

Sole Witness

W hat I could remember. It came in patches. The neurologist said a miracle you can speak at all, it was methamphetamine they forced on you.

Crystal meth: drug of choice in rural Chateauguay County.

Take your time Annemarie. But try.

I knew: these were detectives. I was in a hospital, I was being interviewed. I could not lift my head, I could not move my legs. My arm was fixed in place, a spike through my arm in the soft flesh at the elbow. Another one of them came to stick a needle in my arm, I kicked at her.

Kicking, screaming. No no no noooo.

Drug overdose. Methamphetamine. Remaining in the brain for days, weeks. Flashes, paranoia. I was panicked, I was being suffocated! Clawed at the pillow, threw the pillow onto the floor. So agitated they had to strap me onto the bed, my arms were bleeding from stab wounds. Broken glass inside my head.

Where was Aunt Drewe, I asked them. Was Aunt Drewe in this hospital. They ignored my questions, they repeated their questions to me. *Witness you are our sole witness at the present time Annemarie Straube is that your legal name anything you can tell us to help us find your aunt Drewe Hildebrand.*

Annemarie: that name! No one called me Annemarie, in Chateauguay Springs.

If Drewe heard, she'd be annoyed. Annemarie was the other girl, Marta was the girl I'd become. *My daughter. If I had wanted a daughter which I don't.*

Drewe's laughter, like silk tearing. Soooo shivery that sound of silky Drewe tearing.

Can't budge the goddamned pillow. They must've strapped it onto the bed. Tearing with my teeth, to throw it to the floor. But I can't. And my heartbeat monitored by a machine, if it goes crazy they will come running. How can you believe anything I tell you, my memory is gone.

Sole witness to—what?

Sometime in the night, Drewe entered the room. Stealthy and secret a forefinger to her lips. Drewe takes mercy on you sometimes when you are weak and stammering, other times not. *Smallness of soul. Curse of the ordinary.* Drewe took pity on me laying a cool hard hand on my burning forehead. Drewe hauled me up in her arms that are so strong, you can feel the small muscles bunching. *Out! Out of bed! On your feet Marta! I'll drive us home.*

I wasn't sure if this had happened yet. If Drewe was somewhere in the hospital, in secret. While they were searching for her in Shale River Mountain State Park.

Yes I forgive you Marta. Of course I love you.

Except: the detectives were asking me questions, was it another time? Goddamned nurse poking my arm with a needle to draw more blood. I wanted to make a joke about blood, were they draining my blood, Xenia tried to drain my blood, I kicked and fought, I hoped Xenia would die. One of the detectives was a woman. Could not remember her name. *Annemarie* she said *sometimes you are called Marta is that correct please can you hear me? look at me? try to answer our questions?*

Four days, or five. Night/day. Day/night. Throbbing in my head, can't see. I am trying to answer questions put to me by strangers but I can't remember why, where I am.

. . . from the beginning? said you were upstairs in your room, you heard voices, your aunt often had late-night guests so you didn't register anything unusual until, happened to see it was 2 A.M.?

Yes I said. No. Yes I think. My throat was raw, scraped raw. My face was so swollen/ugly they would not allow me to see it except I can feel it, I can "see" as I feel it like braille. He'd held my head as in a vise, pried my jaws open. Crystal meth I had not known what it was, don't do drugs I am frightened of drugs do you believe me?

No didn't see any faces. Voices, didn't recognize.

. . . skin color? Ages? You must have heard . . .

. . . in the time you were with them, forty minutes minimum . . .

They'd taken my aunt and me in separate vehicles. This, I seemed to know. I knew this. I didn't know where they'd taken my aunt and I would not have known where they'd taken me, I was blinded, I had no idea what was happening, where I was taken, and dumped. Why hadn't they killed me, if they wanted me dead. The "sole witness" dead. Why had they abducted me, drugged me, abandoned me, living, while they hadn't abandoned my aunt . . . It seemed clear, it was assumed that the abductors had wanted Drewe Hildebrand, not Drewe's nineteen-year-old niece who lived with her at Chateauguay Springs. The niece had to be incidental. She'd walked into the scene. Blundered into the scene. Instead of remaining upstairs and calling 911. Instead of helping her aunt she'd confronted the intruders naive and stupid deserving to be punished.

So afraid. They were keeping from me, they'd found Drewe's body. Not a kidnapping but a homicide they were investigating.

. . . *into protective custody, if you can identify them.*

. . . *guard outside your door here, twenty-four-hour watch.*

But I could not. Could not identify them how could I?

It was known, Drewe Hildebrand had numerous enemies. Drewe Hildebrand was known to laugh at her enemies. Many times warned, Chateauguay County isn't New York City. The Village of Chateauguay Springs isn't SoHo or TriBeCa, Manhattan. People here in the Newburgh area, in Orange County, not just right-wing conservatives, not just Christians for Life, numerous others who hate the kind of art she exhibits, promotes. Vandalizing her property, attempted arson. Threats. The men who'd forced their way into the house to overpower Drewe and me had left behind a crucifix on the fireplace mantel.

A crucifix! While I was in the hospital I wasn't told this. Such information was kept from me. Even when I was much improved, able to read newspapers, watch TV, I wasn't allowed, nor were the hospital staff or my visitors allowed, to tell me what the news was, what the police investigation was yielding, facts known to the public.

Sixty hours in the park, before I'd been found. My medical condition, my taped statements, none of this was revealed to me, detectives didn't want their sole witness "confused"—"contaminated."

Questioned about drugs. Methamphetamine?

No I told them. No "drug history."

Nineteen years old. Born 3/17/84, Cattaraugus County, New York. Birth records, they'd checked. Living with aunt, father's sister,

Drewe Hildebrand, since the age of fifteen. No "drug history" prior to the alleged forced overdose of 3/29/03. Maybe they believed me, maybe they did not. No one ever tells the truth about drugs and I was the niece of Drewe Hildebrand living at Chateauguay Springs where it was believed "drug use" was common.

Detectives from both Chateauguay County and Orange County would check into my background. The expensive private schools my aunt had sent me to in Woodstock, New York, and in Connecticut, schools for students with "special needs" where, in fact, drug use was common: ecstasy, painkillers, barbiturates, "horse tranquilliz- ers," anti-depressants, Ritalin, cocaine, even heroin and crystal meth; where smoking pot was casual as smoking cigarettes except I'd always been frightened of drugs, what might happen to my brain.

Slipping over the edge, and you can't pull yourself back.

Like my mother.

My family I'd fled in Cattaraugus. You can't believe how quickly a family can fall apart like a shattered brain.

Shame, shame! My aunt Drewe had hoped to save me such shame.

Annemarie: is there anything you haven't told us?

Anything you've been remembering, you haven't told us?

These long pauses. Nowhere to look. My damaged eyes, my head that hurts. *Annemarie? Try.*

One of the detectives reminded me of my father: that middle-aged once-handsome face going to ruin. Eyes alert and intelligent and lightly threaded with blood. The nose was just perceptibly swollen, a drinker's nose beginning to be disfigured and discolored by tiny broken capillaries beneath the surface of the skin. I did not want to look at this stranger identified as a senior detective with the Chateauguay County Sheriff's Department for he was the one, he was the only one, of all the strangers who'd questioned me, who regarded me with doubt. He did not contradict me, he was courteous, even kindly, you could see that he pitied me, the wreckage of my brain, yet he was doubtful of what I had to tell him, there was something in my faltering words he did not believe. I did not want to look at this man but it was not possible to look away, I was frightened, I was confused, I thought *Does he know me? But how does he know me?* Hadn't seen my father since I was fifteen, hadn't spoken to my father Harvey Straube in nearly that long and so seeing this man, this stranger, somehow he was confused with my father, if this was a dream (and maybe I was dreaming: hallucinating) maybe this detective was my father in disguise or a stranger disguised to resemble my father and at the thought my heartbeat began to quicken, I felt a jab of adrenaline to the heart *Oh oh oh!* I hid my face in my hands, terrified this man would peer into my soul, next thing I knew I was crawling into a burrow, a panicked creature crawling into a burrow to hide.

Nurses were summoned, to restrain me. Where I'd crawled screaming and hyperventilating to the foot of the bed, beneath the covers. The detectives were gone. A doctor was summoned. A needle was inserted in an available vein, to sedate me.

"Going to Live with the Rich Aunt"

June 1999. My father was taken from us to begin an eight-to-fifteen-year term in the State Facility for Men at Oriskany. Our household was falling apart, our family name was disgraced in Cattaraugus. The telephone rang, my mother picked up the receiver crying, "Yes? What do you want?" and it was her sister-in-law Drewe Hildebrand, my father's older sister.

"Send the girl to me—'Annemarie.' Get her out of there."

Get her out of there. My mother needed a moment to recover from the shock. I was in another part of the house, I froze hearing her say loudly, "No. Go to hell. I will *never.*"

My mother slammed down the receiver. For weeks she would repeat to anyone who wished to listen the words so contemptuously uttered by a woman whom she scarcely knew, who had had nothing to do with our family until now.

Send the girl—"Annemarie." Get her out of there.

This terrible time, weeks and months. Telephone calls, sudden outcries, curses, slammed-down receivers. Collection agencies, a grim-smiling officer from Cattaraugus Home Mortgage & Finance knocking at our door. Relatives avoided us, my classmates stared at me in wonder. *Straube* was a name too often in the local papers, on local TV news. Still, I wasn't prepared for my mother fierce as a hornet grabbing my shoulders and shaking me as if she wanted to break my neck. Her sallow face was livid, indignant. "You! Traitor! Going behind my back, are you? Talking to that woman? Your rich-bitch aunt? You and your father, eh? Behind my back?"

I was stunned, I knew nothing about my aunt Drewe Hildebrand. Only the way some of the relatives spoke of her as the "rich" Straube sister who'd left Cattaraugus, run away as a girl and had nothing to do with the family.

"Mom, no. I . . ."

In my confusion I didn't know what my mother was accusing me of, only that I was innocent.

"Betraying your mother with that woman! Because she's rich— because she's 'famous.' Because she looks down on us, on *me*." My mother shoved me from her, sobbing, furious. Her breath was sour from hours of sodden daytime sleep, there was a wet druggy glare to her eyes. "Well, you're not going to live with that woman, Annemarie. We don't accept charity. You can live with shame as well as I can. You're not going anywhere. Stop staring at me like that, I'll tear off your homely face. You're my goddamned daughter not hers, you are staying here with *me*."

I tried to explain to my mother that I hadn't been speaking with my aunt Drewe, I didn't know my aunt Drewe at all. I'd met her only once, years ago. I felt bad about Daddy but I wasn't ashamed (of course, I was ashamed, I wanted to die), I didn't want to live anywhere else. Maybe I said these things. It was hard to speak to my mother in one of her excitable moods, you dared not raise your voice because it would infuriate her but if you spoke in a normal voice, my mother did not hear. Such things my mother said, you didn't know whether to believe them or not. In the past several months she'd become reckless in her suspicions and denunciations. My father's arrest, indictment, trial, conviction and now his incarceration seemed to have taken most of our lives and with the passing of weeks my mother was becoming more deranged. Though, for as long as I could remember, she'd made scornful references to my father's older sister, *rich-bitch sister, wouldn't it be nice if she did something for us?* Seeing a woman on television who was patrician, pretentious, snobbish and snotty, yet undeniably glamorous, she would say in disdain, *Could be your rich-bitch sister, eh?* My mother would laugh to show that she was only joking; she was above such pettiness, if others were not.

But lately it had been revealed, since my father's legal troubles, that Drewe had been "lending" him money for some time, in secret. My father must have contacted Drewe, asking her for help. Maybe she'd even helped pay my mother's medical bills. All that was finished now, Drewe wasn't providing any more money. She would take me in, but refused to negotiate with my mother. My mother protested: "That rich bitch, now she wants to take my daughter. She's already taken somebody's daughter, isn't one enough?"

Somebody's daughter was flung out in reference to an incident that had happened at Chateauguay Springs the year before: a young woman artist had allegedly died of a drug overdose in one of the residences. There had been a police investigation, Drewe had been cleared of any involvement. Still in the collective memory of Cattaraugus, where "Drewe Hildebrand" was so resented, the scandal lingered like a perverse homage.

"She will *not.* You will *not.* You are staying here with *me.*"

My mother's arms, grappling and clumsy as tentacles, I managed to push away from.

She was a sick woman: three days after my father began serving his sentence at Oriskany, my mother was arrested for impaired and reckless driving and made to commit herself into a drug rehabilitation facility in Jamestown. So I was surrendered after all, to live with my aunt Drewe Hildebrand on her ninety-acre estate seventy miles north of New York City on the Hudson River.

The girl who'd died of a drug overdose. The girl I'd heard of, lacking a name only just *the girl, that girl. The girl who'd died.*

One of those childhood memories that come at second- or, third-hand. I had overheard my mother speaking with relatives on the phone, her voice lifting in excited disapproval. *A girl? Drugs? Dead? And Drewe is involved?* My father had refused to discuss it. My father had a way of dismissing rumors with a shrug and a wink at me, the two of us linked against my mother, an excitable woman.

When my father's legal troubles began ("legal troubles" was the favored expression within the family) he refused to allow newspapers in the house, refused to allow us to watch local TV news that only distorted and sensationalized. You could not trust the media in its treatment of *Harold Straube, 41.*

My father spoke admiringly but guardedly of my aunt Drewe. He spoke of driving to visit her, sometime. As if Drewe had invited us, an open invitation, a summertime visit would be best, Chateauguay Springs was beautiful in the summer. Views of the Hudson River, a dignified old manor house with numerous bedrooms, an "artists' colony." There was the Village of Chateauguay Springs (population 1,200) and there was the estate my widowed aunt had inherited, a few miles outside town. On the map of New York State, Chateauguay Springs was a small blue dot on the western bank of the Hudson River between Newburgh to the north and Cornwall-on-Hudson to the south. And south of that, West Point. I had never been in that part of the state, no one among the relatives had ever visited Chateauguay Springs.

I felt a stab of pride, gloating. That I'd been singled out by the rich aunt.

The girl who'd died had been an artist of some kind. She'd been "in residence" at the Chateauguay Springs Artists' Colony. No one in Cattaraugus had much idea of what an artists' colony might be. "Art" itself was viewed with suspicion, scorn. There was the sense, as people like my mother conveyed it, of a fraud, a hustle. "Art" was putting something over on someone, the way politicians did. "Art" was a sorry excuse for not being productive, useful. "Art" was vanity, pretension.

In Cattaraugus, no one would have referred to my aunt as "Drewe Hildebrand" for her name, her true name, was "Eileen Straube." She'd been born here, she'd grown up here. Cattaraugus knew her as the oldest of the Straube daughters who'd been a "difficult"—"high-strung"—"selfish" girl, a "discipline problem" at school who'd "mouthed off" to her teachers, and been "secretive, stubborn" at home. She had the temerity to imagine herself an artist—there were no art classes, no art teachers, in the Cattaraugus public schools to train or test her. She'd barely managed to graduate with the class of 1981 from Cattaraugus High, less for academic reasons than for disciplinary reasons, and, memorably, on the day following graduation she'd disappeared with no warning, taking only a few clothes, a single suitcase, leaving behind a hand-printed note generally interpreted as taunting:

GOODBYE   DON'T LOOK FOR ME
(I WON'T BE THERE)

No one had gone to look for her. She was seventeen, with the poise of an adult woman.

In Cattaraugus, it wasn't known if Eileen Straube had become "Drewe Hildebrand" for professional reasons (she was a "career woman," a designer of some kind, an artist) or if that was the name she'd acquired when she married a man named Hildebrand about whom little was known except that he was a "rich" businessman in some way connected with art.

From time to time, Drewe Hildebrand's name and photograph might appear in publications read in Cattaraugus: *Newsweek, Time, People, USA Today.* The Chateauguay Springs Artists' Colony had been featured on CBS *Sunday Morning,* and Drewe had been interviewed. No one in her hometown could have said what Drewe had done to merit such attention: exhibited "controversial" art? Nurtured young artists? If she'd been an artist herself, she seemed to have set her art aside, or maybe she'd given up. Her personal life was said to be complicated, messy. By the standards of Cattaraugus she was a promiscuous woman. Even her photographs differed suspiciously from one another: her hair changed style and color, her face appeared altered, a kind of malleable sculpture. Only once had she returned to Cattaraugus, twelve years after she'd run away, for her mother's funeral—"Just like Eileen, isn't it, to come *too late!*" My memory of having seen her after the funeral is blurred. Maybe I was frightened of her. A woman I had never seen before, a face that looked as if it were made of something like hammered metal, mask-like, beautiful and impersonal as a face on a billboard. The fleshy red mouth looked disdainful, reluctant to smile. The face was partly obscured by oversized dark glasses, of a kind no one in Cattaraugus was likely to wear, especially on an overcast winter day, and indoors. Aunt Drewe wore black trousers with a sharp crease and a black brocaded jacket of such elegance and luxury, you couldn't help but stare. Her head was wrapped in a black silk turban, her hair was completely covered, a curious sight in Cattaraugus. She looked Egyptian, exotic. Yet she was distracted and unsure of herself, as if the fact of her mother's death was only just catching up with her, like a delayed illness. (It was believed that Drewe had been out of touch with her mother for twelve years. Later, after my father's legal troubles, it began to be speculated that Drewe might have been "lending" her mother money, too, in secret.) I was a shy child, forced by my parents to "say hello" to my aunt Drewe, the imposing woman in black who smiled at me politely, eyes obscured by glasses so darkly tinted they appeared black. This was after my grandmother's funeral service, my aunt was wiping her nose with a tissue, uneasy, clearly wanting to be left alone. But my parents were nudging me forward, with nervous smiles. Other nieces and nephews were being introduced to Drewe, nudged and even shoved at her, with the (unconscious?) hope that the rich aunt might take an interest in their futures. But Drewe Hildebrand wasn't interested in any of us. She especially aroused indignation by declining to stay for the funeral brunch. Conspicuously and dramatically she'd arrived in Cattaraugus in the cushioned rear of a Lincoln Town Car driven by a black chauffeur; it was calculated that she'd traveled more than 350 miles to arrive by mid-morning, but by 1 P.M. she was gone, vanishing into the rear of the gleaming black car.

Like dirty, churning water, anger lapped in her wake: "Thinks she's too good for us! Did you see that look on her face!"—" 'Eileen Straube' is who she is. Wants us to call her 'Drewe,' what kind of a name is that, a man's name?—I had all I could do to keep from laughing in that woman's face!"—"Not even crying, and it's her own poor mother she'd abandoned, and broken her heart."

Maybe. Maybe not. Already as a child I'd learned to question such remarks adults made to one another.

Because you can't. Can't believe. Their words. Even their eyes fixed on you, swearing they love you, never meant to hurt you. Even insisting they are innocent as my father insisted, it was others who committed crimes, not him.

My mother's final words, flung back at me like a curse: "So, you can go to her now! I hope you're happy! You and that rich bitch aunt of yours! Maybe I'll die, where I'm going, you'd like that, wouldn't you! You and *him*."

I stared after my mother. I was numb, unfeeling. There was a terrible cold on my skin, and inside me. I believed that I would never see my mother again, as I believed I would never see my father again.

I heard myself call after her, "Mom, goodbye! I—"

My voice faltered. My mother was speaking now to the relative who'd come to drive her to the Jamestown clinic, complaining, cursing. I ran back into the house, to hide the wild happiness I felt.

Going to live with my rich aunt.

* * *

Aunt Drewe sent the Lincoln Town Car to Cattaraugus to bring me to Chateauguay Springs, chauffeured by the black driver. His name was Sammy Ray Lee. He wore a white shirt, a navy blue jacket, a visored cap. He was good-natured but reticent. Politely he opened the back door for me to climb inside, there was not a thought of my sitting in front with him. Politely he called me, as no one had ever called me, even as a joke, what sounded like *Miss Straube.* I told him he should call me "Annemarie" but he seemed not to hear.

My things—my "possessions"—were in two suitcases and three cardboard boxes in the trunk of the gleaming black car. Our family house had been claimed by the bank that had mortgaged it, the furnishings had been sold, or stored with relatives, or hauled away with the trash.

So ashamed! But my mother was gone, away from Cattaraugus and shame. My father was gone.

You can live with us my aunt Janice said. *You can live with us* my grandmother (my mother's mother) said. *No no! I want to be gone from you all* I kept to myself, I could not scream in their faces.

Miles, hours. Familiar landscapes were changed by the green-tinted windows as if undersea. Then the familiar landscapes vanished, I began to be exhausted.

I slept groggily in the rear of the car. I woke, my mouth was stale, aching with thirst. The driver stopped at roadside gas stations, at a Holiday Inn near Binghamton. I'd brought books to read, a sketch pad, a notebook, but I couldn't concentrate. I thought *Is it too late to turn back, why am I here* in that voice of wonderment that is the most private voice of my soul, a voice of dreams, a voice of perverse solace, *what will happen to me, that I am here?* Often in my dreams of confusion and flight I am naked, or only partly clothed, I'm in an open, anonymous place that feels windswept, but now I kept waking in the rear of the sleek black car driven by a black man intent upon ignoring me and by the time (late afternoon, a sky streaked with fire) we reached Chateauguay Springs my head was wracked with pain, my mouth felt misshapen. Homesickness struck like nausea.

CHATEAUGUAY SPRINGS EST. 1964.
PRIVATE PROPERTY NO OUTLET.

The narrow lane was bumpy, Sammy Ray drove with care.

Trees! So many, I would never find my way back.

We emerged into a clearing. The sunlight hurt my eyes. Sammy Ray continued driving up a grassy knoll, there were buildings ahead. We approached a large house, a "mansion" of a house, with a prominent roof made of what appeared to be smooth dark slate. There was a rose trellis, small red roses were in bloom. There were dense evergreen shrubs close beside the house, shading the lower windows. Out of nowhere a woman appeared, staring in my direction. Then she smiled, she called out: "Annemarie! Welcome to Chateauguay Springs."

Before Sammy Ray could climb out to open the rear door of the car, the woman opened it, seized my hand and hauled me outside, clumsy as a child. She hugged me, hard. We were laughing, breathless. I could not recall ever having seen this woman before. She was nothing like the stiff unfriendly woman swathed in black who'd come to Cattaraugus for her mother's funeral, this was a younger-seeming woman, solidly fleshy, with a sunburnt face, dull-gold hair in a thick braid that swung between her shoulder blades. Her eyes were warmly brown, there were fine white lines radiating from her eyes, fine lines bracketing her mouth. She wore no lipstick, no makeup. She wore khaki shorts stained with paint and a vivid-red cotton T-shirt cut high on the shoulders, as if to display her upper arms that were firm and smooth with muscle like those of a young woman athlete. I felt a thrill of vindication, gloating. *See, Mom? Aunt Drewe is no one you know.*

"This is your home now, dear. I will protect you from harm and shame."

"You haven't brought much. Good!"

It was like playing house. Aunt Drewe helped me put my things away in "my" room. A cedar closet large enough to stand inside, a chest of drawers, a bureau with three large, heavy drawers, that would remain mostly empty. "This is your private space. This view, your private view. Think lofty thoughts, dear! They are the only thoughts worth thinking." My room back in Cattaraugus had been one-third the size of this room, which had a high ceiling with white molding, walls papered in white with fine blue stripes. There were four tall, narrow windows, venetian blinds but no curtains. Aunt Drewe strode about happily, I could barely look at her, at her glowing face, it was as if a blinding light shone in my eyes. Drewe said, "Oh, this house! It's a 'landmark,' it has 'history,' my late husband inherited it, a beautiful house of course, but not a house I would have chosen, or wished to build, but here it is, and here I am, and *here you are.*"

Drewe's voice lifted on *here you are.* We laughed again, breathless as if we'd been climbing stairs.

How strange this is, I thought. How wonderful.

I don't think that I was frightened. I was waiting to be hugged again, and quickly released.

Drewe's hugs, in those early days: spontaneous, warm, hard enough to make me wince, but very quick, giving no time for reciprocation.

No time for a lonely girl to hug back, and burst into tears.

I was a shy girl, it's a fact that shy girls, once they begin talking, talk too much. Shy girls, once their tongues are loosed, have no idea how to shut up.

Drewe's posture: so straight you could imagine a steel rod where her spine was. Sitting on the edge of "my" four-poster bed.

Most of my things were put away, out of sight in the large white-walled room. It was as if I'd been swallowed up. It was as if my clothes, my few books, had vanished. In the bureau mirror my aunt's face in profile, a strong-boned face neither female nor male, and the heavy dull-gold braid, and her broad shoulders, were visible, at an angle; but I could not see myself, there appeared to be no one in the room except my aunt. All this while she'd been smiling but now, I saw, she was frowning; there was a small vexed frown between her eyebrows; for in my headlong flight of words, I'd been telling her about my mother, my mother at the Jamestown clinic, what a shock it was when I'd first discovered that my mother was addicted to painkillers, and Drewe lifted a warning finger and said, "No. We won't speak of your mother at Chateauguay Springs." I felt rebuffed but I understood, I thought: my aunt scarcely knew my mother and could have no interest in her. But when I began to speak of my father, the shock of my father's arrest, the trial, the fact (for it seemed to me a fact) that my father was innocent of the crimes for which he'd been convicted, Drewe reached over to touch my wrist, to nudge my wrist as you'd nudge an annoying child: "No. We won't speak of your father at Chateauguay Springs."

Aunt Drewe smiled at me again. A sudden seductive baring of teeth, a smile of warning.

Don't resist me! Not ever.

I was shivering, I wanted Drewe to nudge me again, or to take hold of my wrist, chiding.

She rose to leave. The bedsprings creaked, surrendering her weight. She was not a small woman, strength flowed in her shoulders and upper arms. Now she did kiss me, lightly, the top of my head.

"One more thing, dear. 'Annemarie' is a servant girl's name. A shopgirl's name. Your new name is 'Marta'—you'll grow into it."

I was fifteen that summer, yes I was growing.

Survivor

━━━

Help me, Marta! You must.

I had, I had helped her. And then I had not.

This fact, I would tell no one. Not one of my interrogators in the hospital at Newburgh.

Newburgh, that aging city on the Hudson River. We'd rarely driven there, it wasn't one of Drewe's cities. The river widens here, perpetually windy, the hue of slate. I stared at the broken waves and rippling slats of light in the water's surface like nerve endings in a gigantic skin.

The small-souled are born to be slaves of the larger-souled, it's a law of nature. Drewe said *Each to each, that's our happiness.*

I shoved at her, in panic. Would have clawed her except my nails had turned the color of old ivory and were splitting vertically.

No! no! Get away!

"Sorry. Time to take a blood sample, Annemarie."

In the hospital at Newburgh my hair came out in clumps, wan

childish curls. I couldn't control waves of paranoia-panic, the glittery white poison had stuck to crevices in my brain.

In a hospital you can drift, your mind blank, like debris in a rushing river, no idea where you've come from or where you are headed.

But I was alive, my white blood cell count was "improving." I sat up in bed, I walked unassisted to the bathroom. Suddenly I was eating solids again, ravenous! A starving animal.

In a few weeks I would regain the ten or twelve pounds I'd lost in the Shale River Mountain State Park where I'd been meant to die.

Fewer strangers. Fewer detectives entering my room to question me. They'd drained from me all that I knew. My damaged brain.

Telling me: "You're looking good! Your color is returning."

". . . an ordeal, but now . . ."

". . . still missing. We're sorry."

". . . search is continuing, police are following 'leads' . . ."

Must be alive, can't be dead! Though I saw.

Felt the skull crack like a layer of thin shale. I think I felt this.

Five days. Six, seven days. I hated being an invalid, hated nurses' aides hovering over me. Finally I was allowed to take a shower in privacy, not standing but sitting on a stool in the shower stall as a nurse's aide waited outside the door, to help me to my feet and dry myself afterward.

Don't touch me! I am capable of drying myself.

I waited for the detective who reminded me of my father to return. He didn't.

Statements were taken, an "investigation" began. Annemarie Straube a.k.a. Marta Hildebrand was not a reliable witness due to physical and mental (i.e., drug-related) impairment but she was the sole witness, so far.

Detectives were investigating my aunt's relatives in Cattaraugus, New York. My relatives.

They would question my father Harvey Straube (incarcerated at the State Facility for Men at Oriskany) and my mother Lori Straube (released from the Jamestown Rehabilitation Clinic for the second time, February 2003).

My father, my mother. They were small-souled individuals, Drewe would say. *We won't speak of them. No!*

Tried to remember a time when I'd loved them. My weakness was, I had loved them. *You hadn't known me then, Marta. You were a child.*

Inside my skull was my brain that had been damaged. CAT scans, MRIs were prescribed. I think I remember being shoved into an immense machine, I shut my eyes thinking *This is death, I am returning.* You learn that the terror of dying is only in resisting, if you cease to resist there is no terror.

Later, you are wakened: lights! My brain was now a series of X-ray negatives, it could be observed, analyzed, discussed like a grapefruit, for instance, the tough rind peeled away, sinewy fruit-sections exposed. There was a "neurologist"—one of the hospital staff—to inform me that no permanent neurological damage seemed to have been done to my brain, the "tentative" prognosis was very good.

"Once the methamphetamine traces are gone."

"But—when will that be?"

"Difficult to say. It might be a matter of just a few more days, or it might be a matter of weeks."

Weeks! I wondered if my memory would return, then. What shreds of memory remained.

". . . digging into my past, private life! Because of that woman, and *you*."

My hand shook holding the receiver. My mother's voice was nasal, aggrieved. She hadn't been feeling strong enough to visit me in the hospital but she'd called several times and not until this morning was I able to speak with her, to hear of her agitation not that I'd been abducted, injured, hospitalized but that detectives from Chateauguay County had come to Cattaraugus to interview her and other relatives. "As if we need more shame. More public attention. Oh I knew, something terrible would happen to you, Annemarie, going away to live with that depraved woman."

As my mother spoke in her lurching, flailing-out way, I felt a tight, impacted sensation behind my eyes. The room's white walls that were smudged, soiled. The chipped metal rail at the foot of my bed. Small blank TV screen across the room. The IV fluid container, the drip into my forearm that was bruised like rotted fruit. I wondered if the crystal-meth poison in my brain was seeping out, into the world. For everything seemed so strange: toxic.

When I didn't argue with my mother, she began to sound less angry. She explained again that she wasn't feeling "strong enough" to make the trip to see me and anyway, she wasn't sure she wanted to see me, or that I wanted to see her. "Oh I was shocked, I was very upset, Annemarie, when the call came, some woman calling herself 'Madeleine'—'Magdalene'?—who works for Drewe Hildebrand, telling me what had happened to you, and sure enough, there it was in the paper, on the front page of the Jamestown paper—'Arts Patron Hildebrand Missing.' And this woman gives me the hospital number to call, and soon as she hangs up, the phone rings again, and it's some person wanting to speak with—"

My mother's voice spilled out of the phone. I was very tired now. I wanted to tell my mother that I was sorry for what had happened, for of course there was no connection between this and her and it was wrong for strangers to question her, but I could not interrupt her. For now she was saying whoever was paying my medical bills there, it could not be her. Understand that! She was paying off debts, she had to qualify for county medical assistance, I was nineteen years old now, not her responsibility. "Maybe that woman has remembered you in her will," she said, meanly. "Everybody here asks me."

I said that I would have to hang up the phone now, I was so tired.

I am alive—am I? I was saved—for this?

"Disgusting, what you read about that 'artists' colony'! This 'Blood Mask' thing that your aunt had made up, to look like her own head, it was on TV, in the local papers, people here are talking and laughing about it, 'Eileen Straube' is how people know her, not that fake name of hers. You can be sure, every time 'Eileen Straube' is mentioned, 'Harvey Straube' gets mentioned, too: and all the shame of that. Now everybody is waiting for her remains to be found, it's expected she has been killed. Or maybe, knowing her,

there's people that wouldn't doubt she staged the kidnapping herself, for publicity, she ran away from home, didn't she? At seventeen? To hurt and embarrass her family, to get attention for herself?"

Now my mother had worked up her anger again, I couldn't follow each twist and lunge in her voice. The last words of hers I heard,
before the receiver slipped from my hand, were, "—one more nail in
my coffin, *you*."

Waking: one of the nurses prodding me.

Time to take a blood sample, sorry.

Her Scots sculptor-lover Xenia had drawn Drewe's blood with a
syringe, he'd stored the blood in canisters, refrigerated. Drewe had
shuddered and laughed, insisting it hadn't hurt.

Well, maybe it had hurt. Xenia's touch wasn't gentle. Xenia
wasn't skilled at drawing blood. Syringes in his studio, underfoot.
Syringes in the trash, Xenia had cooked cocaine, heroin to inject
into his ropey veins and into Drewe's and what of Marta, too?

No Drewe said. *Not Marta.*

Not Marta not yet.

So much you forget, vast patches of amnesia like deserts indicated on maps. No human habitation, nothing to name.

(They were suspicious of me, I knew. Local police. Anyone associated with the artists' colony. Dope was smoked in the resident
artists' cabins, harder drugs were probably in use. And hadn't a
young woman died of a heroin overdose a few years ago, her body
found beginning to decompose in the pine woods?)

Whoever had taken Drewe Hildebrand and her niece, they'd
taken time first to trash Drewe Hildebrand's art, that had been on

display in the house. One of the artworks was *Blood Mask II,* a replica of Drewe's head made of her own dark, frozen blood. It had been removed from its freezer shrine on a pedestal, dumped onto the floor to melt into liquid blood.

It must have been an astonishing sight: Chateauguay County sheriff's deputies entering the house, discovering the melting head, melting-blood-head, in a puddle of blood soaking into the Moroccan weave carpet.

The sculptor Xenia from whom Drewe Hildebrand was "estranged" was being interviewed by detectives. Xenia, who'd become an enemy.

In the hospital at Newburgh, outside the door of my second-floor room for the nine days I was kept there, a uniformed deputy was stationed to "guard" me.

For it was believed that I might be at risk. Whoever had been involved in the abduction might want to hurt me, so that I could not identify them, give testimony against them.

The deputy guarding me wasn't always the same man, there were several, youngish guys with names like Rick, Wylie. They wore neatly pressed pebble-blue uniforms, they were clean-shaven, bored. For nothing happened to warrant their presence, the routine of a hospital is mechanical, lacking in drama. Even death, if there is death, is likely to be low-keyed, routine. The deputy named Rick glanced into my room from time to time but didn't speak with me, I heard him flirting with nurses and aides outside the door, I heard their laughter, felt a pang of jealousy.

I wasn't a normal young woman. I'd been told.

Didn't feel toward men as you are supposed to feel. A young female of my age. I wasn't beautiful. Though Drewe insisted: I had an Old World peasant beauty. Heavy eyebrows, long nose, broad forehead and jaws, but Drewe insisted I had a "strong, sensual beauty" like that of the biblical/vengeful Judith in a famous painting by Artemisia Gentileschi, Drewe showed me in a book of color plates.

My face! My eyes. I looked away, as in an obscure shame.

Of course I had never heard of Artemisia Gentileschi, before Drewe. I had never heard of Caravaggio. In my aunt's eyes I was crude and natural as a peasant, my eagerness to learn pleased her.

No one so faithful to you as me. I promise.

"Marta. You remember me, I hope."

The evening before I left the hospital. He came.

Virgil West. Staring at me with a faint, forced smile. A look of disbelief in his eyes. Dread.

Virgil West had been my aunt's lover, several years before. They were estranged now. He was an artist of some renown, though his reputation had declined, lately. He was a large clumsy man, and it was like him to thrust something at me without seeming, himself, to see it: branches of newly budded pussy willow with raw broken stems that looked as if they'd been torn by hand, a fistful of mud-splattered daffodils very likely grabbed out of the backyard of the man's house in Cornwall-on-Hudson.

"This terrible thing, Marta! *You* are alive at least."

Virgil collapsed into a chair at my bedside. He was wheezing, indignant. His blood-netted eyes stared at me, wonderingly. I had not seen Virgil in nearly two years, he had disappeared from my aunt's life. It was a shock to see him now, close-up, slovenly in paint-stained clothes, smelling of his body, something sweetly liquorish on his breath. He was old now: his hair had gone brightly silver, his head was large and slovenly as the head of a molting buffalo. Heavy cheeks like soiled clay, broken-vein cheeks, webs of wrinkles about the eyes.

"And Drewe? No word? Still 'missing'? Terrible!"

Virgil West was a "person of interest" in the police investigation. He had a tangled history with Drewe, personal as well as professional, dating back to the 1980s. They'd been involved—somehow.

Between us there was a history. In his distraught state, Virgil wouldn't remember.

"When you are well enough to leave this place, Marta, will you call me? I will drive you back to Chateauguay Springs. While Drewe is away, I can help."

Strange to hear Virgil West speak my aunt's name so familiarly: *Drewe.* As if he hadn't hated her, after all.

"Will you? Will you call me? And we will keep in touch? I'm still at Cornwall, you know. Little in my life has changed. I work, I sleep. People come to visit me, a few. Not 'art people'—no longer. The lawyers, all that, between your aunt and me"—Virgil shook his head with a look of extreme repugnance, as if smelling a bad odor—"is dropped, of course. You knew."

I didn't know. I'd known little about what had happened between Virgil West and Drewe Hildebrand, even when they'd been lovers, and friends. I knew that women came and went in Virgil West's life, he had been married several times, he had grown children. He looked like a man in his sixties but was in fact younger.

I had never heard Virgil West speak with such animation, agitation. I had never heard Virgil West so concerned with anyone or anything apart from his art. It was a shock to me, it was a revelation. He
was an ugly man with beautiful eyes. He had snaggle teeth stained
with nicotine, whiskers sprouting from his jaws. But those pale blue
eyes, fixed upon me. When I'd known him, or had wished to know
him, he had rarely looked at me, or even at Drewe; he'd moved in a
trance of self-absorption, preoccupation with his work. For the work
never ceased. Virgil West was a painter of large blunt elemental canvases, the earliest and most celebrated resembled smears of earth or
excrement in which faceless human beings, elaborately imagined yet
lacking identity, nude, sometimes disfigured, floated like clouds.
The paintings were convoluted, mysterious. Ugly at first but by degrees beautiful. As Virgil West was himself an ugly man, a colossal
ruin of a man, but by degrees, if you looked, beautiful.

On his enormous feet, well-worn leather sandals worn with gray
woollen socks. Paint-stained work trousers that, pleated at the
waist, billowed out to accommodate his powerful thighs.

In disgust, Virgil was saying, "The local gestapo! Seeking 'suspects'! Two squad cars pulled into my driveway, Monday morning,
pounded on my door like TV cops calling 'Open up! Police!' It was
a ghastly hour, not seven A.M., I had only dropped off to sleep at
about five A.M. I had no idea what they wanted, my first impression
was such shock: Drewe had been murdered? They tell you little, you
know. They took me to their headquarters in Newburgh to 'interview me'—for seven hours. I know, I know—you are asking why
didn't I call a lawyer, but I refuse to involve a lawyer, to pay a lawyer
when goddamn I have nothing to hide, there can't be 'evidence'
linking me to an 'abduction' because *I am innocent*. Naturally they

found my fingerprints at Chateauguay Springs: Drewe's studio, Drewe's bedroom, Drewe's bathroom even, anywhere. I explained, the prints have got to be old prints, surely they can date the age of prints, it's been at least two years since I've set foot on Drewe Hildebrand's property, any number of witnesses will testify, anyone who knows us, I have nothing to hide. Well, they tried to say that I had 'threatened' Drewe, they had 'incriminating' statements from witnesses whose names they wouldn't divulge, absolutely bullshit and I knew it. Lying to civilians is a legal police tactic in the United States, it's outrageous, if they can't find criminals to match crimes they arrest innocent civilians and try to fit the crimes to them, and all of this perfectly legal. My God, trying to say that I, Virgil West, would wish to 'take revenge' on Drewe for any reason, as if I would wish to injure a woman, and a girl, this is outrageous! 'Kidnapping'—'abduction.' My God." Virgil wiped at his perspiring face with a wadded tissue. His voice had grown loud, reckless; the sheriff's deputy peered inside my room, to see if the old molting-buffalo man in the painted-stained clothes was dangerous.

I caught the deputy's eye. Tried to smile. Only a friend, an excitable friend. No danger.

Virgil continued, in a hoarse, aggrieved voice, "These gestapo bastards, I asked them will you give me a polygraph test, I will prove to you I am telling the truth, but my blood pressure was so high I had to go away and return the next morning, still it was high, it is high, I was sweating like this, maybe worse. A madness comes over me, I am desperate for Drewe, I forgive her every harmful thing she has said to me, every error at the Hildebrand Gallery, I want Drewe back safely, for Christ's sake don't waste time on me I told the police, eliminate me, I am not a 'suspect,' I am telling you the truth.

So I was hooked up to a machine, like a cardiogram. 'Is your name Virgil West?'—'Are you a resident of Cornwall-on-Hudson?'—'Is your birth date 1/21/50?'—'Are you acquainted with Drewe Hildebrand?'—'Have you had an intimate relationship with Drewe Hildebrand?'—'Do you know the current whereabouts of Drewe Hildebrand?'—'Do you know who entered Drewe Hildebrand's house on the night of March twenty-ninth, who abducted her and her niece?'—'Do you know if Drewe Hildebrand is alive?'—'Are you in contact with anyone who knows?'—'Did you in any way conspire to abduct Drewe Hildebrand?'—'Did you speak or see Drewe Hildebrand within the past week?'—'Within the past month?'—'Within the past year?'—*no no no no no* was my answer, I knew they were trying to trick me somehow, to upset me, but I refused to be upset, and when the test was over, and analyzed, d'you know what the bastards told me: 'The test is inconclusive.' "

Virgil laughed loudly. He fumbled for my hand, gripping it hard. Virgil West's hand that was twice the size of mine, a coarse hand, calloused, nails broken and edged with paint. Beneath the hospital gown I was naked. I was shivering, my breasts felt soft and unprotected, the nipples were hard as unripened berries. It was believed of me that I was abnormally passive for my age, "immature," I knew that I had disappointed Drewe in certain ways yet it was so, my body sometimes frightened me, I could not comprehend what relationship was appropriate with it, my soul trapped in this female body, peering out of bewildered eyes. Virgil West stared at me, suddenly stooping to grasp my head in both hands, his mouth pressed against mine was abrupt and hurting, anguish in such a kiss, you wouldn't call it a kiss but a wet frantic sucking at another's life.

"Ah, Marta. Where has she gone to leave us!"

The kiss had stunned me, like a blow. In the time I'd known him Virgil West had never touched me. Now, the look in the man's face, I saw fear, I saw desire. And anger. *Where has she gone to leave us.*

I felt a stab of jealousy, Virgil West was still in love with Drewe. He'd kissed me, unable to kiss her.

"Eight days, Marta. Do you know, is there something you have not told? *Is* she . . . ?"

Is she alive, is she dead. Where is she.

The kiss seemed to have been forgotten. It was time for Virgil to leave. Without noticing he'd knocked a pussy willow branch to the floor, a broken daffodil. Now he'd sucked up all the oxygen in the room he was on his feet, daring to smile at me.

That ghastly stained-tooth smile, of hope.

"Ah but Marta!—they haven't found her yet. It isn't over, yet."

Here was news: Drewe's Jeep had been found.

After days of searching locally, the Jeep had been found in fifteen feet of water in the Shale River, two miles upstream from where I'd been found.

It was Magdalena, my aunt's housekeeper, who called me with the news. Quickly adding, "There was no body, they said. Nowhere near where the Jeep went in. They are dredging the river there, but—no body has been found, Marta."

Meaning Drewe might still be alive. It isn't over, yet.

* * *

On a gurney with a creaking wheel I was being transported along the corridors of the old building, couldn't see whoever it was pushing the gurney, in the night after the detectives left after I fell asleep I must have died for I was paralyzed now, flat on my back on the cold stainless steel cart, my arms and legs heavy as lead, now that my heart has ceased beating I am not so frightened, I am able to think *This is not so hard after all, it will be over soon.* But the basement morgue is cold! As soon as the gurney with the creaking wheel is pushed inside I begin to whimper, such icy-cold entering my bones. I think that I must be younger than I was when I'd been alive, for my aunt Drewe is standing at the foot of the gurney, younger than I've seen her in years. Drewe is still angry with me, Drewe is not one to be easily placated, yet her face is so strangely luminous, her skin gleams and glitters with a look of fine-hammered silver, her hair is dark, loose on her shoulders, her eyes shine with that look of hunger, rapacity that makes my heart clutch. Only when Drewe's lips part, only when Drewe bares her teeth in a slow seductive smile I can see that the teeth are caked with blood.

Yes I forgive you, Marta. I am all you have.

The Return

━━━

Next morning I was discharged from Newburgh General Hospital.

Nine days. I had not died, and Drewe had not returned.

Not on a gurney with a creaking wheel but in a wheelchair pushed by a nurse I was brought to the rear of the hospital where my aunt's driver had come to pick me up to bring me home to Chateauguay Springs.

A wheelchair! I stared at it, I was filled with dread.

"Please. I can walk. I've been walking. I don't need a wheelchair, this is ridiculous."

The nurse intent upon pushing me in the wheelchair smiled as if she'd heard such protests before. Pleasantly she said, "It's hospital procedure, a matter of insurance. All our discharged patients are wheeled to the door, there you can get up and walk away."

Magdalena Olenski, my aunt's housekeeper, had come to the room to help pack the things I'd accumulated in the nine days. The nurse spoke to include Magdalena, too, for Magdalena was clearly the older, mature woman, the mother, the grandmother to whom one might sensibly appeal at such a moment.

I said to the nurse, "You mean I can walk from the door out of the hospital, turn around and walk back inside the hospital?"

"Yes. That's right."

"But I can't walk downstairs to the door? I can't take the elevator downstairs by myself, can't walk through the lobby to the door, I have to be pushed in this wheelchair?"

"Yes. That's right."

I hated the way the nurse smiled at me to humor me. I wanted to slap her face, a flame of pure wildness passed over me. But Magdalena touched my arm gently, saying, "Marta, do as the nurse asks. You must want to leave this place, don't you?"

Forcing myself to think *Drewe isn't here, that was not Drewe in the morgue. That was a dream.*

Medicated thoughts come shattered and scrambled but if you stand very still and breathe very slowly the moment will pass, the madness fades.

Magdalena said, "Noah is waiting outside. I have a hat for you. Noah and I, we will protect you. We have to continue as Drewe would want us. We're waiting for Drewe to return, she would want you to be brave, Marta, while she's away."

This was so: Drewe would want. Drewe had her ideas about Marta, specifically stated.

A hat? Was this Drewe's hat? A beige rain cap slightly too large for my head, Magdalena laughed as we both pulled it down onto my forehead, tucking wisps of hair inside.

"All right," I told the nurse, "I'll sit in the wheelchair. So don't tip me over."

I sat. The strength in my legs drained away in an instant. I fought down panic, that I would never be able to stand again.

As crawling in the underbrush on the bank of the Shale River and beneath the park services shed in dirt and litter I'd been panicked that I would never be able to stand again, never be able to straighten my spine again, I'd become a broken-backed snake.

Briskly the nurse pushed me in the wheelchair, out into the third-floor corridor, past the nurses' station and to the elevator, into the elevator, down to the busy hospital lobby, I was crouched in the chair, the rumpled beige hat pulled low over my forehead yet still I felt strangers' eyes drift onto me. And stare at me. There had been so much local publicity some of these strangers had to know *That's her. The girl, the one who'd been abducted and left for dead, niece of that woman Hildebrand.* I shrank in the chair, my heart beat sullen and hard.

Magdalena's hand was on my shoulder. Magdalena murmured, "We're almost there, Marta."

Magdalena had come frequently to see me in the hospital. In the wake of what had happened, we were drawn closer together.

Magdalena Olenski was Drewe's oldest staff member, for almost thirty years she'd overseen the "manor" house at Chateauguay Springs. She was fiercely loyal to Drewe as you might expect not of a mere employee but a blood relation.

Drewe had said dryly *Magdalena thinks she's my mother, I don't have the heart to tell her the last thing I want is a mother!*

Drewe didn't believe in the old, tired tyranny of family life. At Chateauguay Springs there was a newer kind of "family" to which you didn't belong by blind biological chance.

I believed this, too. I believed most things my aunt Drewe told me even those things I had reason to think were untrue.

Magdalena's hand on my shoulder was intimate, comforting. A fleshy wedge of a hand. Never in the several years I'd known my aunt's housekeeper at a little distance, had she touched me in such a way; never would there have been such an occasion.

For years Magdalena had looked younger than her age, now, in her late sixties, in this upheaval in her ordinarily routine life, her face was waxen, raddled, her eyes bloodshot and ringed in fatigue. She was a stout soft-bodied woman of about five feet two with a large sloping bosom, a hopeful manner. When she'd called me the previous evening to tell me that Drewe's Jeep had been pulled out of the Shale River, Magdalena had interpreted this to mean that Drewe must not have been in the Jeep when it had gone into the river since her body hadn't been found with it.

"She's alive. I feel it. I feel *her.* Every minute day or night I'm near a phone, I think that, as soon as she can, Drewe will call me."

So many of us, who loved Drewe, imagining that, if Drewe could get to a phone, she would call *us!*

I was touched that Magdalena had taken pains to look attractive this morning, despite her obvious exhaustion. She wore a light, lavender trench coat, her silvery-gray hair had been fastened into a neat, tight coil at the nape of her neck. She'd powdered her unnaturally pale, creased face. She smiled, she was being brave. Magdalena had become one of that vast army of older women invisible to most eyes even as I was still, at nineteen, one of those younger women at whom people glance with interest, especially men, even if, repelled by something hostile and unyielding in the set of my "sensual" mouth, they look quickly away.

In the wheelchair I was being pushed into, and through, the large slow-revolving automatic door at the rear of the hospital, emerging now suddenly in chilly sunshine. At once I knew that something was wrong. I saw the long black gleaming Lincoln sedan at the curb, there was Drewe's driver beside it holding the rear door open for me. I lunged from the wheelchair, desperate to get inside. Voices lifted like cries of predator birds, Magdalena gripped my arm to steady me.

"Hey! Hello! 'Annemarie'—"

" 'Marta,' is it?—'Marta Hildebrand'?"

"—WCLX-TV Channel Six Action News, can you speak to our viewers for just a—"

"—anything about your aunt Drewe Hildebrand's whereabouts?—anything the police haven't released?"

"Any idea who—"

"Any idea why—"

"Marta! Do you think—is Drewe Hildebrand alive, or—"

Magdalena had given me the hat to pull low over my face, she'd warned me that reporters, photographers, TV cameramen were waiting outside the hospital. Somehow they'd learned that the niece of Drewe Hildebrand was to be released from Newburgh General this morning. I had been warned yet somehow I wasn't prepared, not for the strange exultant tone of the voices, the way in which I felt physically threatened by strangers pressing toward me, sudden explosive camera flashes. Drewe's driver Noah Rathke intervened: "Leave her alone. She isn't going to speak to you. She's just out of the hospital for Christ's sake. Get back." Noah helped me into the rear of the car, I half-fell clumsily, panting. Magdalena climbed inside with me. Noah slammed the door shut behind us but the voices persisted:

"Is it 'Marta'? The niece—"

" 'Annemarie Straube'! Did you know Tania Leenaum?"

Suddenly, with no warning, Noah Rathke erupted in fury. This normally reticent stiff-backed man hired by Drewe to replace Sammy Ray Lee was pushing at an aggressive male reporter with the flat of his hand. It was amazing to see, my aunt's driver moving swiftly on long legs like a pair of walking scissors.

"I said, you bastards—*get back.*"

Noah was tall, lanky, whittled-looking with finely cut lips that were rarely shaped into a smile, and a wedge of muscle beneath his lower lip that gave him a combative expression. His skin was slightly coarse, of a texture like sand. His eyes were dark, wary, watchful and evasive. His hair, stiff as a brush, was the wan hue of wood shavings, lifting in two distinct wings from his pained-looking forehead. He was no age I could guess: mid-thirties, late twenties? There was something mysterious about him, withdrawn. In Drewe's presence he was politely reticent, for Drewe liked to tease him, as she teased certain of her employees for whom she obviously felt some attraction, and Noah was easily embarrassed. But sometimes I overheard Noah talking and laughing with Magdalena, when Drewe was nowhere near.

There were shouts outside the car. Something, or someone, fell against the window beside me. Hospital security guards in navy blue uniforms had entered the fracas, trying to separate individuals. Noah's raw voice was distinct, over the shouts and protests of the others. The incident would be broadcast on local TV channels that evening, but I would not see it.

Cursing, Noah slammed into the sedan, shut the door hard, kicked down on the gas pedal. The car leapt forward, reporters leapt out of the way as in a comic TV sequence. "Damn bastards. Vultures." Within minutes Noah was driving us out of Newburgh, turning south on the river road. In the rearview mirror, Noah Rathke's eyes were fierce, aggrieved. ". . . want to steal your soul."

I thought *But I don't have a soul. It was taken from me.*

"Tania Leenaum."

At Chateauguay Springs, anywhere within Drewe Hildebrand's hearing, this name was never spoken.

Tania Leenaum was the young woman who had died of a drug overdose on Drewe's property in August 1998. It had been a malicious question to put to me, if I'd known Tania Leenaum, for of course I had not, I hadn't come to live at Chateauguay Springs until the following year.

"How could I have known her! How could there be any connection between us."

The drug connection, maybe. In the news release it had been stated that I had suffered a drug overdose, inflicted on me by unknown assailants.

"Look, I don't do drugs. I have no 'drug history.' There is no connection between Tania Leenaum and me."

Though I knew the name, I'd been told. Not by Drewe but by others. Tania Leenaum had been young, only twenty, a resident artist at the colony, initially a friend/protégée of Drewe Hildebrand, living in one of the cottages in the woods. Allegedly, they'd had a falling out. Allegedly, Tania Leenaum turned out to be a heroin user, involved with a local dealer; because of Drewe's prominence, her death had been luridly publicized by New York– based tabloid media. FOX News had broadcast a half-hour "exposé" of the artists' colony as a haven of drug users, sexual predators and perverts, anti-American political sentiments, decadent "avant-garde" artists. Tania Leenaum's death had been investigated by both county and state police and no charges were ever brought against Drewe Hildebrand.

At the time, I'd been in eighth grade in Cattaraugus Middle School, hundreds of miles away. I knew nothing of Tania Leenaum, I knew very little of the glamorous woman to whom my mother alluded with such disdain and disapproval.

Rich aunt rich aunt your rich-bitch aunt.

Wouldn't have given a thought to Drewe Hildebrand if my mother had not been obsessed with her.

Somebody's daughter, she has taken. But she won't take mine.

At the hospital, Magdalena had overheard the name "Tania Leenaum" flung at me. She was saying, poor girl! poor pathetic girl! why bring her name up now, as if whatever had happened to Drewe had anything to do with . . .

I knew that Magdalena was protective of Drewe, she would never talk "behind Mrs. Hildebrand's back" as she called it. I'd asked others at Chateauguay Springs about Tania Leenaum but I had never asked Magdalena. From an older staff member I learned that the Leenaum family who lived in a small town in northern Pennsylvania had tried to sue Drewe Hildebrand and the Chauteauguay Springs Foundation for millions of dollars on the grounds of their daughter's "wrongful death" but the lawsuit had been dismissed by a county judge.

The irony was, Drewe hadn't even been in Chateauguay Springs at the time of Tania Leenaum's death, but in London.

Swiftly now we were driving away from Newburgh, on the road above the river. The massive width of the Hudson River looked lava-like, molten. Light reflected on its surface in sullen, broken waves. It was one of those days when you couldn't tell in which direction the river was flowing. Magdalena was leaning forward to speak to Noah in her hurt, incensed voice, as Noah drove without acknowledging her, staring straight ahead, his big-knuckled hands gripping the steering wheel tight. There was a tightness in Noah Rathke, his neck, muscled shoulders, a posture of barely concealed rage. At the hospital, he'd been furious on my account. I thought it had to be on my account. But Noah was upset, Magdalena had told me, because he'd been away from Chateauguay Springs at the time of the abductions, he'd been in Montauk at the easternmost tip of Long Island, at Drewe's instruction. She'd sent him in a minivan to pick up a number of paintings from an artist's studio, for an upcoming exhibit at Chateauguay Springs; Noah had driven out, was staying in Montauk overnight, to return the next day. But when he'd returned to Chateauguay Springs, police officers had set up roadblocks in both driveways, he'd been asked to climb out of the minivan, to identify himself, to answer questions.

As Drewe's driver, Noah was given an apartment over the garage. He seemed content to live alone, a solitary life, not mixing easily with the artists' colony staff. Because Drewe was away so frequently, Noah worked intermittently. But I had no doubt he was well paid.

If Noah had been home on the night of the abductions, he'd have heard screams. He'd have heard a vehicle or vehicles drive up. Maybe, Drewe wouldn't be missing now. Maybe, I wouldn't have been found dazed and deranged huddled beneath a shanty in Shale River Mountain State Park.

I hoped Noah didn't blame himself. I hoped his absence from

Chateauguay Springs on that particular night didn't strike detectives as suspicious.

Magdalena was saying hotly, "Noah is right, those people are vultures! The way they rushed at you, Marta. As if you haven't had enough of a shock. Before I went inside I saw them, I tried to speak to them, 'Can't you have mercy? Please go away.' So they took my picture, every one of them, the TV crew asked to interview *me*. What they hope is for Mrs. Hildebrand to be . . ."—Magdalena paused, faltering—". . . hurt, for the sake of the news. Always the news, 'breaking news,' a raging fire no one can put out, always it has to be fed. It makes me sick to read the newspapers, can't watch TV news, even a decent paper like the *New York Times,* they all seem to be blaming Mrs. Hildebrand for what happened. 'Controversial'— 'provocative'—'inflammatory.' Even the detectives who say they want to help ask such questions, the suspicious way they ask about 'art,' you can see that they blame Mrs. Hildebrand. Oh, God, if only . . ."

I told Magdalena not to blame herself. Never!

"But, if I'd wakened . . ."

Magdalena's shame was she'd slept through what police were calling the "home invasion"—the "abductions." Her room was at the rear of the large house, she was partly deaf in one ear, medicated for high blood pressure and for poor circulation in her legs. Unless Drewe needed her, Magdalena was in bed and asleep most nights by 9:30 P.M.; most mornings, she was up by 6 A.M. Except for Drewe's largest and most lavish parties, Magdalena prepared most of Drewe's meals; she oversaw teams of cleaning women, lawn men, repairmen. She oversaw laundry, dry cleaning, she ordered groceries, she shopped for home supplies. She had nothing directly to do with the administration and maintenance of the artists' colony, Drewe had a director and a small staff to handle this, but she was a liaison between Drewe and Drewe's numerous employees whom Drewe usually hadn't time to know. When Drewe was traveling, Magdalena spoke with her frequently. Magdalena Olenski was her eyes, her heart, her link, Drewe claimed, with the "real" world.

Not the art world, but the other: the "real" world, that could sometimes intimidate Drewe Hildebrand.

Magdalena was shaken, shamed. If Drewe didn't return safely, I guessed that she would never forgive herself. To console her, I fumbled for her hand.

Wanting to tell her *But you can't blame yourself! There is so little evil in you.*

I thought it might be good to have some measure of evil in myself, like antibodies in the blood. The stronger the autoimmune system, the more likely to ward off enemies.

Magdalena had been the one to call police, at about 7 A.M. on the morning of March 30. She had wakened at her usual time unaware of what had happened in another part of the house. She could not have noticed that Drewe's Jeep was missing, that was usually parked in the garage. When she entered the kitchen she would have noticed that the house was quiet, but then the house was usually quiet at that hour, for Drewe rarely came downstairs before noon; her private quarters were on the second floor, a loft-sized office/studio/bedroom with French windows and a deck overlooking the river. If there were houseguests, Drewe's houseguests invariably slept in, having been up talking/partying most of the night. (That night, Drewe had had no houseguests.) So it wasn't until nearly 7 A.M. that Magdalena ventured into the front, more public part of the house, into the long, sparely and elegantly designed living room with its vaulted ceiling, recessed lights, white brick walls and hardwood floor, that more resembled an art gallery than a conventional room. (Drewe's personal art collection was always in flux, she kept few things permanently. What seemed "beautiful" and "profound" to her in one season often didn't seem so in the next. In March, at the time of the abduction, Drewe had had in her living room several large paintings and silk screens, metallic sculptures, several small TVs primed to play artists' DVDs when switched on, and, prominently displayed, her own head eerily replicated in blood, Xenia's *Blood Mask II,* in its freezer-Plexiglas case on a white pedestal.) Magdalena had been stunned to see furniture overturned, art objects on the floor, a coagulated puddle of dark blood that had melted from the clay bust of Drewe Hildebrand's head.

She'd begun screaming: "Mrs. Hildebrand!"

She staggered to the foot of the stairs but hadn't the strength to climb the stairs to the second floor, to my aunt Drewe's suite of rooms. She stumbled to a phone and dialed 911.

Assuming that Drewe was in the house. Possibly injured, but in the house.

(Had Magdalena given a thought to me? I had to think, no.)

It was 7:30 A.M. when Chateauguay County sheriff's deputies arrived, approximately five hours since Drewe, and I, had been taken from the house.

It wasn't until hours later that, led by detectives into the living room/gallery, lighted now by blinding lights, Magdalena saw what had been propped up boldly on the fireplace mantel: a six-inch crucifix made of black plastic and cheaply gleaming metal.

Other objects that had been on the mantel, a nineteenth-century pendulum clock, several blown-glass figures, candles and brass holders, had been knocked to the floor.

The crucifix was a sign, a warning. Drewe Hildebrand's enemies.

Now Magdalena was saying, "If only I hadn't been asleep. If only I'd heard. You and Mrs. Hildebrand must have called for help, there must have been voices, I can't forgive myself, I might have prevented this from happening. I might have saved—"

"Magdalena, no. You might have been badly hurt, yourself."

Magdalena was gripping my hand. No one had touched me with such warmth and spontaneity in some time except Aunt Drewe but sometimes Aunt Drewe's touch had been less than warm, sometimes Aunt Drewe's touch had been hurtful, cruel. I felt a wave of emotion sweep over me, in that moment I loved Magdalena knowing *The wound is as deep and raw in her, as in me.*

In the rearview mirror, Noah Rathke wasn't watching me now. Magdalena and I might have been alone, giving comfort to each other.

Twenty minutes later the car turned off the highway, into a dense pine woods, following a narrow gravel lane beside a sign at the entrance warning

PRIVATE PROPERTY   NO OUTLET

Impaired

━━━━━

I love you Noah. But the eyes were gone from the mirror.

Want to love you.

They'd given me newspapers to read. The pages were carelessly scattered across my bed. I was staring out a window. I was tugging at a window, to open my room to fresh, chill air. Must've kicked off my shoes, pulled off my clothes that stank of the hospital. *The morgue. Where Drewe had touched me calm as death.* The river was slate-colored, shot with light. Glittering blades of light that cut my eyeballs like razors. At the window lapsing into a dream, an open-eyed dream, it was the poison in my brain, I'd come to love.

Something terrible had happened, I could not remember.

Always it was a surprise, the river. You felt it in your sleep and heard it murmuring and querulous in your sleep but still it was a surprise, the width of water, a solid wedge of what's called "water" lethal as molten lead in ceaseless motion. Directly below my window I could see land jutting out in a grassy peninsula, I could make out the shore below, the frothy-choppy surf, a surf that emitted a sound like hissing laughter, it wasn't a shore, still less a beach you could walk along but rock-strewn, a confusion of briars and underbrush.

Fifty feet to the river, a fall to kill.

━━━

Drewe and I had hiked along the cliff above the river, years ago. When I'd been younger, when Drewe had liked me more.

Race you, Marta! Run!

Her voice was in the room, playful and taunting. But I knew better than to turn, to look for her.

To break out of the small soul Drewe said grand vistas are required. Drewe had provided grand vistas, Drewe had provided so much it wasn't possible to think she might be gone.

Drewe was dead, I had no doubt. I'd told no one this.

But how can you know? You, who'd been abducted, too. Fed poison and a filthy canvas pulled over my head, to suffocate.

Downstairs Mr. Heller was waiting to speak with me. Mr. Heller who was Drewe's director of the arts colony. Magdalena had said so far as she knew, our lives would continue "like normal"—that is, "as close to normal as we can be"—for the present time. Drewe would return to us, we had to think so. And if Drewe didn't return, there was the Chateauguay Springs Foundation, directed by Marcus Heller.

A giant tree can be devastated at its top, struck by lightning or shattered by wind. Still, the tree can survive. The tree's trunk, its myriad powerful roots sunk deep in the soil, to the approximate depth of the tree's height. We had to think so.

Detectives would want to speak with me, too. Now that I was discharged from the hospital. Presumed to be "well."

The sky was like dirty canvas, slow-collapsing into the horizon. In Newburgh it had been sunny, blinding. Now mist was rising from the river like twilight. Someone was waiting to speak with me, already I was forgetting. I wasn't in love with Noah Rathke, that was ridiculous.

My shame had been, that my aunt's driver would see me in that wheelchair. That was why I'd been so upset. My punishment would be losing the strength in my legs, when I'd tried to stand I would fall to the pavement and Noah would leap forward shocked and pitying, to help me. I'd been ashamed, and I'd been frightened, but then I was disappointed, I think. For it could not be said of me *The niece? Crippled girl, brain damage? Couldn't have had anything to do with her aunt's death.*

Someone had left a window open in my room. I was sweaty, and I was shivering. I went into the large drafty bathroom that opened off my bedroom, my fingers fumbled opening a bottle of oxycodone tablets the neurologist had prescribed for me.

Pain relief. Once every four hours as required.

A dull haze of pain enveloped my head. I seemed to be walking with a limp favoring my right leg. My face was sore as if I'd been punched. My eyes looked underwater. I was ashamed, Noah Rathke had seen. Maybe this body wasn't mine, it was a body I'd been injected into, while my brain was shut off.

"I don't know. I couldn't see their faces. I couldn't hear their voices. I don't remember."

I remembered his name: Armsted. The man who'd reminded me of my father. Who'd watched me closely as I spoke. My clumsy words, evasive eyes.

Couldn't remember now: had I taken one of the coarse white pain tablets since returning home? Maybe it's wrong to deaden pain, you can't then know how much pain you are meant to feel.

"She's here, somewhere. Has to be."

In the car, as Noah drove us through the woods on the private, narrow lane, Magdalena gripped my hand, I could hear her breathing quickly in a kind of excited dread.

". . . can't believe she won't be waiting for us. Oh God."

Magdalena spoke these words. I think.

Lovely, dark and deep is a line of poetry. "Stopping by Woods" I'd memorized at the school in Woodstock where Drewe had sent me, my heart was broken to be sent away so soon. But the woods at Chateauguay Springs hadn't seemed lovely to me after nine days away, too dense and confused, too many trees, a surprising number split and broken, part-fallen, dying, dead. Acres of trees yet not uniformly dark, riddled and splotched with light as the brain is perforated with light after injury. And the woods isn't deep, only endless. If you turn in a circle. Lost.

My aunt's lover Virgil West had quoted the French philosopher Pascal: *Not that these things are eternal and infinite but that the finite things are repeated infinitely.*

He'd been my aunt's lover not mine. Yet he'd kissed my mouth, a wet desperate kiss. I had to think hard to recall it had not been in the morgue, that kiss. I hadn't been able to push him away, the kiss came so swiftly.

In the ER at Newburgh my body had been examined. The limp female body, pried open between the legs to discover if I'd been "sexually assaulted" and I had not.

When I reentered my room I was surprised to see newspaper pages blowing across the floor. Someone had left a window open, the air was cold and damp as spit. I squatted above the pages, shivering.

Magdalena had given me the newspapers she'd accumulated during my absence but my eyes were too jumpy to read anything smaller than headlines.

POLICE SEARCH FOR ABDUCTED CHATEAUGUAY SPRINGS WOMAN, 47
Controversial Arts Patron Missing Since March 29

POLICE SEARCH CONTINUES FOR UPSTATE ARTS PATRON
Drewe Hildebrand, 47, Abducted from Estate

SUSPECTS QUESTIONED BY POLICE IN HILDEBRAND ABDUCTION
"Provocative" Arts Patron Received Death Threats
No Ransom Demand, Authorities Say

On the front page of the *New York Times* Metro section:

HUDSON VALLEY ARTS PATRON ABDUCTED, MISSING 8 DAYS
Police Question Upstate "Militant Christians"
Arrests Imminent, Police Say

In the accompanying photographs "arts patron" Drewe Hildebrand appeared remote, glacially beautiful, sometimes smiling, sometimes without expression, half her face hidden by a pair of dark glasses. Her hair was pale blond, or brunette; her face was smooth and un-lined, or beginning just perceptibly to age; she wore casual clothes, or formal clothes; she might have been an athletic young woman in her twenties, or a thicker-bodied woman well into middle age.

In only one of the papers did I discover an article about myself:

ABDUCTED NIECE OF ARTS PATRON
FOUND BY HIKERS
19-YEAR-OLD WOMAN HOSPITALIZED
IN NEWBURGH
Victim Assaulted, Forced to Ingest Drug

I stared at the accompanying photograph of someone called *Marta Hildebrand.* This wasn't me! Someone had given the newspaper a photograph of a girl with a faint, naive smile, worried eyes, heavy dark eyebrows and untidy windblown dark hair. She was wearing bib overalls and a T-shirt, her arms were crossed tightly beneath her breasts as if she were cold, or uneasy. The picture must have been taken at Chateauguay Springs on the occasion of an exhibit opening in the big barn; you could see that it had been cropped, a shadowy presence to the girl's right had been cut away. I wondered who had supplied the newspaper with this erroneous photograph: Magdalena? (But Magdalena wouldn't have made such a mistake.) It must have been someone in the office. I was certain, this girl wasn't me!

But Marta, of course that's you. Those eyes.

Not me! Nothing like me.

"Marta?"—someone was knocking on the door of my room. I'd lapsed into a trance squatting above the newspapers. The strong muscles of my things ached and throbbed with the strain. "Are you in there, Marta?" It was Magdalena, her voice worried. Like a brattish twelve-year-old I called back, "No! No one's here." Clumsily I gathered up the newspapers, crumpled them and tossed them into a wastebasket. My arms and legs felt heavy as if I was struggling in an element denser than air. Damn Magdalena she'd been waiting for me to come downstairs, Mr. Heller was waiting to see me, Marcus Heller wanting to commiserate with me, stricken by the terrible thing that had happened that no one could comprehend, a devastating explosion that hadn't yet come to an end, and might have no end. I knew that Marcus Heller would stare into my eyes wanting to know if I knew, what did I know, was Drewe living, was Drewe not-living, where was Drewe? *I don't know. I've told you. I've told the detectives. I don't know and what I might know, I can't remember.*

Hearing my muffled voice, probably not hearing my words, Magdalena opened the door hesitantly. I felt a stab of sympathy for her, it was Magdalena who'd had to deal with this household in an upheaval, Magdalena who wasn't young, whose loyalty to Drewe, and love for Drewe, were so fierce. "Marta, are you all right? Mr. Heller is wondering if . . ."

I shook my head no. Like a dog shaking its head. No no!

". . . then, you should have something to eat, then maybe lie down, this is your first day out of the hospital and you shouldn't strain yourself. The detectives will call us if there is any news . . ."

Hurriedly I'd been pulling on clothes, kicked my feet into shoes. I hadn't known how desperate I was to get out of this room, out of the house. Nine days since I'd been outdoors. Nine days since I'd hiked along the cliff above the river, at the edge of the woods. Nine days, I hadn't been able to breathe.

I told Magdalena no, mumbled I was going outside. I was a clumsy girl with "impaired" social skills, my sexuality was "impaired" like an organ that hasn't fully matured. I wore shapeless shirts, I wore bib overalls loose as tents. My hair was matted and frayed from the underbrush, in the hospital it had come out in clumps, or maybe I'd been pulling at hairs, to punish. Magdalena stared at me in alarm. If this woman loved me, I didn't want this woman to love me, or any woman, or anyone. I tried to push past her, not so gently I pushed away her arms that would have caught me in an embrace.

"Marta, where are you going? You're not well, Marta please!"

Downstairs, by the back stairs. Avoiding the man who wanted to speak with me. Run, run! I was favoring my right leg. I was out of breath almost immediately. Armsted was the detective's name: he had seen something in my face. He'd heard something in my faltering voice. *Don't know! Don't remember! I am impaired.*

The back stairs, a back door opening off the kitchen. I hadn't seen the living room since returning home from Newburgh. Hadn't seen the room where Drewe had been attacked, overcome; where I'd been attacked, overcome. I hadn't seen what I knew to be an enormous bloodstain on the hardwood floor and soaked along the edge of a stone-colored Moroccan carpet, from the melted *Blood Mask II.* I hadn't see this, why should I see this?—Magdalena was arranging for a cleaning service to remove the bloodstain, to repair damage in the living room that could be repaired, what couldn't be cleaned or repaired would be thrown out, now the police had taken away what they needed.

I ran stumbling from the house not looking back. Run, run! And in the wind, my hair whipping in the wind, tears blown from my eyes like fugitive drops of rain out of nowhere. On the trail above the river, the wind off the river, steel-colored water beneath a sky that looked like thunder, freezing-cold though it's April, I wasn't dressed for the cold, I was Drewe's niece of whom it was said out of earshot a sweet girl sometimes but unpredictable, impulsive, has she ever been diagnosed as autistic, some sort of neurological impairment but out of earshot, we didn't hear, Drewe scorned to hear. I would run along the overgrown path above the river until my strength gave out. Until someone came for me, where I'd fallen. It's a fifty-foot fall to the river, a kill of a fall, except it's rocks you would fall into, rocks and underbrush with leafless limbs like spikes, you wouldn't hit the water, not even the frothy surf. Drewe said it's a single moment, our entwined lives are a single moment, a match flame flaring up, burning and then it's extinguished. Drewe said *We can't be frightened of what's inevitable—can we?*

II

Pure, Empty

Marta is my niece. Marta is living here now."

Proudly Drewe introduced me to the many strangers who were her friends, who smiled at me, peered at me, curious. It was Drewe's style not to explain why I was living now at Chateauguay Springs, where I was from, what had happened to my parents, even how precisely we were related.

"Marta and I look alike, I think. Around the eyes. In the eyes. I think we do, yes."

Drewe spoke with such extravagant enthusiasm, touching my cheek, stroking my hair (at times, plaited like hers to fall like a heavy hemp rope between my shoulder blades), though what she said wasn't true, no one would have dared object. Even the most belligerent of Drewe's artist-friends wouldn't have said *You and that girl look nothing alike. Especially in the eyes.*

"Are you an artist, Marta?"

"Will you be going to school here?"

"What will you be studying in school?"

"Marta, don't move: keep that pose."

A camera flash. Teeth bared in a smile. "Marta" has become someone's property: a photograph.

* * *

So self-conscious! The more you are stared at, the less your eyes see, as in a blinding light. I had not stammered in Cattaraugus even during the terrible long months of my father's arrest, indictment, trial, conviction, but I stammered at Chateauguay Springs as Drewe looked on. My face burned with a painful sort of pleasure as if, before a crowd of staring spectators, my face had been slapped by the tall beautiful shining-faced woman who was my aunt Drewe Hildebrand.

Especially in the eyes. Marta and me.

It was a time, that first summer at Chateauguay Springs, when I was so happy waking in the morning in the large high-ceilinged light-filled room overlooking the river that my soul floated like cottony milkweed seed borne by the wind. So happy my skin was always slightly feverish and my heart beat at a quickened pace as when I'd been hiking along the cliff or running in the fresh damp air the muscles of my legs thrumming with strength. So happy as Drewe's newest and youngest "staff person" I never cried except in my sleep, and then only in those dreams in which there was someone who wasn't me in some place I'd never been and could not recognize. This first summer in 1999 when I was fifteen years old, when I never gave a thought to the woodframe house with the synthetic-white aluminium siding that glared in twilight, my parents' house in Cattaraugus that had been sold, nor did I think of the prison at Oriskany I had never visited and would never visit. Yet there was my aunt crouched beside my bed in the night her hair unplaited, loose and disheveled over her shoulders, Drewe breathing quickly, a film of perspiration on her face that loomed large above me as a medallion-face, her eyes luminous in light reflected from the window, waxing and waning light as clouds were blown across the face of the battered-looking half-moon above the river, as by day Drewe's touch on my shoulder, my forearm, my wrist was likely to be roughly affectionate, a touch that was a claim, a rejoinder, so unexpectedly by night Drewe's touch was hesitant, as if something about me as I lay in bed, in a tangle of bedsheets and my frizz-hair splotched across the pillow, something about my startled eyes and fevered skin alarmed her, Drewe was asking if I'd cried out in my sleep? if I'd been crying in my sleep? and I tried to sit up drawing the sheet around me, tried to tell my aunt no, of course not, why would I be crying, I never cried and why would I be crying when there was nothing to cry about, when I was so happy here at Chateauguay Springs, but my words were stammered and indistinct, a childish terror must have shone in my eyes. Drewe said, "Marta, I know, I know what it is, this kind of happiness, so raw," holding me in her arms that were surprisingly strong, tight-muscled though lean, stroking my hair, the back of my head, urging me to hide my warm face against her neck, to breathe in the warmth and comfort of her body, "I know, dear Marta, I am the only one who knows."

This was a time, too, when Drewe was becoming disenchanted with her New York City life. I was made aware of my aunt's reputation in art circles by articles, reviews, interviews that appeared in glossy art publications as well as in the *New York Times, New York,* the *New Yorker.* Drewe owned the Hildebrand Gallery on Prince Street, one of the premiere galleries in SoHo, she'd inherited the gallery and some of its artists from her husband, but other, younger and more controversial artists Drewe had acquired in the 1990s by the force of her aggressive personality and the sums of money she was able to advance, to invest in individuals in whom she had "faith"—"conviction." She owned properties in SoHo, she owned a beautiful restored brownstone on Perry Street, she spent much of her time in the city where there were, she said, too many people she'd known too long, and too intimately. Within a year she would sell the brownstone and buy a smaller place, a condominium in the East 50s, on the East River, she would spend more time in the country, as she called it, at Chateauguay Springs. She would have to be merciless, she said, casting off "dead weight"—"too much history." Among her wide range of acquaintances were individuals of reputation whose lives had begun to disintegrate, they had drug problems, career problems, marital/divorce problems, financial problems, health problems, sexual problems, Drewe would cease to see them: "D'you know what 'debridement' is, Marta? A medical term meaning to remove gangrenous flesh, so the healthy flesh can live." Though I wasn't meant to know this, for Drewe never spoke to me in specific, personal terms, she was terminating a lengthy affair with a prominent artist with whom she was also involved professionally, a man whom she'd met on April Fool's Day 1987, at a memorial service for Andy Warhol.

Andy Warhol! Even in Cattaraugus, at the far western edge of New York State, some of us had heard of Andy Warhol. As a beautiful and adventurous young woman in New York City in the mid-1970s, Drewe had become acquainted with Warhol, at a distance; she'd been a participant in several films made under Warhol's direction; she'd been included in the promiscuous, ever-shifting, cocaine-suffused Warhol entourage of the 1970s and 1980s, ending abruptly with Warhol's death in 1987. Drewe spoke of Warhol with clinical detachment yet a kind of nostalgia: "He was an utterly empty man, a vacant space. One of those large vacant lofts where your voice and footsteps echo. There can be greatness in such emptiness, I think. It was the spiritual emptiness of that era. In Andy, a kind of martyrdom. Andy's eyes were dead behind his smoked schoolboy glasses, his oversized wig was glued to his bald scalp, his breath smelled like ether. It's fitting that Andy died in his sleep, since he lived in his sleep."

I had never heard my aunt speak in such a way. I'd never heard anyone speak in such a way. I felt a curious thrill. *This is how you might be. This is possible!*

In her private art collection Drewe had a number of Warhol's silk screens of what looked like crude comic strip characters in smudged colors, reproductions of painted crosses strangely stitched together like flaps of skin, reproductions of skulls, Chairman Mao, Marilyn Monroe, Andy Warhol himself as "The Shadow" and Greta Garbo as "The Star." There were silk screens from the series *Endangered Species*: an African elephant, a bald eagle, a bighorn ram. There was Warhol himself as Jesus in *Last Supper* with the blank look of a man longing for crucifixion, or for something, a way of bringing emptiness to an end.

These silk screens Drewe displayed on the pristine white walls of her living room. One of them, crudely smudged, sleazily erotic in the way of a lurid comic book, was of a girl with long straight hair falling below her breasts, a thin girl with shadowed, staring eyes, knobby wrists and ankles, wearing just a lopsided black T-shirt. The girl's face and hair were over-exposed, bleached-out, you could vaguely see her features. "Aunt Drewe, is that you? *You?*"

Drewe laughed, enigmatically.

"You were so young . . ."

"*You* are so young."

I understood that, being shown Drewe's Warhol collection, I was meant to respond. I was meant to say something, but I didn't know what to say. What I saw was flat, banal in execution, like comic strip drawings, or cartoons. I hadn't the vocabulary or the poise to object *Isn't art meant to be beautiful? If art is uglier than life, why would anyone want to look at it? Why would anyone want to create it?*

Drewe had been watching me closely, now suddenly she took hold of my shoulders and kissed me, a hard wet kiss at the edge of my mouth.

"You will help me, Marta! You, with your pure, empty soul."

No Outlet

PRIVATE PROPERTY NO OUTLET was the warning.

Chateauguay Springs (the estate, the artists' colony) was hidden from the road by acres of pine trees. Driving south from Newburgh in the direction of West Point, veering away from the Hudson River, about midway you would pass a densely wooded property posted at intervals NO HUNTING NO TRESPASSING PRIVATE PROPERTY. At the front entrance was a small sign CHATEAUGUAY SPRINGS EST. 1964. PRIVATE. A quarter-mile farther, nearly hidden from the highway, was a narrow driveway marked PRIVATE PROPERTY NO OUTLET. This was the direct route to Drewe's residence bypassing the art colony's administration building and the artists' cottages scattered through acres of woods and linked to one another by woodchip trails.

Always it was a shock to emerge from the speckled light of the pine woods into the open air, after a turn in the lane to see the large looming English Tudor house on a grassy knoll overlooking the river. I thought *It must be abandoned, no one can be living there.*

Even after I was living in the house myself. Even after Drewe had taken me into her home.

The Hildebrand house, as it was called in the New York State Historical Register, was the largest private house I'd ever seen close up, let alone entered. (Though, compared to other Hudson Valley houses of its era, built by wealthy New Yorkers in imitation of eighteenth- and nineteenth-century European estates, the Hildebrand house wasn't one of the largest or most luxurious. This fact I would learn from Drewe herself.) My first impression was of its size and beauty and the authority of its beauty which was intimidating to me, to whom all beauty carried authority, and the threat of authority. Only later, after I'd been living at Chateauguay Springs for some time, would I see that the house had become shabby, in need of repair: sections of the slate roof were discolored, some of the timbering had begun to rot. The buff-colored stucco was streaked in places as if with rust-tears. In the latticed windows on the third, closed-off floor, several panes were cracked. There were cracks in the panes of a greenhouse attached to the house. The grounds close about the house were usually kept mowed and free of visible weeds but elsewhere tall grasses grew like swirling broken waves, there was storm debris at the edge of the woods, piles of dead leaves. Outside my bedroom window in a clogged rain gutter young green saplings grew to a height of at least ten inches, straight as rulers.

Drewe despaired of the house, the cost of its upkeep, its "ridiculous prestige" that confirmed a kind of cachet upon the art colony, and the art created at the colony, but drained the Foundation's financial resources. Drewe said, "The 'manor house' is an artifact of a civilization in ruins. But I must live here."

It was her husband's wish, Drewe believed. He'd been an idealist who'd inherited money, and Chateauguay Springs, which he'd established as a retreat for artists in 1964, in the throes of a countercultural repugnance for U.S. military aggression abroad and repression at home. Drewe was fiercely attached to the art colony, if not to the house, for which she felt commingled pride and exasperation; she was convinced that local contractors and repairmen were exploiting her as a "rich, stupid" widow from the city, she couldn't bear dealing with them in person but delegated authority to her housekeeper Magdalena Olenski to see what needed to be done and to arrange for it to be done without Drewe's involvement. Plumbers, electricians, painters, carpenters, roofers, masons, lawn crew, snow removal: "Magdalena, don't tell me! Here's my checkbook! I've signed the checks, you can fill in the rest." If Magdalena tried to appeal to her, Drewe pressed her hands over her ears and stomped out of the room.

"I know, I'm irresponsible. But I can't bear it."

A few years before she brought me to live with her, Drewe had undertaken a major renovation of part of the old house: she'd had interior walls knocked down, windows and skylights added, a loft-sized space created for her living room/gallery and a similarly large space converted into a studio-bedroom for herself on the second floor. She'd spent hundreds of thousands of dollars, she said, of her own money (not Foundation money, kept in a separate account) without seeing a single bill or invoice, or filling out a check apart from signing her name with her distinctive flourish. "Magdalena, I trust you with my life. You won't take advantage of me, will you?"

Magdalena blushed. She seemed of another species beside tall poised laughing Drewe Hildebrand who stooped impulsively to hug Magdalena.

It was Drewe's way to hug, impulsively. She rarely kissed any of us but she hugged us often, quick and hard and stepping back from us in the same gesture.

By *us* I mean Drewe's staff of employees, "assistants." With her friends from New York, her professional associates in the art world, her legal and financial advisors (for certainly Drewe wasn't naive as she pretended, in money matters she put her faith in professionals), and the numerous men (and sometimes women) with whom she was involved, Drewe behaved with more discretion.

Her problem was, Drewe said, caressing the nape of my neck as she spoke in her throaty, caressing voice, she liked to *touch*; yet not to *be touched*.

If you turned into the main entrance at Chateauguay Springs, and drove for about a quarter-mile through the woods, when you came to a clearing you would see, straight ahead, the Big Barn: an enormous stone and stucco barn that had been converted into an administrative building with a showcase gallery, a dining hall, a studio for resident artists at the rear. Brochures for the art colony always featured photographs of the Big Barn, that held exhibits through the year, by both established and lesser-known artists. In the art world, an exhibit at Chateauguay Springs was very nearly equivalent to an exhibit at a premiere gallery in New York City, especially since Drewe Hildebrand oversaw the exhibits.

The resident artists lived in cottages, as they were called: log cabins, sparely furnished, winterized, built at a small distance from one another in the woods. They had fireplaces, or wood-burning stoves; they had minimal kitchen facilities. Most of the time there were fifteen artists-in-residence for periods as brief as four weeks and for as long as twelve months. So few positions, for which hundreds of young and not-young artists competed! Artists who were chosen were provided room and board, the community of Chateauguay Springs and the patronage of Drewe Hildebrand, or its possibility;

they were given grants of about $1,000 a month. Drewe disguised her powerful role behind a panel of professional art-critic judges, but she chose the winning artists herself.

Chateauguay Springs was a mission, Drewe said. Conrad Hildebrand's mission and now her own. "To help others create art, if I can't myself."

When she'd run away to New York City as a girl of seventeen, Drewe had hoped to be an artist, a painter. Within a few years, as Drewe ruefully recounted it, she'd had to change her plans.

"Why did you give up, Aunt Drewe?"

This was a clumsy question. As soon as I asked, I wished I'd said *Why did you stop?*

But Drewe wasn't annoyed, or hurt. She sighed, she ran both hands through her lush, uncombed hair (now an iridescent strawberry blond) that fell partway down her back. "Oh, Marta. 'Why' is such a big word, let's just say 'how': I gave up when life intervened."

I thought of the wan, painfully thin girl with the long straight hair and over-exposed features in the Warhol silk screen hanging on a wall of Drewe's living room.

"Wasted"—"strung-out"—" junkie."

Was this so? Had Drewe been involved with drugs at that time, as a young woman? I knew that she'd been involved with a sequence of lovers, one of whom, older than Drewe by twenty years, she'd married.

In her mid-forties, no longer young, Drewe was still adventurous, if not reckless: she drank, she smoked pot, she may well have done drugs in the company of her friends, in her life apart from me. None of this was a secret exactly, though Drewe would not have confided in me.

I was jealous of her, I think. My aunt whom I knew now and my girl-aunt living in an era before my birth.

At Chateauguay Springs all illegal drugs—"controlled substances"—were forbidden. Over the years, raids by the Chateauguay County Sheriff's Department had occurred; there'd been arrests, "scandalous" publicity. (And a young woman had died, of a drug overdose. But no one who'd been at Chateauguay Springs at the time wished now to speak of it.) Drewe admonished all incoming residents to abide by the law but in the privacy of their cottages, even in the Big Barn when the administrative offices were close, individuals smoked pot, got high. Of course they drank, they partied. They were artists, temperamentally inclined to rebellion, and to excess.

I was a minor, I wasn't included. I wasn't the type of girl who might have been invited to join them.

Her? That's the girl who lives with Drewe.

Martha, Drewe's niece. Or—Marta.

Mostly I was an invisible girl. In the summer I was a "summer intern" (among college-age girls, aspiring artists) and the rest of the year I was an "assistant" (Drewe's staff of assistants was ever-shifting, usually about twelve individuals who took orders from both Marcus Heller and Drewe). I was socially awkward, stricken with shyness (so much worse, since leaving Cattaraugus, I couldn't understand why), it came to be thought (not unkindly) that there was "something wrong" with me (family background, neurological, psychological, and maybe I was "dyslexic" too). I became tongue-tied when people spoke to me in the hearty ebullient way of certain adults, women especially, there were many of these in the camp-setting of Chateauguay Springs, or I smiled too quickly, nervously. My aunt gave me funky, funny, glamorous clothes to wear purchased at her favorite TriBeCa shops, some of the clothes were castoffs of hers, or exact replicas of hers, but most of the time I wore shapeless khakis or jeans, oversized T-shirts, sweatshirts embossed with the Chateauguay Springs logo of a clenched fist above the words ART POWER! Stubbornly I wore baseball caps so that I could pull the rim down over my eyes, I wore sun-visor hats to tamp down my bushy hair the color of faded leaves. I was almost as tall as Drewe Hildebrand— who was five feet nine, with a regal posture—but I slouched self-consciously, folded my arms across my breasts, my female body seemed irksome to me as a large clumsy dog, a sheepdog maybe, that accompanied me everywhere, tripping me. Drewe loved to tease me in the presence of others, I blushed so easily. Especially around men I became edgy, anxious, if I saw that the men were aware of me, looking at me too deliberately, as if I might matter: as if I existed! Now and then a man tried to speak with me beyond what the situation required, smiled at me, eased in front of a door to block my exit even as he smiled, called me *sweetheart, honey.* But of course I was allowed to slip away if I seemed genuinely frightened, such flirtations were only casual, playful, I was Drewe Hildebrand's niece.

A few days after I'd come to live with her, Drewe took me to lunch in the dining hall in the Big Barn, introduced me to dozens of people, took me through the artists' studios (skylights, streaming sun, a startling cacophony of rock music), singling out some of the art with her excited praise, she strolled with me into the woods to drop by a few of the artists' cabins, afterward saying, "Now Marta! If anyone here bothers you, male or female, if there are 'unwanted advances,' tell me immediately. A place like this, a good deal of sexual activity occurs, it's only natural, but you're young, you might not understand. You don't seem to realize that you're an attractive girl, not pretty perhaps but—who gives a damn for 'pretty'?—a very sensual—sexual—girl. Of course it's wholly unconscious in you, you're only fifteen, but other people, you can bet most men, can pick up instinctively on what's unconscious, I've already seen some of them staring at you, and it isn't the way they stare at *me*. At least, not any longer."

Drewe laughed, the look in my face. I wanted to hide my face in my hands but I knew that, if I did, Drewe would pluck my hands away.

"My family! My needy children."

Drewe loved her resident artists, sometimes she became emotional speaking of them: former residents who'd remained close friends, artists who were represented by the Hildebrand Gallery, new arrivals to Chateauguay Springs from as far away as New Mexico, Vancouver, Alaska. Though there were usually a few older, more established artists in residence, most were young, at the outset of careers, struggling and ambitious. They were painters, sculptors, photographers, video artists, "conceptual" artists. There were audio-artists who worked in sound, there were light-artists who worked with lights. There were innovative potters, weavers. All artists at prestigious Chateauguay Springs were judged to be "uniquely talented," and they were obviously highly competitive, or they wouldn't have been chosen by Drewe Hildebrand. Yet still they were edgy, uneasy. For Drewe clearly favored some of these artists over the others, once she came to know them; some works of art Drewe singled out for extravagant praise, but not others; a few artists invariably proved disappointing, or in Drewe's lethal judgment, "boring."

As Drewe said, crinkling her nose, "But it's so boring, being around needy people. You can't breathe."

Working in the Big Barn office, I came into frequent contact with resident artists, especially those with problems, complaints, worries but after the first exhausting summer I gave up trying to learn most of their names, or to associate names with faces, and with their work. As a senior staff member said *They come and go, Marta. We aren't responsible.*

Still, they persevered! Some of them. Those whom Drewe had initially praised, if/when Drewe lost interest in them, hadn't followed through on her lavish if vague plans to introduce them to New York art-world people, sign them on at the Hildebrand Gallery, often in desperation approached me: to ask, as if innocently, how Drewe was?—was Drewe "distracted"?—"busy"? I saw the anxiety brimming in their eyes, I was stricken with embarrassment yet a kind of elation, for Drewe would never withdraw her interest in *me:* I was her niece.

"Marta."

I looked up, a bewhiskered youngish man whose first name was Derrick, from Galveston, Texas, a "light sculptor" who in fact my aunt had several times taken to New York with her to gallery openings, parties, was approaching me, as I sorted mail one morning in the office, and my heart clenched, though Drewe never confided in me about such private matters, I knew before Derrick spoke in an elliptical, guarded, resentful way, that he wanted to ask about Drewe, and so he did, and I fumbled the mail, dropped envelopes onto the floor, onto my feet in waterstained sneakers, though it was morning

I could smell beer on the man's breath, I could feel the fury quivering in his muscular forearms, I stammered I didn't know, didn't know my aunt's schedule, yes I thought she was in New York most of this week, yes I'd tell her "Derrick" hoped she would return his cell phone calls which evidently she had not been returning, I felt my face burn in a kind of shared shame unable to utter what was obviously true *Once Drewe Hildebrand loses interest in you, it's over.*

Before Your Time

Months, years at Chateauguay Springs. I was fifteen when I arrived, I was nineteen when it ended. There is no way to compute how four years could seem like so much longer, or no time at all.

Exhausting. Yet I was filled with elation. In my aunt's presence you were drained of your strength but made happy, a kind of radiance flowed from Drewe to you.

I asked about the girl-who'd-died-of-an-overdose whose name was Tania Leenaum. Not Magdalena who'd have been offended at such a question but my staff supervisor who was accustomed to speaking frankly with me except she glanced up at me startled and frowning and said, "Her? How'd you hear about her? She was before your time."

Daughter

▬

V*irgil West.*

The name was a near-illegible scrawl in a corner of a massive canvas on a wall in Drewe's living room/gallery. In fact you would have to know the artist's name before you could decipher it amid swirls and clots of earth-colored paint.

Drewe said, "Exactly like the artist! To take no care for his own name. Probably he hadn't remembered to sign the canvas, his dealer had to remind him."

When Drewe spoke of Virgil West, her voice quivered and there was an involuntary tensing in her jaws. She'd known the painter for years, there was a kind of history between them though West was something of a recluse, he loathed the New York art world.

I felt a stab of jealousy for all that my aunt knew, that I would never know of her.

The painting in my aunt's house was titled *Earthflesh 1989,* one in a series by the artist. On a trip to New York City, Drewe had taken me to the Whitney Museum where we'd seen two other canvases in the series, both like and unlike the one Drewe owned. As other paintings were rotated onto and off Drewe's high white walls, to be placed elsewhere at Chateauguay Springs, or returned to the

Hildebrand Gallery in New York to be offered for sale, *Earthflesh 1989* remained untouched.

(Like the Warhol silk screen of the waif-like young girl with her features partly erased, that Drewe invariably showed to visitors, to see if they recognized the model.)

Of the paintings on my aunt's wall it was *Earthflesh 1989* that seemed to me the most powerful. I didn't know much about art, of course my eye was untrained, though at school (Drewe was sending me to the Woodstock Academy, sixty miles away) I was taking a "studio" course in art, but *Earthflesh 1989* exerted a spell over me: crude, unframed, with patches of bare, soiled-looking canvas, it must have measured six feet by eight. Nude figures, female, male, seemed to be emerging out of the earth, or fading into it, fleshy and solid, as if blood pulsed warmly beneath the surface of the thick-textured paint. Most of Drewe's art collection exuded a cool, minimal, faintly jeering aura as if mocking you for leaning close and taking it seriously, but *Earthflesh 1989* was raw, sincere. You could say that it was ugly as physical beings are ugly up close, or you could say that it was beautiful as physical beings are beautiful up close.

Excitedly Drewe told visitors, "Virgil West! He's a magician of the earth. A kind of shaman. He's crude, primitive. Where most artists imagine themselves geniuses, who'd be damned lucky to be blessed with just a little talent, Virgil West is a genius utterly unaware of his worth. His paintings are ambitious, yet the man has no ambition in his life. His 'career' just grows and proliferates like a weed he can't be bothered to tend. I've tried to convince him, as his only friend who isn't out to exploit him, that, if he respects his own art, he must be more conscious of its placement in the world."

Drewe spoke vehemently as if Virgil West were in the room with her, stubbornly needing to be convinced. She spoke in the way of one who has been carrying on a one-sided quarrel for some time.

Once, a visitor inquired mildly if Virgil West was represented by the Hildebrand Gallery and Drewe said sharply, "No. He is not. That has nothing to do with it. Virgil West has a dealer to whom he remains 'loyal' out of indifference, or ignorance. You'd think the man had a private income, he's so oblivious of money."

Virgil West. The name was exotic to me, magical.

" 'Tania,' eh? Is it?"

Quickly Drewe interceded. " 'Marta,' Virgil. My niece's name is 'Marta.' "

Virgil West loomed over me, his smile was broad and snaggle-toothed, rudely intimate. He was well over six feet tall and must have weighed 240 pounds. His manner was both slovenly and digni-fied, regal. He said, "Drewe has told me about you, dear. 'The daughter I would wish, if I wished a daughter.' "

Drewe laughed as if Virgil West had said something outlandish, to be immediately dismissed. I saw that she was embarrassed. And I was embarrassed.

(Like a small gem slipped into the palm of my hand. I would open my hand later, in secret. Thrilled, I would contemplate this riddle: my aunt thought of me, an individual so utterly unlike her as she was now or had been at my age, as a *daughter?* The thought left me light-headed, it did not seem possible.)

(And yet: Drewe' s qualification had been *If I wished a daughter.*)

Virgil West and his wife had come to my aunt's house for dinner, it seemed that they had recently moved into a "stone ruin of a house" not far away in Cornwall-on-Hudson. Among the artists-in-residence at Chateauguay Springs there'd been a flurry of excitement for days, that Virgil West was expected, but West had told Drewe that he didn't want to meet anyone, especially not artists, the last thing he wanted was the adulation of the young, he laughed at Drewe's extravagant praise. "Enough, dear! You care too much for the vanities of this world. Art is material, like anything else. Especially my art, it's earth: a kind of excrement."

West laughed, such a stricken look in Drewe's face.

Virgil West was a massive man in his late forties, his head unusually large, his face boiled-looking, swollen pug nose, stained teeth. Immediately he entered Drewe's house, the focus of attention fell onto him, as if a blinding light had been switched on. The air seemed to quake, the hardwood floor quavered beneath him. I watched in fascination as West drank Drewe's Scotch whiskey, oblivious of how it spilled down his fingers, glistened on his stubbled chin. He wore a grimly tweed coat over a grimy sweater, no shirt beneath; grizzled gray hairs sprang at the base of his throat like briars. Stained work trousers, hemp sandals with thick gray wool socks. Like a landslide in motion West sank into a chrome-and-leather designer chair that shuddered beneath his bulk. He sighed, he wheezed. He laughed frequently, and loudly; you wanted to make him laugh, you wanted to see those cruel teeth. He interrupted others, even Drewe. He took no heed of the woman introduced as his wife. I offered him mixed nuts, brie and smoked salmon on small pieces of dark bread he devoured hungrily. He thanked me, he caressed the back of my hand with calloused fingers. "Marta, eh?" Here was the exotic artist, I thought. Here was magic. I was appalled, I was mesmerized. Slovenly dressed, carelessly groomed as a molting bison, yet Virgil West exuded an air of richness, authority. Booming voice, burnished-looking skin. His eyes were a pale, pure blue, brazenly he winked at me.

"Niece, eh? That's so?"

Drewe said, "I told you, Virgil. Yes."

"But you have no living relatives, Drewe. No brothers, no sisters." Now Virgil West leaned over to nudge my aunt's shoulder in the way of an older relative, or a lover of many years, gently chiding.

Drewe said, faltering, "It's—come to light recently, Virgil. Just last year. In fact I do have an older brother. I mean, had . . ."

Drewe was staring at Virgil West, oblivious of me. I realized that she'd fabricated a family history and was fabricating even now.

West laughed, his hand still on Drewe's shoulder, roughly caressing. "No sooner 'come to light' than the long-lost brother has become past tense. What a lethal woman you are, Drewe Hildebrand."

Amazing to see my aunt who was usually so self-assured now uncertain, hesitant. I'd never seen Drewe in the presence of anyone who was her equal, still anyone of Virgil West's stature. She had made herself up elegantly: her now ashy-blond hair was brushed back into a chic chignon, her mouth was a rich dark moist red. Her skin looked poreless as a young girl's skin, there was a kind of electric intensity in her eyes. I saw a pale vein, unless it was a near-invisible thread of a scar, at her left temple, disappearing into her hairline. Drewe wore silky black trousers, wedge-heeled shoes that looked as if they'd been carved out of a hard black wood. From one of her downtown Manhattan boutiques she'd acquired a new black top of some fine puckered material threaded with gold, that fitted her solid torso so tightly that her midriff was outlined and the nipples of her breasts were prominent as unwinking eyes; the sleeves were cut up onto her shoulders to display shapely, well-developed biceps. It was an extreme style for a mature woman, and Drewe had to be in her mid-forties.

Virgil West was saying, as Drewe leaned near gazing attentively at his face, "You know that I believe in greatness, grandeur. I believe in the possibility of mankind. But I don't much care for individuals, in history. Caravaggio! Modigliani! Picasso, I would despise. Even the great-souled are stained by the epochs in which they live, it's like living out your life on a toxic waste dump. You can't escape contamination."

Drewe said eagerly, "I think you can. You can try."

"To try is not to *do.* To be contaminated is to be unaware of your condition."

"But you must try." There was something wistful and subordinate in the curve of my aunt's spine, as she leaned near Virgil West, slouched in the sagging chrome-and-leather chair. She glanced at me, with the same look of yearning. "We can change our lives, we can lead other lives. We can 'die' in one place if we must, and 'come alive' in another."

Virgil West laughed, swallowing a large mouthful of whiskey. His stubbled chin glistened. He said, teasing, "In the Factory you didn't learn that, did you? Warhol was all about emptying-out, vacating."

Drewe said stiffly, "I left the Factory fifteen years ago. I left before Warhol died. Damn you, you know that."

"To have never been in the Factory would have been better, as the philosopher says, 'To have never been born.' "

"This is a new life, here. In the country. 'Chateauguay Springs.' It has become far more successful than my husband could have guessed. I wish you'd wanted to at least say hello to a few of our young painters, it would have meant so much to them. 'Art colonies' are scorned by ignorant people, they don't realize how the artist, in America, needs a community, a family. Chateauguay Springs is a worthy cause, it will outlive me."

"Outlive Drewe! I hope not."

"All right, I make myself vulnerable. You can laugh at me, if you want to. It's only smallness of soul that I dread. The small-souled are the slaves of the large-souled, it's a law of nature."

"And are we 'large-souled,' dear Drewe? Is a soul measured like one's girth?" West stroked his barrel-torso, his swelling belly. He seemed well satisfied with his girth. In a teasing voice he said, " 'Not that things are eternal and infinite but that the finite things are repeated infinitely.' "

Drewe laughed, and gave a little cry as if she'd been wounded.

"Who said that?"

"Pascal. In the *Pensées*."

Drewe protested, "But there is change, there is progress. All around us are untried lives. I mean our *own*."

West said, "There are no 'untried' lives, only the lives we've tried. This is what we have." He sighed, for a moment quiet, contemplating. "Well, I love it how you've tried to soar above the toxic dump, Drewe. Your strong bravely beating wings, I adore." The man was suddenly drunk, sweetly maudlin. It seemed to have happened within seconds.

Drewe said, her mouth downturned, bitter, "And you: you've flown nearly out of sight."

During this conversation West's wife, or the woman who'd come with him, was prowling restlessly about the room drinking whiskey and peering at Drewe's art collection. She paused in front of the Warhol silk screen, as if impressed, or disdainful. Her name was "Daisy"—I knew that Drewe would sneer at such a name. " 'Daisy!' Exactly." She was probably twenty years younger than Virgil West but lacked West's vigor and animation. She seemed irritable, edgy. Her skin was sallow, her eyes had the glassy belligerence of my mother's eyes in the final days before she'd entered the Jamestown rehabilitation clinic. Between her and West there was an air of strain as if they'd been quarreling before they'd arrived; Daisy glanced repeatedly in West's direction, but West was scarcely aware of her. At last Daisy said in a small grating voice, "Vir-gil."

West continued speaking, oblivious. Nor did Drewe seem to hear.

"Vir-gil: I want to leave now."

Daisy was a "designer in jewelry." She wore a long hobbling skirt in a stiff material like felt, a velvet caftan that strained at her hips, many necklaces and bracelets, some of them carved of wood. It wasn't clear if Drewe had expected this woman, who clearly wasn't happy at seeing Drewe. As she approached us she collided with a spindly-limbed metallic sculpture: "God *damn*." Drewe leapt up to help Daisy detach her skirt from the metal and Daisy said spitefully, "Don't worry, Mrs. Hildebreth, I haven't hurt the ugly thing! It isn't bent any more than it was, anyway if it is who'd fucking notice?"

Drewe said quickly, "Of course it hasn't been damaged. But you've cut yourself."

"I didn't cut my*self*. The ugly thing was in my way."

"I think, actually, it wasn't. I think you went out of your way to walk into it."

Drewe spoke coolly, turning away. I saw Daisy's surprise at this response, her look of a naughty rebuked child. Virgil West hadn't moved from the straining chrome-and-leather chair. He said, amused, "Poor Daisy is accident-prone. And yet, there is design in her accidents."

Daisy insisted she wanted to leave, her face was flushed now, her fingers twitching. I recognized the symptoms: a junkie missing her meds. She appealed to Virgil West in her grating little-girl voice until abruptly he drained his whiskey glass and heaved himself to his feet as if he'd forgotten why they had come to Drewe's house, which was for dinner. Drewe was hurt: "You can't leave so soon, Virgil. Magdalena is about to serve us dinner."

Daisy plucked at West's tweed coat, West brushed her away. He was at least one hundred pounds heavier than Daisy but boldly, daringly Daisy pulled at his arm, scolding and whining. West told Drewe he had to get back to his work, his mind wasn't right: "Like a fire that's burning somewhere, that no one is monitoring."

Drewe pleaded, "But Magdalena and I spent time on the menu, Virgil. Your favorite, braised beef shanks, portobello mushroom soup, bread pudding—" and West said, striking his forehead, "Where is Magdalena? I'll tell her. I'll explain what a selfish bastard I've become, she'll forgive me." West careened off toward the kitchen, he seemed to know the large house well.

There was an awkward moment, Drewe and Daisy left together.

Daisy said meanly, "His children are leeches. You know them, I'm sure. They're selling Virgil's paintings he gave them, any price they can get. He won't believe me, you tell him."

Drewe said quietly, "You're mistaken, Daisy, if you think that Virgil would take personal advice from me."

" 'Daisy'! Don't you call me that, you're not my friend."

Daisy looked like a woman bracing herself against a strong wind. In another part of the house there was laughter. "I want my coat, where the hell is my coat," Daisy said to me, so I went to fetch her coat, and Daisy stumbled after me, in the front hall I helped her struggle into the sleeves, there was a strange sudden intimacy between us, fleeting as the flaring-up of a match. Daisy sobbed, "You! You're young, you don't know." Her glassy eyes tore at me, I felt as if I'd been cut. "You're his daughter, aren't you. That woman, and Virgil. Aren't you."

Daisy stumbled outside. I returned to Drewe, we watched headlights outside, then red taillights, as Daisy drove the van away, blundering down the long driveway between banks of snow. It was past nine o'clock, very dark except for the whitely glimmering snow. West still hadn't returned from the kitchen, Drewe went to fetch him.

Her voice quavered in triumph. "Your 'Daisy' has driven away. She has left us with you."

The stained snaggle-teeth flashed in a smile. West was seated at a kitchen table, Magdalena in her apron stood at the stove, her cheeks flushed with pleasure as a girl's. West snatched at Drewe's hand, lifted it to his lips and kissed it wetly.

"You will be hospitable, I hope."

The fire flows from them, protects them. If I come too near, I will be burned.

Homesick

It was midwinter 2001. I was sixteen, my aunt had sent me to the Woodstock Academy sixty miles away from Chateauguay Springs: north, inland from the Hudson River, in the snowbound foothills of the Catskills. So beautiful, the air so piercing-cold, you wanted to suck it deep into your lungs, to die.

I hated Woodstock. I hated my exile. Desperately I'd wanted to remain at home and attend Chateauguay Springs High School, but without knowing a thing about it Drewe had pronounced the school "inadequate to our needs."

Needs! I have no needs. If I have you, I have no needs.

I was growing into Marta, though. Growing into strength and cunning.

"Marta, smile!"

My roommate, pitiless as a party balloon careening at me in her good cheer, buoyancy. Though she, too, cried in secret. I saw the evidence in her puffy reddened eyes and chafed nostrils, unless it was evidence that, like other classmates, in secret, giggling together in one another's rooms, she was sniffing cocaine smuggled back from party weekends in Manhattan.

Coke was the most prestigious of the numerous drugs used by my classmates at the Academy, *it really clears your head.*

At Woodstock time passed in a haze of loneliness, melancholy. The more crowded my days with classes, "activities," the deeper the loneliness, melancholy. I skipped classes, I had difficulty concentrating on my course work, my grades hovered at B–. (Woodstock was a private school geared to the "special needs" of many of its students, where grades below B– were rare as non-smokers/non-drug users among the student body.) In Cattaraugus with classmates I'd known all my life, the previous year I'd been distracted by what was happening to my father but this year in my new life as Marta, I rarely thought of my father and yet more rarely of my mother. Obsessively I thought of my aunt Drewe.

I adored Drewe and was fierce with pride of her, and of Chateauguay Springs. Though sometimes I hated the "colony" of resident artists, for the attention Drewe lavished upon them, when she was in the mood. And sometimes I hated Drewe.

On my cell phone I called her. Sometimes several times a day. She wasn't a person to carry her cell phone with her, she was careless, indifferent. She was gone from home often (I knew: I communicated with Magdalena, too) away overnight, away for days at a time, in New York, in London, in Paris, Venice, Rome . . . She was traveling with Virgil West, they were lovers now were they? Late at night my plaintive voice was preserved in Drewe's voice mail. *I miss everybody at home. I'm so lonely here. I wonder if you are home, I want to come home this weekend! I want to come home.*

My e-mails to Drewe went unanswered. My aunt used e-mail only for business purposes, never anything personal.

At Woodstock, I was Drewe Hildebrand's niece. My parents were *was*. They had no names, no one inquired after them. Aunt Drewe was *is*.

Among the faculty at Woodstock, "Drewe Hildebrand" was a known name. Also "Chateauguay Springs."

Except to some, this was the art colony *where the girl died, drug overdose wasn't it?*

Quickly I murmured no. I had never heard anything like that.

My art instructor persisted. He was middle-aged, fattish with a wispy goat-beard, goat ears bristling with hairs. His eyes fastened on me, on the first day of classes in September he'd seemed to know exactly who I was. Asking about Drewe, asking about Chateauguay Springs, even about Virgil West. And *that girl who died a year or two ago what exactly happened there?*

Don't know. Don't know. If there'd been anything, it had happened before my time.

Before I'd started school at Woodstock, Drewe had taken me into the city to a TriBeCa salon to have my "unruly" hair cut. She'd outfitted me with "appropriate" clothes, chic-somber downtown colors, fabrics of stiff, unusual textures, jackets, sweaters, shirts, a pair of leather boots. A quilted coat with a thick lining, a faux-fur collar. My look was to be "bold, defiant." The "peasant strength" of my face, my "good bones," the "spiritual beauty" of my eyes. Within a few weeks at Woodstock I was wearing my old jeans, pullovers, ART POWER T-shirts, I slept in T-shirts, sweatshirts, white cotton underpants and wool socks. It would come to be known that Drewe had arranged for me to room with my roommate, the girl was the daughter of an art-circle friend of Drewe's from years ago in New York, a "kindred spirit" Drewe believed though she'd never laid eyes upon Halli and probably had not seen Halli's father in fifteen years. I hated my roommate tormenting me *Smile, Marta!* I hated her taking up most of the space in our room. I hated her for crying in toilet stalls, sometimes in our room. I didn't cry.

Calling Drewe on my cell phone that glimmered blue in the dark, cupped in my fervent hand. *Is he with you? Virgil West? Right now? There are strange people here, people who ask me about you, Aunt Drewe can I come home this weekend?*

Sometimes Drewe called me back. Sometimes she asked Magdalena to call me back, to explain: not this weekend. Sometimes no one called me.

Didn't cry but my pillow was streaked, stained. Turned it over but the pillowcase on the other side was even more soiled.

I'd never told Drewe what Virgil West's wife had said to me.

His daughter, aren't you. That woman, and Virgil.

I tramped in my expensive boots out back of the Academy, beyond the playing fields heaped with snow, breathing hard, expelling steam, sweating inside my big quilted coat. In my mind pierced with cold like the "ice" sniffed, swallowed, smoked by the more adventurous of my classmates, a form of crystal meth, I began to think yes it was plausible, if I was Drewe Hildebrand's daughter it was plausible that Virgil West was my father for they'd been lovers seventeen years ago, I was sure.

"Smile, Marta!"

My roommate's face was puffy and blotched from too much starchy food, her eyes were bleary, bloodshot. There was a laser-twitch to her mouth meant to be a smile, a hurt smile, a weeping smile, a smile that cracked the lower half of her face in two. And later that night when Halli was too excited to sleep, twitchy-nervous missing her meds and breathing like asthma, I left my bed to sit with her, on the edge of her rumpled bed I sat with her, listened for two hours as Halli told me terrible things about her family, laughed shrilly and wiped her nose on the edge of her hand, Halli's eyes were rimmed in red and her nostrils were raw, as she cried I stroked her hair clumsily, her hair that was matted like my own, I heard myself murmur to Halli the comforting nonsense words my aunt Drewe sometimes murmured to me *It's fine, you'll be fine, this is just a bad time, you'll be fine, this will pass.* So I realized that I didn't hate my roommate, I guess I liked my roommate, my roommate was a girl like myself, I thought we might be friends, maybe; except my roommate left school a day early for Christmas break and returned several days after classes began in January and the first weekend overdosed on a drug ("X," ecstasy, the rumor was) in a senior boy's room and she had to be rushed by ambulance to the nearest emergency room in Kingston where she was put on life support (her boyfriend, or friends, hadn't reported her collapsing right away, hours were allowed to pass) but recovered and was eventually shipped home to New York City so I never saw my roommate again and when her half of the room was emptied out, which was in fact more than half of the room, I missed her, it was so quiet, I couldn't concentrate on my schoolwork, couldn't sleep so I called my aunt repeatedly on my cell phone until at last (at 12:05 A.M., a Monday in February) she picked up the call sounding irritated, impatient, I had to wonder if Virgil West was close beside her, or another man, or if she was alone, and where she was, I was trying to keep my voice calm, a mature voice not a brattish frightened voice, I told Drewe, "Hi! I'm a little homesick, I guess I'm missing everybody there, Aunt Drewe, I'm wondering if I could come home? I mean home to stay?" and Drewe said, "Marta, look: we've been through this, you must give yourself more time there, to adjust," and I said, "More time! Seems like I've been here forever, it's been winter forever, I miss you, I miss Magdalena, I miss my room," and Drewe said, "You were just home for winter break, only a few weeks ago," and I said, "I hate it here! I'm so lonely, I don't have any friends," and Drewe said, an edge to her voice, "But you must be educated, Marta. You are sixteen and not a child, you're an intelligent girl if you try, certainly you could make friends if you tried," and I said, "I don't want friends, not here," and Drewe said, annoyed, "But that happens to be where you are, Marta. You make friends where you are which happens to be the best place for you, I think, God knows it's expensive enough," and I hesitated, I was tugging at a hair, pulling at a hair until my scalp hurt, strange how you can pull out a hair so quickly you don't feel pain but if you tug at a hair slowly it brings tears to your eyes, in a rush of words I said, "Halli is gone, Aunt Drewe. Halli OD'd on a drug some guys gave her, last weekend Halli almost died and Halli is gone from school now, I miss her," and Drewe could not speak for a moment, Drewe must have been surprised, I liked it that I'd surprised my aunt, maybe I'd shocked my aunt, in a faint voice Drewe said, "My God! That's terrible. I'll have to call her father . . ." and I said, sensing my advantage, "Aunt Drewe, please can I come home? Halli was my only friend, I miss her and I want to come home, I'm afraid that what happened to Halli might happen to me," and now Drewe spoke sharply, "I'll pretend I didn't hear that, Marta. How dare you say such a thing to me," and I couldn't think how to reply, I began to stammer, "I mean, I only mean— I don't do drugs, Aunt Drewe, but I'm so lonely here, I—" and Drewe said angrily, "That's right, you don't 'do' drugs at that school, and you don't 'do' drugs anywhere, let's get that straight," and I wanted to protest *But you do! I know you do!* and Drewe was saying, "Your hateful mother calls me, leaves her hateful messages, your mother is practically blackmailing me, not that she wants *you,* she simply wants money, but I refuse to be blackmailed, you'd better believe that. Now you, you are trying to blackmail me, emotional blackmail, you'll learn that you can't do that, Marta, not with me, now I'm going to hang up and next time I speak with you we'll have forgotten this entire conversation, do you understand?" and meekly I said, "Yes, Aunt Drewe."

Later that night in bed planning that, if I killed myself, I would take drugs first to make it easier, then it wouldn't matter that I'd taken drugs. At once, I began to feel better.

The Adventure

Come with me, Marta! It will be an adventure for you."

Cornwall-on-Hudson, a weekend in May 2001: wild-growing wisteria, a part-collapsed wall of aged brick, loose window screens that thumped and clattered in the wind. In his makeshift studio the painter was oblivious of his surroundings, he was at home anywhere, or nowhere. He painted from his gut, there was no romance to it.

He lived in a tumbledown ruin of an old stone house (formerly a tavern, in the mid-1800s) at the edge of town, with a view, at a steep incline, of the river that flowed past the windows of Drewe's house eleven miles to the north at Chateauguay Springs. The house was poorly insulated, with warped door- and window-frames, a chimney in partial collapse, antiquated heating, plumbing. The driveway was rutted in spring, you had to park in weeds beside the county road a hundred yards away, and hike to the house. Drewe had several times suggested that West live at Chateauguay Springs, at least during the pitiless winter months, of course he'd have private quarters, an utterly private studio, the Foundation would provide him with assistants, with expenses, even with meals, but naturally West refused, the very offer was insulting to him. He wasn't a struggling young painter, he was fifty-one years old, nearing the prime (he believed) of his painting life. He wasn't poor, he spent money frugally, his needs were few, his former wives had been granted settlements, not alimony; his children were grown, no longer his legal responsibility. At least, Drewe said, exasperated, he might allow her to send Magdalena to put his household in some sort of order, Magdalena knew the repairmen to be trusted, the husky Russian/Ukrainian girls to be hired for heavy housecleaning, Drewe would pay for such services herself: "You can't possibly be doing your best work, Virgil, in such chaos." But Virgil West refused.

"No intruders. I hate intruders. I hate even intruding thoughts. It's enough for me to make an exception for you, darling, and for"— the protuberant blue eyes shifted to me, the stained teeth smiled, in that instant my name had been mislaid—"your niece, but no one else."

Eventually, Drewe would talk West into allowing rudimentary repairs, a thorough housecleaning, when she and West were away together for two weeks in Mexico. My aunt's strategy was indirection, tact.

The woman who'd been living with Virgil West, whatever her status, whatever her name, had departed Cornwall-on-Hudson, no one spoke of her. In West's house one weekend Aunt Drewe enlisted me in erasing the woman's presence, in triumph she pulled open bureau drawers in which solitary objects (lipstick tubes, stubs of eyebrow pencils, carved wooden beads the size of walnuts) clattered, in triumph she emptied closets of the lone items of women's apparel that remained, dumping everything into cardboard boxes. "The 'designer of jewelry' is no more."

I wondered if Daisy had died, or been killed.

We sneered at her together, Drewe and me. For, in Drewe's company, a sneer was a kind of inverted smile, that bonded.

In secret harboring in my heart the drunken flung-out words *His daughter, aren't you. That woman, and Virgil.*

Crucial pieces of furniture were missing from Virgil West's household, the fleeing woman must have carried with her. The front room was nearly empty, in the floorboards a border of grime showed where a carpet had been. Lighting fixtures were missing cords, windows were missing blinds. Cracked panes had been repaired with duct tape. It was Drewe's strategy to say nothing to Virgil West, she simply hauled furniture from Chateauguay Springs, nothing so conspicuous that West would take note, and object. She bought new lighting fixtures, blinds. Beautiful old brick fireplaces in several of the rooms were heaped with ash, Drewe cleared out herself. She teased West: "This house! A woman has to live in a cave with you."

West's large eyes glanced about, as if unseeing.

"No one forces them. It seems to happen."

Though it was crowded and confused in its clutter as a rat's nest, the most habitable room in West's house was his bedroom. The waterstained walls were covered with art, shelves were crammed with books, there was a brass bed with a sunken mattress covered with a hand-sewn quilt. Virgil West spoke of long hours of insomniac reading in the room, in the bed, propped up against pillows, his bedside tables were stacked with books, art journals, newspapers. I'd only glanced into the room, I'd never dared to enter it. Smells of tobacco smoke, bedclothes needing to be changed, mildew. Yet a more subtle smell of my aunt's cologne. I knew that Drewe took special care with this room because it was the room in which, when she was away from Chateauguay Springs overnight, she sometimes stayed.

Yet Virgil West exulted in aloneness, he thrived in isolation. Alone for days at a stretch, indifferent to a ringing phone, unconnected to e-mail, he worked in his studio, he rarely bathed. Whiskers brittle as wires sprouted from his thick jaws. Though he seemed to feel a powerful attraction for my aunt in her presence, he seemed also capable of forgetting her, that she existed, and meant something to him. Drewe adored the man, the artist in the man, she joked of Virgil West as "my Philip Guston," why should such a man be aware of *her*? It was enough, Drewe believed, that she was aware of him, she alone really understood the worth of his art.

"He's impossible! He's a saint. I'd follow him anywhere, I want only to serve him. I want nothing for myself."

Drewe made such breathless declarations not only to me, but to others, visitors at Chateauguay Springs. Her ardor for Virgil West was shocking to some, embarrassing. I believed that Drewe meant what she said sincerely, at the time of saying it; though I knew, too, that Drewe was eager for Virgil West to sign on with the Hildebrand Gallery for his upcoming exhibit, to leave his gallery of many years and "move up."

"No one can help Virgil West as I can. He's languishing in a second-rate gallery. Oh, impossible!"

Virgil West's new paintings were "sumptuous"—"gorgeous"— "monumental." Drewe was one of the artist's few friends who'd been invited to view them, in his studio at Cornwall-on-Hudson, so far.

The studio was a crudely converted shed at the rear of the old stone house. A leaky skylight had been fitted into a sloping, rotting shingled roof. A long rectangular window faced east, on clear mornings it was flooded with light, a glitter of wide water beneath where the Hudson River flowed. West thrived in discomfort, physical difficulties, like a beast shrugging off impediments that would paralyze lesser beings. Debris on the floor he kicked aside, oblivious. In

winter (windy, bitter cold, temperatures low as minus twenty degrees Fahrenheit) West conceded a need for reasonable comfort, he
dragged two space heaters into the studio, painted in layers of
sweaters, an overcoat, a hat. Often he smoked a pipe as he painted,
he "swilled" black coffee, he was in the mode of Balzac, he acknowledged: "Obsessed, incurable, doomed." He was so immersed in the
new sequence of paintings, he painted in a kind of trance, tireless,
thrilled. We were allowed in the studio that afternoon in May only if
we promised not to speak. Not a word!

The new paintings were as large as those in the *Earthflesh* sequence of the 1980s, that had brought Virgil West to prominence.
They were more vividly colored, dreamlike, with large floating
shapes, seemingly human yet lacking identity, even sex; they were
linked to one another by a network of fine veins, or nerves, or roots.
It was West's way to work on several canvases at the same time, in
his trance of concentration. "Oh! So beautiful." Drewe whispered in
my ear, Drewe squeezed my fingers like an excited child. I dreaded
that Virgil West would hear her, speak sharply to us, ask us to leave.
Drewe had been excited for days, I knew the symptoms of her
over-excitement, that could shift to anger, sudden exhaustion. At
Chateauguay Springs several times when I'd happened to be home,
when West was staying the night, I'd heard them quarreling in
Drewe's room upstairs, sharp exchanges of words, flaring up quickly,
subsiding. West had a way of provoking other people, as if teasing,
or taunting; Drewe wasn't accustomed to being teased, she reacted
emotionally, wounded. When Drewe was critical of others she was
calm, sarcastic; it was rare for her to become emotional. Only Virgil
West had the maddening power to unmoor her. Behind shut doors
the man's voice was murmurous, insinuating, the woman's voice was

shrill, the quick-jabbing beak of a bird. *I hate you! How can you say such things! To me, the only person who knows who you are.*

How West responded to such cries, I didn't know. I hoped, for my aunt's sake, he didn't laugh.

When they quarreled like this I stood very still in the corridor outside Drewe's room, listening. I was reminded of other adults quarreling behind shut doors. A man's low provoking voice, that was a voice of mystery; the woman's sharper voice, the jabbing of the beak, the frenzy, the humiliation.

Long ago, a time so distant it seemed I hadn't yet been born.

"So beautiful. Isn't it!"—so Drewe whispered in my ear as if daring the painter to overhear, to turn to her. But Virgil West was painting in his trance of concentration, oblivious of us as he was oblivious of his physical surroundings, kicking aside debris without taking notice, sucking at a pipe that had gone out. In her trance of adoration my aunt looked on, I slipped away to leave the adults alone together.

"I love it here! Nobody needy in sight."

The kitchen in Virgil West's house: a low smoke-stained ceiling, a large brick fireplace, bare floorboards worn smooth with the footsteps of decades. The warmest room in the house, where, when he wasn't painting and wasn't in bed, West mostly lived. He'd propped open a back door with a brick, flies and other insects drifting companionably inside. A rich odor of blossoming wisteria drifted inside. Atop an old, vibrating refrigerator was a small TV set. The stove was old and squat, with scorched gas burners that flickered blue when they were lighted. Drewe had brought food from Chateauguay

Springs, a rich beef and vegetable stew prepared by Magdalena, sourdough bread baked by Magdalena, vivid green asparagus spears, dark, nutty-tasting rice, a black pudding (molasses, butter) known to be one of West's favored desserts. Drewe had chosen a particular Italian red wine she'd bought in New York, for she and West took wine very seriously.

"Ah! Delicious."

I saw the pleasure in my aunt's eyes, when Virgil West lifted his glass, sniffed, tasted, and made this pronouncement.

It was dusk. A wisteria-fragrant evening. We heated Magdalena's supper on the gas-burning stove. Drewe barefoot, in slightly soiled white cord trousers, a cotton T-shirt that showed her bust, hair (now streaked blond, brown, wheat-colored, glossy) fastened back from her face with silver clasps, wavy and unruly as the hair of a young girl. At a distance, you would mistake Drewe for a young girl. She'd removed her rings, she was wifely at the stove, stirring Magdalena's stew with an outsized wooden spoon. She wasn't a cook, Drewe insisted, but she appreciated good food. In our honor, Virgil West said, he'd not only showered but shaved—"To a degree." His damp hair fell in blade-like strands cross his large forehead. Even his ears looked clean, pink as a pig's. He too was barefoot, his feet enormous, very pale, gnarled, the toenails discolored. As West poured wine into three glasses, Drewe dared to speak of his new paintings which were, she believed, his strongest work. "What an impact they will make, Virgil! I'm very excited."

West grunted, preoccupied with the wine.

I set a table for us, in what was called the front room. From out of a closest Drewe had located a tablecloth made of some dark material stiff as sailcloth, I draped over a table with a rickety leg. Carefully I set out mismatched forks, spoons, knives. In a drawer I located candles of varying lengths, all of them used. At twilight we sat down to eat, candles burning. A misty-green light suffused the room. Drewe was effervescent, her skin glowed. She was saying, "—of course he's an old friend, you are famously loyal to your old friends, but there must come a time of reassessment, Virgil. Frankly, he's no good for you now. Your reputation. As he sinks, his artists sink with him. Everyone asks me about you and I say, 'Well. Virgil is loyal to a fault.'" West was eating hungrily, inclining his head toward his plate, chewing. Veins stood out in his forehead, he hadn't eaten since early that morning, he was famished. I cut thick slices of Magdalena's bread, I passed to him. We were seated very close together at the table. This was nothing like the formality at Chateauguay Springs where, even when Virgil West was a guest at dinner, a very different atmosphere prevailed. Beyond West's shoulder I saw, on a window sill, a stack of waterstained sketchbooks, on a nearby table were scattered piles of bills, unopened envelopes addressed to *Virgil West*. There is something wonderful in such indifference to one's surroundings, I thought, and there is something terrifying about it, a deep ravine into which you might fall.

Drewe persisted, "But you must care, Virgil! For the sake of your art. Think of Rothko: a great genius, a saint, yet incapable as a child of dealing with life. It isn't the 'career' I mean. I don't mean that. But the art, that needs to be revered, Virgil, and, to be revered it must be seen, properly." Half-listening, scowling, West wiped the rim of his bowl with a piece of bread, and ate. He grunted a vague assent, his expression showed annoyance, yet I saw him pause, thinking. Something in Drewe's words had struck him. "It's survival, I suppose. A law of nature."

This stray remark, seemingly casual, spoken with a shrug of West's shoulder, had the effect of lighting up Drewe's face. Her eyes widened, for just a moment. She glanced toward me, her lips were parted in surprise, and in pleasure, as if we were conspirators, made happy. But she knew to change the topic, to speak lightly. "Isn't this meal delicious! And Magdalena has such a good heart, she's more than I deserve."

West said dryly, "People like us are often surrounded by people we don't deserve."

"And the air here," Drewe went on, as if unhearing, "the day, the hour, the smell of wisteria—the very river smells different in Cornwall-on-Hudson, than it does at Chateauguay Springs. I love it here, there's nobody needy in sight."

Quickly I looked down, hoping Drewe wouldn't notice me. Nobody needy!

Brimming bowls of stew, steam rose into our faces. We were hungry as a family that has been toiling together through the day. Drewe was urging me to drink the red wine.

At the Woodstock Academy away in the woods, in the foothills of the Catskills, where we all had "special needs," most of my classmates drank: not expensive wine but beer, smuggled into the residences. They drank to get "smashed," "wasted." Smoking pot, snorting coke, they were eager to get "stoned."

I thought of my mother, her slide down that had been slow at first, then quick. My father had been a drinker, too: a "career drinker" he called himself. Drank but never (appeared) drunk. He had not fallen exactly, he'd lost his balance and stumbled, finally skidding down, down a steep incline, desperately clutching at scrub bushes, tree limbs, to break his fall.

Drewe had no interest in them, her shamed brother and sister-in-law. She'd forbidden me to speak of them and so I never spoke of them and rarely thought of them for their outlines were smudged, fading like aged Polaroid prints.

In Cornwall-on-Hudson, my aunt Drewe didn't want to think of Chateauguay Springs. She would never have confided in Virgil West that she was embroiled in a conflict with one of the resident artists, and that a legal squabble was developing. (Drewe's former protégé Derrick had become a problem drinker, a drug user allegedly supplying drugs to other residents; he'd made harassing threats against a young woman painter as well as against Drewe herself; he'd been asked to vacate his quarters on the property and leave immediately though his residency extended for another month. Sighting me one day as I crossed the grounds he'd stared at me, unshaven, belligerent, saying what sounded like, "You! What's-your-name! Tell your bull-dyke-bitch aunt she'd better stay out of my way.") Drewe herself refused to speak with the young sculptor, this was the responsibility of Marcus Heller, staff members, the Foundation's legal counsel. Such vulgarity disgusted her. Such "small-soulness."

In her lover's romantic ruin of a house Drewe's manner was purely vivacious, untroubled. She knew how women—wives, mistresses—and his children had weighed heavily upon Virgil West, Drewe would not make such a mistake. Speaking to him, Drewe touched West's brawny arms, stroked the coarse hairs. She lifted West's gnarled fingers to kiss as if unconsciously, impulsively. Nothing about West repelled her, his slovenly manners while eating, his occasional impatience with her, his indifference to her praise. Frequently, she touched my wrist. She touched my hair. She said, as if this had been a topic of discussion, "Marta will model for you to-morrow, Virgil. This new work of yours . . ."

West said, "I don't require models any longer, Drewe. Rodin said there's a time when you've seen enough human bodies. You re-call all you need to know from your gut."

I felt a shiver of relief. As if I would "model" for anyone.

My fellow art students at the Woodstock Academy sometimes volunteered to model in our figure-drawing class, fully clothed of course. But never Marta.

I knew: Drewe had once modeled for Virgil West, in some long-ago phase of their lives to which Drewe alluded obliquely. I won-dered if Drewe's image was preserved in one of the female nudes of the *Earthflesh* series. It wasn't difficult to imagine Drewe posing naked, she wasn't at all shy about her body, but I couldn't easily imagine Virgil West as a younger man, taking such pains with any-one, anything, in the world outside his imagination. Drewe was say-ing now, "Well, I don't model any longer. Obviously."

West said, "Don't be stupid. You're a beautiful woman, so far as that goes. But beauty is boring, no one cares for beauty any longer."

Drewe said quickly, "No. We care for something more profound: 'spirit.' "

West laughed, scratching at his chest. "Fuck 'spirit.' Body. Body is all there is, and more than we can comprehend."

Drewe nodded, Drewe was eager to concur.

West had opened a second bottle of the tart red wine, somewhat clumsily, wine ran down his fingers. He splashed more liquid into my glass though I hadn't finished what was in the glass. All of our glasses were cut crystal I'd located in a kitchen cupboard, and all of the glasses were chipped, with scummy rims. Neither Drewe nor West noticed. In her festive mood, Drewe prodded me to drink. "It's really quite delicious, Marta. You should acquire a taste for good wine."

I lifted the glass to my mouth. The taste was strong, smarting. It wasn't delicious. Yet the inside of my mouth felt like a flower opening into sudden bloom.

It was Drewe's way to persist in a subject. She wasn't accustomed to being rebuffed. She spoke again of my "modeling" for West, to bring "new life, vigor" into the new paintings. She said, "And Marta might learn from you, Virgil. She is on a kind of quest, I think: she requires guides."

West asked politely if I was studying art in school?

West had asked this question before. Several times he'd been told by Drewe, by me, that I was taking art at Woodstock, but of course he never remembered. He had trouble remembering my name, I meant so little to him. There was a comfort in this: knowing that, whatever I told this man, no matter how Drewe wished for some reason to impress him with me, he would quickly forget.

His daughter, aren't you. That woman, and Virgil.

I told West that I was taking a studio course, sketching, drawing, painting, but it would probably be my last art course.

West grunted, "Good."

Drewe asked, "Why 'good,' Virgil?"

"Because art is too much effort. Why pursue it if you have not the compulsion."

My instructor at the Woodstock Academy was the middle-aged man with the wispy goat beard and goat ears who'd asked nosy questions about Drewe Hildebrand and Chateauguay Springs. He'd taken an interest in my work, I hated his attention, I hated most of the work I'd done in the course, the drawings that were so worked-over, earnest and amateurish. Drewe had given me books of color plates by the Renaissance artists Caravaggio and Artemisia Gentileschi, I'd tried to be influenced by these great artists sketching in charcoal and pencil, but the results were disappointing. The contemporary artists my aunt most admired, her stable of artists at the Hildebrand Gallery, and Virgil West, had pushed beyond replicating the world, scorned replicating surfaces, West painted out of his gut-memory, as he said. In serious art there were few recognizable landscapes, still lives, portraits. At our prep school art students toiled at replicating a world others had left behind. Our instructor encouraged us all, rarely criticized, as instructors at the Woodstock Academy invariably encouraged their students, with their "special needs." A few days ago I'd torn up most of my laboriously assembled portfolio, in disgust. The instructor stared at me, dismayed. "Marta, what have you done?"

Marta what have you done echoed in my ears. I wanted to laugh, what did I care what I'd done, maybe I'd fail the course, maybe I would fail all my courses and Aunt Drewe would withdraw me from the Woodstock Academy and let me attend Chateauguay Springs High.

That way, I would see more of Virgil West, too. I thought so.

It was a relief, to have destroyed my "art." I could never have shown it to Drewe, who'd promised to come to class day at the end of the term, Drewe would have been mortified to see that her niece was so untalented, had so little imagination. I'd learned that it was wisest, safest, not to compete. The resident artists at Chateauguay Springs were all talented, ambitious, driven to succeed, yet few would succeed, very likely none. To them, Virgil West was a major artist.

Drewe herself had given up on art when she'd been only a few years older than me. Mysteriously she'd said, life had intervened.

I drained my wineglass, Drewe replenished it. A warm sensation in my throat, chest, belly. My eyelids drooped, I was getting sleepy. Drewe was telling Virgil West how she'd taken me to the Whitney to see his paintings, what I'd said, I was embarrassed and covered my ears with my hands, for why should Virgil West care in the slightest what an ignorant young girl thought of his work . . . Drewe pulled my hands away, laughing. " 'Like the inside of a dream,' Marta said. She was very moved." Drewe framed my face in her hands, that were warm, dry, strong as a vise. "Such an interesting face, eh? Like Judith after the beheading, you know the painting, Gentileschi, the one in which Judith is younger, vengeful yet spiritual, even ethereal. In the eyes . . ."

Virgil West had pushed away his emptied plate, was teetering back on two chair legs, resting his wineglass against his fattish chest. Frowning, he looked at me as if for the first time.

"Yes. The eyes."

So strange! To hear such remarks made about me by these powerful adults, as if I was invisible. Naively I thought *They will protect me.*

I tried to stand, my legs were weak. Was this drunkenness? Falling, sinking. I couldn't seem to keep my balance, yet it was a comforting sensation. Such a clumsy girl! Drewe laughed, lurching toward me to kiss me wetly at the edge of my mouth. Her breath was sweet with wine. Somehow I was managing to stand, leaning on the back of my chair. Drewe said, "She needs to sleep, Virgil. Help her."

West said, "You must help her yourself, Drewe. The girl is your niece."

"She is! Marta is! Marta is, my niece."

Drewe walked me from the front room along the hall, one of her strong arms circling my waist, the two of us swaying and giggling, we were in the bedroom at the rear of the house, waterstained ceiling and walls crowded with art, unframed canvases, photographs, a cascade of books, shelves crowded with books, a smell of pipe tobacco, grimy carpets. This cozy nest of a room, the big double bed with the sunken mattress, a single lamp burning. Clumsily Drewe helped me onto the bed, tugged off my shoes, dragged a quilt over me, for the night air was cool now. Urgently she said, "Marta! We can love more than one person, our love only increases. You'll see." Drewe's breath was so sweet, I wanted to kiss her, to suck at her lips, except my head rolled heavily on the pillow, I hadn't any strength. Drewe pulled off my shoes, lightly tickled the soles of my bare feet as you'd tickle a young child, then she was gone. At a distance I heard the adult voices murmurous, melodic. I could hear no words only voices. I could not imagine why I'd been so unhappy away at school, so lonely often I had wanted to die, childish and spiteful wanting to die when Drewe hadn't wanted me to come home for a weekend, hadn't answered my plaintive phone messages, now my heart swelled with happiness, I thought *She has never said love to me. Never before.*

Someone had come to the doorway, a large shambling figure with disheveled hair, hoarse quickened breathing. Through my shuttered eyelids I saw. I think I saw. He stood in the doorway watching me without moving. The bulk of the man, the large heavy head, I was asleep yet my mind functioned with perfect clarity telling me *You are expected to make a sign to this man, your aunt wishes this.* But I did not. I did not open my eyes, I did not move my mouth that was rigid as if paralyzed. Stiff and unmoving and not breathing I lay on my side with my knees drawn up toward my chest cold and still as death until finally the hulking figure turned away, the hoarse breathing was gone.

Two years later Virgil West was a "person of interest" in the police investigation into whatever it was that had happened to Drewe Hildebrand. Two years later Virgil West would grab my head in his hands and kiss my astonished mouth.

Aging Eros

—

When Virgil West's exhibit of eleven new paintings opened at the Hildebrand Gallery on Prince Street, New York City, in mid-October 2001, I was 120 miles away at school north of Pittsfield, Massachusetts. I had not been invited.

After the "adventure" in Cornwall-on-Hudson. What was un-spoken among us. The three of us.

Soon afterward they'd gone away together, Drewe and Virgil West. I had not been invited then, either. Fifteen days in Mexico, in Yucatán after Virgil West was satisfied he had completed the new paintings, he'd "painted out his guts" and nothing remained inside him.

So Drewe had said. Not to me (for Drewe rarely spoke to me of Virgil West any longer) but of course I'd overheard her speaking with others. An edge of excitement in her voice, the smallest sliver of apprehension.

Pride, too. Boastfulness.

It was news in the art world, noted even in the *New York Times,* and other publications: Virgil West had left his gallery of twenty-three years, to sign on with Drewe Hildebrand. His "New Paintings 1991–2001" were eagerly waited.

Then, out of nowhere, came 9/11. It might have been an earthquake, a tidal wave swamping lower Manhattan. It might have been a comet crashing to earth. Out of nowhere it seemed to come, so many deaths, such destruction, so swiftly. It would come to be called 9/11, for there was no adequate word with which to designate it: a terrorist attack on the United States, that had imagined itself invulnerable to such attacks, a nation blessed by God. Even those who did not believe in God and who understood the political reasons for the attack had lived with the assumption of invulnerability, it was a wholly American sort of faith. Five weeks later, less than two miles north of ground zero, Virgil West's exhibit opened. Acres of devastation in lower Manhattan, the air still stank of ashes, sludge, incinerated human flesh. On overcast days a kind of chemical yeast or malaise coated the lining of the sinuses, the interior of the mouth. It was not a time for "New Paintings 1991–2001." It was not a time for patience, sympathy, attentiveness to such art, it was a time of politics, raised voices, blunt primal emotions. Who could care about obsessively intimate "figure" painting, the sensuality of a middle-aged Caucasian male artist who'd made his reputation in another era? *Been There, Done That: Aging Eros in an Age of Terror* was the jeering headline of the *Times* review, I stood reading, trying to read, in the common room of my residence at the Pittsfield School.

The review was a half-page, dense columns of newsprint. There was a small photograph of Virgil West, the large molting head, prominent eyes amid a face like crumbling masonry. There was a photograph of one of West's long horizontal paintings, huge sprawling nudes, a swirl of color. The reviewer identified himself as a one-time admirer of Virgil West, in the 1980s. Now in post-9/11 America he was recoiling from his own "outmoded"—"neo-romantic"—"high-decadent-Modernist"—taste. The review was cruel, condescending, as if "easel painting" was a quaint custom, no matter how gifted the artist, such art in a time of political crisis was self-indulgent, retrograde. The reviewer wrote as if Virgil West was an adversary, it was the reviewer's duty to eviscerate, destroy. My hand shook, holding the newspaper. I was anxious that someone would drift into the common room and discover me, the look in my face.

My aunt Drewe had not spoken to me about the upcoming exhibit, she hadn't even shown me the catalog, still I was well aware of it, of course. I had expected a very different sort of coverage in the art pages of the *Times,* where the Hildebrand Gallery often advertised. I had expected to show the West review to my roommates, a few of my classmates, teachers. I would speak of knowing Virgil West, I would not be boastful but modest, I would say that I'd seen some of the new paintings in the artist's studio, West was a friend of my family. Above all I'd expected to telephone Drewe this morning, to share her excitement at the review, and to suggest that I come home to Chateauguay Springs for the weekend, and go to New York City to see the exhibit. But now, none of this would happen.

I stood stunned, staring at the review. At Virgil West's face that was unsmiling, brooding. I thought *I must have loved him, this hurts so.*

The Pittsfield School, est. 1879. "Historic New England campus"— "scenic Berkshire Hills." I hated it here, I was lonelier here than I'd been at the Woodstock Academy. So stupid: I had only myself to blame, now I was farther away from Chateauguay Springs than I'd been at Woodstock.

I had complained to my aunt about my art instructor asking questions about her and the artists' colony. His allusions to *that girl who died there a few years ago? Drug overdose?* Naively I'd hoped that Drewe would be furious and withdraw me from Woodstock so that I could come back home and attend the local high school but of course it didn't work out that way. (Drewe had warned me not to try to manipulate her. I knew it had to be risky.) Yes, Drewe was furious with the Woodstock Academy, she'd called the headmaster to complain, she'd insisted that her niece be allowed to withdraw from the art course without receiving a grade ("That bastard isn't going to punish you by failing you"), she arranged for me to complete the academic year at Woodstock but not to return in the fall. Except there was no question of my attending Chateauguay Springs High School.

"As if I would send you there! With such people."

For the first time my aunt conceded, there were "prejudiced individuals" in rural Chateauguay County, some of them our neighbors, who disliked the artists' colony; disapproved of the "modern art," and of the "morals" of the artists. In the late 1960s, Chateauguay Springs Artists' Colony was believed to be a "hippie commune"—a "Communist hangout." Local tradesmen and workmen profited from the artists' colony, Drewe Hildebrand behaved cordially and generously with her neighbors when she encountered them, yet it didn't seem to matter—"Prejudice against art runs deep in the American soul. Chateauguay County is Caucasian-Christian, seventy-five percent Republican in the last election." Drewe said she didn't want me to confront, at school, the sons and daughters of such people, who hated her.

Immediately I objected, "Aunt Drewe, nobody hates you! Nobody who knows you could hate you."

Drewe laughed. "Marta, how naive. Nobody who knows me could love me."

Like stepping swiftly back from an embrace. Before the embraced one can reciprocate.

Since that evening at Cornwall-on-Hudson, Drewe wasn't nearly so affectionate with me as she'd been. Often I saw her contemplating me at a distance, as if assessing me. Her niece Marta had grown taller in the past year or so, my body maturing, breasts, hips, a new fullness to my face, still I was physically awkward, shy, lacking the social personality Drewe wished for me, that way of speaking, smiling, laughing with others that is a kind of grace, impossible to be learned. Where bright bubbles of conversation drifted and burst above my head I sat self-conscious and wishing to be gone, hiking through the woods or above the river, upstairs in my room. "Marta, try. As I do, try." It was true, there was something stubborn in my habit of withdrawal, something willful in opposition to my aunt. Sometimes glared at me as if to warn *Don't disappoint me! You will regret it.*

Drewe wanted to be perceived as generous, emotionally uncomplicated, yet she was quick to detect any attempt to manipulate her. So long she'd been a rich widow, a powerful "patroness" of art, she was easily suspicious. She loved her needy children except when she became bored and impatient with them.

"No. You're not going to Chateauguay Springs High School. You will go to a private school, Marta, appropriate to your situation."

My situation! I wondered what this was.

The Pittsfield School in northwest Massachusetts was quaintly beautiful in the way of "historic" white clapboard New England.

There was an austere chapel with a bell tower, there was a rectangular "green," well-weathered iron gates and fences, views from high windows of the "scenic" Berkshire hills dense with trees. Three hundred students about equally divided between girls and boys, most of them from New York City and its affluent suburbs. They were my Woodstock classmates with slightly different names, faces, "special needs." Some were alarmingly precocious for their ages, some were socially, maybe even mentally retarded. I had two roommates, so I couldn't worry about losing one and being alone again. We'd all transferred to Pittsfield from previous prep schools that hadn't "worked out."

At Pittsfield, I was the shy-sullen-stubborn dark-haired girl in sweatshirt and jeans who sat in classes with arms folded over her chest, who stared at the instructor as if listening intensely, yet rarely volunteered to answer a question, rarely smiled, seemed distracted, melancholy. Teachers smiled at me encouragingly as you might smile at an invalid.

My fault, I knew. I'd disappointed my aunt. Drewe was my entire family now, I thought of her constantly. Many times I relived that last day at Cornwall-on-Hudson which I could not have known would be, for me, the last. *Love* Drewe had said dreamily, earnestly. *We can love more than one person.*

I'd been afraid, though. Lying on Virgil West's bed paralyzed, knees drawn up to my chest. *No no no no no.*

Since that night, Virgil West had dropped away from my life entirely. One day I realized I hadn't seen my aunt's lover in weeks, hadn't heard his voice that was so often booming, teasing. I hadn't heard Drewe speak his name to me. The three of us no longer shared meals together. But I knew that Drewe was seeing West, of course.

Often I lay awake in my room thinking *She is with him. She is with someone she prefers to me.* I was rarely invited into the city any longer to attend art openings with Drewe, visit museums, see plays and friends of Drewe's, stay overnight in the luxurious condominium apartment overlooking the East River, all that had ended.

Yes but you know why. Don't pretend to be naive.

My aunt spoke of me as a sensual/sexual being. Or had spoken of me in that way. I wasn't sure what "sensual/sexual" meant, exactly. I did have sexual feelings, I suppose: dim, fleeting, unfocused. But these feelings weren't associated with men, or boys. Or women.

The prospect of being sexually touched by any man or boy was frightening to me. I was thrown into confusion, how I should react.

Easier to keep my distance. Easier to withdraw.

The trip to Mexico, in June! Several times Drewe had spoken of taking me to Mexico, now suddenly she left without me, not a word of explanation, only a careless goodbye. I was hurt, I hung out in Magdalena's kitchen wanting to know: where exactly has Aunt Drewe gone? How long would she be gone? Is Virgil West with her?

Magdalena felt sorry for me, the left-behind niece. Magdalena recognized in Marta one of her employer's needy children, ever more boring as she is ever more needy.

Cheerfully Magdalena said, "Well, Marta! You know Mrs. Hildebrand, sometimes she decides she wants to travel somewhere, already she's made reservations, has tickets. But she'll be back soon and while she's gone she will keep in touch with you, I'm sure."

A single postcard from Yucatán, that didn't arrive until after Drewe had returned. A handwoven bag, in bright parrot colors. A heavy, heart-shaped silver ring to be worn on the middle finger of my right hand.

Gifts my aunt brought back for me, souvenirs of a trip I hadn't taken with her.

Now there were often trips, weekends when Drewe was absent from Chateauguay Springs and I was left behind like any staff member. I was a "summer intern" and earned a small salary. In the Big Barn, I felt a thrill of pride, adults seemed to trust me. I thought *They will tell Drewe what a good worker I am, how reliable and devoted.*

For weeks I waited for Drewe to tell me about the exhibit, scheduled for October, of Virgil West's new paintings in her gallery, but she never did. In Marcus Heller's office I discovered page proofs of the catalog, an introduction by a prominent art critic at Yale, beautiful full-color reproductions of paintings I'd seen at Cornwall-on-Hudson. I dared to ask Drewe if I could attend the opening and Drewe said, frowning, "You have school, Marta. The opening is on a Thursday evening."

"School! I can miss a day of school."

"You'd end up missing two days. No."

"But, Aunt Drewe—"

"No."

I was close to tears. I was hurt, and I was angry. Drewe's face was flushed with annoyance, she disliked confrontations, especially she disliked willful naïveté. Certainly I knew that, if Drewe hadn't spoken to me about the opening, I wasn't invited. I wasn't wanted.

This was the season, shortly before September 11, when, for some impulsive reason, Drewe had had her hair dramatically darkened, straight-cut and severe. The look was Asian-exotic: her face was made up ivory-pale, her mouth small and red as a blister. She wore brightly colored silk kimonos, she wore layers of gauzy fabrics inside which her breasts swung heavy and loose. Her eyes shone defiantly, her perfume was strong. I couldn't believe that Virgil West was charmed by such costumes, if he noticed them. I had to wonder if Drewe was seeing another man, or men.

Love more than one person, our love only increases.

I didn't believe this. What I knew of love was that it made me jealous, not generous.

In a rush of words I said, "I want to see him again. I miss Virgil West. I miss—"

Coolly Drewe said, "Virgil isn't interested in you any longer, Marta. 'Babysitting bores me,' he has said. So, sorry."

Drewe turned away, her cell phone was ringing.

I folded up the *New York Times* clumsily and replaced it on the table. Thank God, no one had come into the common room to discover me.

I slipped away undetected. My heart pounded in resentment, shame. I had no wish to see others, I would avoid the dining hall through the day, I would cut most of my classes. Beyond the school playing fields were trails through the woods where I could wander for hours. Halfway I hoped I'd become lost, or hurt myself in a fall and be unable to return.

Been There. Done That. Aging Eros. I hadn't known how printed words can hurt, burn, slash. I felt sickened, as if I'd been the one to be insulted. Why had the reviewer said such things? Why had he decided to hate Virgil West? He might as easily, as plausibly have admired him, for the reasons he'd given for disliking him.

I seemed to know: this was only the first of such cruel reviews of "New Paintings 1991–2001." No matter the beauty and power of

Virgil West's work, or the effort that had gone into the work. It was the small, mean mood of the time: a wish to punish.

Babysitting is boring. I'd never believed that Virgil West had made such a remark, only Aunt Drewe could have thought of such a remark, to silence me. Not Virgil West upon whom I'd made so slight an impression.

"He is a great man. A great artist."

It was a cool October day, a gray haze hung over the Berkshire hills. The gaudy autumn foliage was muted, fading.

I carried my cell phone everywhere with me, in the hope that Aunt Drewe might call, now I placed calls to her several numbers and left messages. *Aunt Drewe? Just me. Checking in. Hope you can call me back.*

Of course I called Magdalena, whom I called frequently, in any case, for Magdalena was always happy to hear from me, unless she was too busy. I asked about my aunt and Magdalena said "Mrs. Hildebrand" was in the city, she didn't know when she'd be back.

I wondered if Magdalena had heard yet about the review in the *Times.* I didn't think that Magdalena read the newspaper or gave much thought to reviews.

Everyone involved in the arts colony would know, certainly. Word would have spread in the Big Barn.

I called the Hildebrand Gallery, asking to speak with Aunt Drewe. The receptionist knew me, or should have known me: her employer's niece Marta, whom she'd met several times, though had not seen recently. Politely the young woman said, "Mrs. Hildebrand isn't taking calls right now. But I'll tell her—is it 'Marta'?—has called." I said please, it was urgent that I speak with Aunt Drewe, and the receptionist said, "I'll tell Mrs. Hildebrand that you called, Marta. I'm sure she will want to speak with you."

She didn't, though. Not for the remainder of that day, and the night that followed, and most of the following day, until early evening.

And not for weeks would I see her, not until Thanksgiving recess when I was allowed to return home. Lifting my eyes to Drewe's, anxious and eager to know if I was loved, if I'd be hugged in the old way, in arms that were strong enough, if she wished, to crack my ribs.

"My family. My friends, and my family. *I love you.*"

It was Thanksgiving 2001: twenty-two guests at the table in Drewe's house in Chateauguay Springs. Drewe stood at the head of the table dramatically lifting her champagne glass in a toast, that spilled over onto her fingers.

Dazzling in a minutely pleated crimson kimono, her dark scissor-cut hair swinging about her face that was pale as a geisha's. Her wrists glittered with bracelets, her hands trembled. Much of the evening she'd been drinking with her guests of whom several were staying the night. I'd been introduced to them, their names had flown past. Maybe I'd met them before, in New York. No one seemed to remember me.

"This time of 'thanks-giving,' after tragedy, we give thanks for one another simply to be . . ."—Drewe faltered, gazing out over the candlelit table as if searching for someone not there—". . . alive."

Others lifted their glasses. It was a festive occasion. It was difficult to hear much that was said, voices were so loud. I was grateful
that Drewe had included me.

I was seated at the farther end of the long table, with several of
Drewe's staff members, including Marcus Heller. We sat on mismatched chairs not cushioned chairs like those nearer the head of
the table, our elbows collided, we were giddy with laughter. I was
the youngest of Drewe's Thanksgiving guests. I wondered if she'd
included me out of pity, or because, despite my failings, she still
liked me.

" 'Marta'? Drewe's niece? Very nice to meet you."

My hand was shaken, my name was spoken. Quick assessing
looks were cast my way. I felt my face redden in an unattractive
blush.

Drewe's glamorous friends! Except some of them were defiantly
unglamorous. They were artists, or individuals associated with the
"art world." Most of them were male.

(Derrick, the light-sculptor who'd caused such trouble at
Chateauguay Springs, who'd threatened Drewe and ended by trash-
ing his cabin, had at least vanished from her life.)

Since Virgil West's departure from Drewe's life, her new male
friends tended to be younger than West, of a generation younger
than Drewe's own. I wondered which of them was Drewe's lover. If
Drewe had a lover. I tried not to stare. I tried not to fumble and spill
my wineglass onto the white linen tablecloth.

Here was terrible news, I don't think I was supposed to know:
since the disastrous opening of West's new exhibit, he had broken
with the Hildebrand Gallery, or was trying legally to break with it;
he was suing to annul his contract. Lawyers were involved, litigation.

Still, Drewe was determined to have a festive Thanksgiving. There was a tradition at Chateauguay Springs of such Thanksgivings, with many guests. Drinks before dinner began at 5 P.M. and continued until nearly 9 P.M., more guests kept arriving. Magdalena and two helpers had prepared a sumptuous meal: roast goose. There were large platters of food. There was Champagne, and there was wine, numerous bottles of wine. Up and down the lengthy table like wildfire, talk ran. Much was hilarious. There were shrieks, interruptions. Talk of art: art in the "shadow" of 9/11. There were solemn speeches, there were arguments. Drewe's face seemed puffy, her skin sickly white. The flickering candlelight was not flattering to many of the guests. Drewe seemed sometimes not to be listening to the conversation, her gaze drifted away, bored. The roast geese were carved by one of Drewe's New York friends, a stranger to me with whom Drewe seemed on familiar terms. He was a handsome youngish man with a shaved head, pierced ears, pierced eyebrow, pierced upper lip. The long sharp knife blade flashed in his fingers. Jagged pieces of goose fell from plates onto the tablecloth, there were gravy stains, wine stains. More food was passed, more wine bottles were opened. Embarrassed, Magdalena was summoned out of the kitchen to be applauded. Drewe lifted her glass in a toast: "To those we don't deserve! Dear Magdalena, we thank you."

Arguments began to flare up, like flash fires. My face felt feverish, I helped Magdalena and the other women clear the table. No one was leaving. The wax candles were burning down, dripping onto the table. One of Drewe's male friends spoke contemptuously of the hypocrisy of the United States government: "All of the world says, 'They deserved it.' Except us, unable to see ourselves." Drewe said, incensed, "It has nothing to do with the 'terrorism' of the Middle East, it's our own terrorism, our self-loathing. In New York it's a feeding frenzy." Smiling bitterly Drewe said, "I'm thinking of selling the gallery. I want to live in the country and lick my wounds. Fuck the gallery. Fuck art. Fuck 'soul.'"

Laughter. As if Drewe meant to be funny.

Shortly afterward Drewe rose from the table, swaying as she left the dining room. She'd kicked off her glittery high-heeled sandals and was barefoot. Her departure was abrupt and unexplained but her guests were talking loudly among themselves and took little notice. I'd been helping Magdalena clear the table, now I followed my aunt upstairs at a discreet distance. I hoped that no one else would follow.

Drewe stumbled to her room, muttering to herself, shut the door, hard. Uncertainly I waited in the corridor. From downstairs came voices, laughter. Loud bawling laughter. It was after 11 P.M., dinner had begun late, had straggled on for hours as it often did at one of Drewe's dinner parties, most of the guests were drunk. I summoned courage to knock at Drewe's door. "Aunt Drewe? Are you all right?" There was no reply. Beneath the door, I saw a dim light. I waited a minute or two and knocked again. Earnestly I said, "It's me, Aunt Drewe. Can I come in?"

Drewe's voice came quick and muffled through the door. "No! Go away. I'm very tired."

I slumped against the door. My back against the door. My knees drawn to my chest. I would protect her, I thought. Or maybe this wasn't a thought. Asleep against the door of my aunt's bedroom, my head lolling and mouth open like a dead girl's.

The Hike

―――

"Marta?"

Next day. Dark-windy-November. Hiking along the cliff above the river. Drewe was impatient with weakness, her own as well as others. She'd drunk too much the night before, she said. Disgusted with herself now needing to clean—cleanse?—her head. Did I want to join her she'd asked.

"Yes! Yes, Aunt Drewe."

Eager, scrambling like a puppy. *Yes yes yes yes yes Aunt Drewe.*

Here was an astonishment. Here was disbelief. For Aunt Drewe seemed to love me again. She did!

For five months we hadn't walked together. Hadn't hiked in the woods, or along the cliff above the river. Since Cornwall-on-Hudson when I'd disappointed her. Oh I was excited, confused. I would not remember what happened exactly. It was the day after Thanksgiving. It was afternoon. It might've been dusk, the sky was heavy with thunderhead clouds, not a day for hiking along the cliff above the river. A taste of snow in the air. The sky, and the river the color of lead. Drewe's houseguests had departed. Drewe had asked them to leave. Drewe wanted to be alone. Yet Drewe had knocked on my door: "Marta?"

Laughing at me, the look in my face so puppy-eager.

Maybe she knew. Probably yes. How I'd fallen asleep slumped against the outside of her door. That morning I'd wakened sprawled on my bed. In my room. Clothes loosened, shoes removed. Someone must have carried me away from Drewe's door. I think this is what happened. So tired!—I could not have crawled away by myself. My eyelids so heavy. Not-wanting yet wanting Drewe to discover me. Never would I know who carried me away to my room. Which of the strangers had laid hands on me.

Drewe's (male) friends. It was the start of all that, I would not realize at the time.

That day, after Thanksgiving. The day of our hike together.

Astonishing to me, as in a dream where too much of what you've wished has come true. Already when Drewe knocked on my door she was wearing hiking boots, warm trousers, a quilted jacket with a hood. Her hair that had become dramatic-dark was flattened and had been brushed back carelessly from her face that wasn't made up like a geisha's in ivory-pale powder, her face was exposed to the light, showing its age, slightly puffy, a faint yellowish tinge to the skin, the eyes. But the expression in the eyes was tender, I thought. Laughing at me, at clumsy Marta, but tender.

Does she forgive me? In my excitement I could not remember what it was for which I had to be forgiven.

The house was quiet except for the wind. A creaking in the windows, high in the roof. Where braying laughter had been now there was this quiet. A lingering odor of cigarette smoke, hash. Some of the guests had smoked hash. An odor of roast goose. We would avoid that part of the house, we would take the back stairs. Drewe's footsteps heavy on the stairs. Wouldn't go near the public rooms of the historic old house: dining room, living room/art gallery, front foyer with its marble floor, chandelier. The elegant old house, even with its front rooms made to look contemporary, one of the Thanksgiving dinner guests had asked Drewe if the house was haunted?

Wittily Drewe had said all places are haunted, if there's a human head nearby.

Memories, you mean.

Doesn't need to be memories, even. Just a human brain inside a head.

"You and me, Marta. Fuck the rest of 'em, see?"

Drewe clapped her hands to hurry me. I grabbed a canvas jacket from a peg in the back hall, kicked my feet into my hiking boots. At school often this fall I'd been walking by myself, hiking along hilly trails, needing to be alone with my thoughts, my legs had grown hard with muscle. Outside, I had to hurry to keep up with Drewe. This woman was nothing like the glamorous Drewe Hildebrand but another woman entirely, sucking in the fresh air, exhilarated. I saw how the glowering November light exposed lines in her face, deepened the shallows beneath her eyes. Drewe caught my glance and laughed. "Aunt Drewe looks her age, eh? Well, good! I hate hypocrisy, Marta. I hate dinner parties and don't know what kind of madness comes over me, giving them. I've decided: never another fucking 'dinner party'— no more fucking 'houseguests.' I hate drinking and I hate 'getting high' and I hate people sucking up to me, a sow with too many teats."

I laughed with sheer happiness, hearing these words.

We were crossing the back lawn, through winter-stiffened grasses, toward the river. Wind rushed at us fierce and cold, tasting of snow. Oh I wished I'd worn a heavier sweater beneath my jacket! I had to hurry, keeping pace with Aunt Drewe's exuberant strides.

So long the shadow of Virgil West had fallen between us, not to be acknowledged. Never would I have dared to speak of him except suddenly Drewe said, "*He! Him!* A ridiculous old man. 'Only a whore cares about money,' he said. 'That's what you wanted from me, wasn't it—money.' I told him he was insane, to say such things. I told him he had to know that I loved him. But his vanity had been wounded, nothing else mattered. A man's vanity is his soul. A man's vanity is more precious to him than his cock. I realized then, he never knew me. None of you do. I pass among you, you see nothing. I offer my love to you, you spurn it. He wanted to believe that the reception of his art in the world would not matter to him, Virgil West is superior to such things, and the shock of it was, it did matter. Oh, it mattered! In his art the man is a genius but in his life he's become a ridiculous vain old man. That is what he can't forgive me for seeing."

Drewe spoke angrily, derisively. I was shocked she'd confided in me like this. For she would regret it, and despise me.

She'd had too much to drink the night before, very likely she'd gotten high (not hash but high-quality cocaine brought by her Manhattan friends was Drewe's drug of choice) and the effects lingered: her eyes were threaded with blood, tiny broken capillaries that gave them an unnatural glisten, a kind of frantic enthusiasm seemed to drive her forward. Experienced hikers know to conserve their energy but Drewe was determined to keep a fast pace though breathing hard, through her mouth. Inside my clothes I was beginning to sweat, despite the cold wind on my face. I supposed that Drewe had told no one where we were going. The trail was increasingly overgrown, rocky. Stones and small pebbles were loosened beneath our feet, miniature avalanches that caused me to lose my balance, fall to one knee. Luckily I was able to break the fall with my hand. I thought *At least we can't become lost here, there is only one way back.*

After about forty minutes, at the top of a lengthy, exhausting hill, Drewe finally paused, to rest. Hesitantly I said, "Maybe we should go back now, Aunt Drewe? We've come pretty far." I couldn't see Chateauguay Springs in the distance behind us: Drewe's house, the Big Barn. Drewe said indifferently, "Go back if you want to. I'm fine."

Below us the river rushed, as if driven by the wind. There was no barrier, no fence, if you stepped carelessly forward, you could lose your footing, begin to slide, fall from the trail down the steep cliff and into the rocks, maybe into the swift-flowing current, below.

I didn't want to leave Drewe here. I could not.

Drewe asked what was across the river and I told her, I thought it was Hudson Highlands State Park. A few miles to the south, lights were flickering. The river had to be a mile wide at this point. There were no houses, no human habitations in sight. Water rushed whitecapped, pocked and heaving with wind as if the tentacles of a giant sea-beast were writhing below the surface. It was growing dark, a premature dusk. Snow flurries had begun in mad swirling patches. A pale sun appeared as a crack of flame in the thunderhead clouds. Fleeting rays of light in the lead-colored river like flame. Drewe groped for my hand, suddenly excited, euphoric. Raising her voice to be heard above the wind, "Marta! Darling! I know now why I've been summoned here today: to realize that I don't want to die. In my very misery I want never to die. Isn't that remarkable, Marta? Isn't it? Only just to 'die' in the broken, vain self, and to be reborn in another. To slough off the old, putrifying skin, to come alive in another skin. The suicide terrorists understand this, this is their mission. We believe they are deluded. They die, but are not reborn—we might die, and be reborn. This is why I've been summoned, Marta. And why you have come with me."

I had no idea what Drewe was talking about. Words seemed to spring from her of their own volition. She seized my head in her hands, kissed me hard on the mouth, a kiss like an exclamation, a quick hard impress of teeth. In the next instant she pushed me from her.

"He's old, I am not. He can choke on his own vomit, I will not."

Hawks circled overhead, riding the wind. Smaller birds, that might have been gulls, flew above the river, wind-buffeted. The kiss would burn on my mouth, I stood breathless, confused.

Abruptly now Drewe turned back, she'd had enough of hiking for the day. I followed behind her slipping and sliding, panting. My knee must have been injured, blood was seeping through the fabric of my trousers. Sharp pains radiated downward from my left knee into my leg. Pausing to rest, to catch my breath, seemed to have been a mistake, now I was limping. My aunt drew farther away, not glancing back. I didn't want her to see: she despised weakness. And then I slipped, and turned my ankle, and fell.

Immediately scrambling to my feet. My right hand stung, as if frozen with shock. My right ankle throbbed with pain.

My aunt Drewe was nearly thirty years older than I was, yet I could not keep up with her on the trail. I could barely see her, tears flooding my eyes. Finally I had to call: "Aunt Drewe! Aunt Drewe! Wait." My voice was piteous, pathetic. Wind blew away my cries. I wondered if Drewe heard me and was deliberately abandoning me, out of contempt.

I thought you'd forgiven me. I thought you loved me again.

The wind! There was mockery in the wind, loosening the hood I'd fastened over my head, blinding me with tears.

Suddenly, I was on the ground. My legs had given out, I fell heavily again, striking my head against an outcropping of rock. I had not been able to protect myself, my arms had moved too slowly. I might have lost consciousness for a moment. Something trickled down the side of my face. My heartbeat was wild, erratic. I was crying, pleading. When I'd first come to live with my aunt she'd told me *In you, Marta, I hope to rediscover life. What life is, not just what happens in life.* But I had failed her, I thought. I had not understood at the time, I didn't understand now. But I knew that I had failed, I was of no worth.

"Marta?"

How many minutes had passed, I wasn't sure. Drewe had returned and was leaning over me, staring into my face. Her look was incredulous. "Marta? What have you done? Hurt yourself, have you! Bleeding! Oh, look at you: your face! I've been wondering where the hell you were, how fucking slow, this is ridiculous, you aren't even half my age." Disgusted, Drewe squatted beside me, hauling me up into her arms. She was furious with me and yet tender: rocking me in her arms. She dabbed at my bleeding face with a wadded tissue. She comforted me as, helplessly, I cried. I begged for Drewe to forgive me, I knew she hated weakness, hated tears, but Drewe said, sighing, "What can I expect. My peasant-girl-niece, from Cattaraugus. Maybe you aren't beautiful. Maybe you aren't even very attractive. Maybe you're just an ordinary girl, you might as well attend the local high school, make your friends there. You are to help me, are you! Why, it's a joke. I will have to haul you home."

I didn't hear this. Not most of this. I heard the scolding, and I heard the disgust, but I heard the tenderness beneath. That day after Thanksgiving 2001 hiking with my aunt Drewe on the trail above the river. After she was gone, I would remember this. Not my aunt's words but the way she'd held me, rocked and cradled me in her arms. They would ask where she'd gone, who had taken her. Which of her enemies had taken her. I would remember only her arms holding me, sheltering me from the wind, until strength from Drewe flowed into me and I was strong enough to stand, and limp back down the trail, Drewe's supporting arm tight around my waist. I would remember thinking in elation *She loves me, she forgives me.*

I would remember happiness.

"Happiness"

Months later: therapist asks why do I believe I am having such protracted "problems of adjustment" at school and the reply is a small politely baffled smile, twining my fingers in my hair, giving a surreptitious tug that brings quick tears to my eyes though my poker face shows nothing, as usual. Mumbled words issue from my mouth: "I don't know."

Sometimes adding, "Sorry."

Dr. Beagle, or Beedle, therapist/psychologist. She is called, calls herself, conspicuously, "Doctor."

Meaning not Doctor of Medicine but Ph.D. As if the two are equivalent.

Which of my teachers at the Pittsfield School advised weekly sessions with the resident therapist, maybe it was all of my teachers. The headmaster as well. Headmaster called Drewe, speaking of her niece's protracted "problems of adjustment" now we're well into the spring term, I didn't want to imagine what my aunt's response was.

Sitting quietly in hard-backed chairs facing adults. Quickly I'd run my fingers through my matted hair, washed my face chafed and windburnt from hiking outdoors, I'm embarrassed to be blowing my nose. I try to be polite but baffled, unyielding. Possibly I'm seen as sullen, sulky. My eyes have a tendency to drift to the lead-paned windows.

Outdoors: alone. Hiking, alone. Or just walking, wandering.

Always I carry my cell phone with me. If someone wishes to call.

Of course the headmaster at the Pittsfield School knew who Drewe Hildebrand was, immediately. (I'd recently discovered that through my aunt's professional association with an alum/trustee of the school, she'd arranged for me to be admitted after the deadline for applications the previous spring.) The headmaster has told Dr. Beagle, or Beedle, who is warmly friendly in these sessions with me, not wishing to pry, wishing "only to help, Marta," wary of offending the rich-patroness aunt who is paying my tuition.

I don't tell Dr. B. that I'm unhappy at school because I want to be somewhere else: home. That I'm counting the days until the next weekend Drewe will allow me to come home. Counting the days until the end of the term.

Dr. B. is a middle-aged woman with a sweet, pained, earnest squint, somehow I know that Drewe would be contemptuous of her. I hear myself tell her that I will try to be "more detached" from home.

Dr. B. asks if I am unhappy at the Pittsfield School?

Unhappy? How could I be happy, here? I bite my lower lip, to keep from laughing.

"My aunt Drewe doesn't believe that 'happiness' is very important."

Dr. B. blinks as if she has never heard such a remarkable statement. "But, Marta—what do you think?"

"What do I think?"

The question stumps me. *What do I think?*

"Yes. What do you think? If 'happiness' isn't important, what is?"

Desperately I try to remember: what has Drewe said? But Drewe has said so many extravagant things . . . Happiness is having a large, not a "small, stunted" soul; happiness is "taking risks," not "playing it safe." What this means exactly, I don't know.

Surreptitiously, I give one of my long straggly hairs a tug, and pull it out. Soon a coin-sized thinness will appear just above my hairline at my left temple. Think! What do I think!

Dr. Beagle, or Beedle, repeats her question. "If happiness isn't important, Marta, what is?"

"Happiness," Cont'd.

But we were happy, Drewe and Marta! For a time we were happy.

I remember this, I think.

When I was seventeen. Stricken with flu in the infirmary at the Pittsfield School. It was mid-winter. Half the school was sick. A week, ten days. The infirmary wasn't large enough to accommodate so many sick students. Magdalena tracked Drewe down, wherever Drewe was, possibly traveling with a new (male?) friend, and Drewe spoke with me on the phone, Drewe chided me at first for "catching some bug" then began to sympathize, my fever was running at 101°F, Drewe arranged for a "real" doctor from Pittsfield to examine me, not trusting the credentials of the school's resident doctor; after which I was allowed to return home to Chateauguay Springs to recover, a car was sent for me driven by a newly hired driver (Noah Rathke, but I was too sick to take note of him), I wept with gratitude, with love, allowed back to the warmth and comfort of my room on the second floor of Drewe's beautiful old house.

When Drewe was home, we watched videos together on the flat-screen TV in her loft/studio/bedroom. When Drewe wasn't spending the weekend in New York, or Chicago, or "taking the red-eye" out to L.A., we had Chinese takeout, pizzas, fetched for us from Newburgh by the newly hired driver. "Isn't this fun! I missed adolescence the first time around." Drewe had become bored with her Asian-exotic high-couture look, she'd had her hair cut punk-style, cut short to her skull, dyed maroon that glistened like shoe polish.

(Drewe had considered having my hair cut in punk-style, too, and dyed to match. Except, studying me critically, she'd had to concede that I lacked the cheekbones for the look, my face was too "earthy-peasant.") Drewe dumped onto my bed the most exciting art brochures, museum catalogs from her trips. Drewe gossiped with me about her "crazy friends" whose names meant nothing to me. Drewe bought me books, cascades of paperback books: art books: travel books, memoirs, novels, poetry. Sylvia Plath was her favorite poet, she said. I made an effort to read most of these books until I began to realize that Drewe hadn't herself read them, not even Sylvia Plath, with much care. I wondered if art didn't appeal to her because it was something you saw, not something you had to read; something you saw immediately, could react to immediately, not something you had to take time with.

Drewe tossed onto my bed a slender book titled, simply, *Andy Warhol.* Saying, "So that's what Andy was doing! I never knew. 'He couldn't stand "old" art.'"

The Pittsfield School had granted me a "medical leave" but recovery was slow. I was supposed to be keeping up with schoolwork via e-mail and teachers' web sites but somehow I fell behind, it seemed that I was always "relapsing," catching chest colds from leaning out my windows, running from the house to the Big Barn without taking time to put on a jacket or sweater. Finally, in April, it was too late for me to catch up with my courses, I'd missed too many tests, papers. It was planned then that I would take summer courses at Pittsfield to make up as much as I could but somehow, that failed to happen, too.

Drewe laughed, running her fingers through her punk-style hair in exasperation. "Marta-girl, I'm not happy with this. I perceive that you've been messing with my head as I've told you I don't appreciate. You know you need to be educated. In another year or so you'll want to go to college and won't be able to get into a decent school with your grades."

Pouting, I said she hadn't gone to college. And she was the smartest person I knew.

Such brazen flattery was allowed: Drewe could construe it as a joke.

Also, it was true. Aunt Drewe was the smartest person I'd ever met.

"Well, that's me, Marta. That was me. In the mid-1970s, when things seemed somehow easier. Before you were born."

"Why's it different now? I don't need damn old college, I can learn from you. Things you tell me, things you bring me. The art I see out here, and at your gallery. Aren't I your 'intern'? I could be your assistant. I could help mount shows. Nobody would be so . . ."—searching for the right word, the perfect word, to convince, to seduce—". . . faithful to you as me, Aunt Drewe. I promise."

Because I am your niece. Your blood relation.

For a long moment Drewe stared at me. With a strange wistful smile saying, "It's so, we want to discover life through others. We can only savor life the second time. Except . . ." Her voice trailed off, there was an awkward silence.

Like a child pressing my advantage I said I didn't need college, why did I need college! I didn't even need school.

"I'm seventeen, I don't have to go back, ever. Anywhere."

"Marta, don't be ridiculous. You are not going to quit school at seventeen."

"Aunt Drewe, please. *Please please please.*"

We were sprawled on my bed. Pizza crusts lay strewn about us. Drewe seized a clump of my hair in her fist, gave my head a shake. "Didn't I tell you, girl, not to mess with me? Not to try to manipulate me? I warned you, didn't I?"

I stuck out my tongue at Drewe. Laughing, shrieking with laughter, snatching up a pillow to hide behind, that Drewe punched with her fists like a boxer hitting a heavy bag.

Please please please please please.

Aunt Drewe never said yes, but Aunt Drewe never said no. And somehow no arrangements were made for me to return to the Pittsfield School in September. Or to enroll at any other school, anywhere.

So happy! I couldn't believe my good luck, messing with Drewe Hildebrand's head.

After Xenia

You can touch it, Marta! Like this."

Laughing, Drewe reached for my hand. I felt a wave of childish revulsion, panic. Close by, the "Scots" sculptor stood watching us, with a lewd smile. For it was his head, the "blood-masked" replica of his head, my aunt was insisting that I touch.

Like his sex. A man's sex. I won't. I hate it. My fingers will smell of it, afterward.

It was a blustery November evening. Three of us alone together in the Hildebrand Gallery. The gallery's doors were locked for the day, lights had been dimmed. Xenia had been telling us, lecturing to us: only biological identity (cells, molecules, DNA) abides, all else is ephemeral, lost. He'd had to extract his blood from his veins over a period of several months because he couldn't find a medical worker willing to extract blood for such a purpose. Xenia was filled with contempt for "the tribe" that knows nothing about art yet presumes to judge art, and artists, by their own blind standards. Drewe smiled, brandishing the key to the freezer-display case where *Blood Mask I* was kept on a pedestal. The blood-masked head was on display in her gallery but it was not for sale, for Drewe had bought it for her private collection. She said, "The most profound art, I think. 'Bio-art.' Xenia is a pioneer. To make of ourselves, our material selves, such blood masks to outlive us."

Drewe's voice quavered with pride. Her hand weighted with rings drifted onto the big-knuckled hand of the sculptor. A blind woman's hand, groping.

Why did she want me with them! Why must Marta be a witness.

It was a sexual thing, I knew. I just didn't know why.

Weeks I'd been hearing about the Scots sculptor Xenia who had taken a name nothing like his "tribal" birth name. In the most advanced art circles Xenia was revered as *radical, visionary, a revolutionary,* in other circles Xenia was denounced as *monstrous, exploitative, sensationalist, sick, depraved.* He was *courageous,* he was *outrageous.* In Britain, his anatomical sculptures had received a range of responses: *disgusting, trash, worthless, ingenious, deeply disturbing, exciting, groundbreaking, of a rare, tragic beauty.* In an influential art journal that had been dismissive of Virgil West's paintings, Xenia had been heralded as *a twenty-first century Hieronymus Bosch.*

"Xenia" was a biological term: having to do with the effect of genes introduced by a male nucleus on structures other than the embryo. I didn't pretend to know what this meant. I wondered if it was the (male) conquest of nature.

Drewe was urging me to touch the head: "It's frozen solid, Marta! You can't damage it."

Drewe chided, teased. The sculptor looked on, amused.

In Drewe's firm grip, my reluctant fingers were made to brush against the top of the head that was layered in frozen blood, in a texture to suggest thin, flattened strands of hair on the scalp. It seemed to me in that instant that my fingertips were burnt, in fact the blood mask was frozen solid, it was icy-cold I felt.

So ugly! The shuttered eyes, lined cheeks and fleshy lips set in a disdainful expression that was a mirror of the sculptor's usual expression. The frozen blood mask looked like raw tissue with its skin peeled away. Coagulated and frozen, the blood had become a deep rich crimson that appeared earthy, sulphurous.

The neck was unusually thick. As if blood-engorged.

I shuddered, in revulsion. The adults, looking on, laughed.

She wants me to touch him, too. Love him.

Unlike Virgil West, Xenia was well aware of me. Marta, the niece. His eyes moved on me insolent and assessing. No, I was not beautiful, not with my clothes on, anyway. But yes, I was young.

". . . these opportunities, how mysteriously they happen, that can alter our lives permanently. Chance encounters, a door opens and if you have the courage to step through . . ."

Drewe spoke urgently. I didn't meet her eye. I seemed to know: after Xenia, my life with Aunt Drewe would never be the same again.

Hate him! The way my beautiful aunt gazed adoringly at this troll-man who was hardly her height, with his paunchy round-shouldered body inside a sleek Armani jacket that fitted his torso too tightly, how frequently she touched him as she spoke, deferred to him, as once she'd deferred to Virgil West. But Xenia was no one like Virgil West.

In turn, Xenia spoke to Drewe with condescending familiarity, as if taking the rich American woman's patronage as his due.

". . . and feel here, Marta! The eyes, almost you can feel the eyeballs inside quickening with life . . ."

So often the Scots sculptor had been told he was a "genius"—
"diabolical, but a genius"—how could he doubt it?

Xenia laughed often, showing blunt stubby teeth. He had a sallow skin, faint acne scars, thin sparrow-colored hair. His close-set eyes had a sparkly confidence, glittered with a sort of manic life, I hadn't yet understood was cocaine-fueled.

The man's throaty Scots accent. The way he called Drewe "darlin' "—"love." Even as he glanced at me, with a snaky smile.

"There! You see, Marta, it didn't hurt, did it?"

Drewe released my hand and I drew it quickly back as if I'd been burnt.

Drewe persisted, "Well, Marta: did it?"

Did it what, I wondered. My lips mumbled *No*.

"Of course it didn't hurt. The texture is fascinating: human blood, sculpted like stone. A new kind of beauty."

For weeks, Drewe had been excited about the newest art: *bio-art, bio-anatomical-art*. The "old, petrified" way of "art materials" like stone, clay, paint employed in the service of "replicating" the physical world was finished, Drewe proclaimed. Now, the physical world would be the art itself, the artist had become a kind of god, transforming biological materials, i.e. bodies, blood, tissues, organs, skeleton into permanent works of art, that were scientifically treated to resist decay.

"It will be our new immortality. I mean, it will be immortality—in art. For there is no other."

Drewe had commissioned a blood mask of her own head, to be sculpted out of her own blood, from Xenia. In an arts column in the *New Yorker* it was noted that the commission had been for an "undisclosed high six-figure sum."

Noted also, that Drewe Hildebrand had "snapped up" the "hot new Scots sculptor Xenia" for the Hildebrand Gallery.

"Xenia" was actually "MacSweeney, Gregor." Born in Edinburgh in 1959. He'd never finished university but had worked in advertising, television. He'd had a long slow meandering career as an artist in a traditional mode (easel painting, figure sculpture) until in the 1990s he'd reinvented himself as an anatomical-art sculptor aligned with the London Arts Alliance, a group of radical artists in turn taken up by the Rizzi Gallery where in September 2002 Drewe had met him at an exhibit opening. She'd been immediately "devastated" by Xenia's confrontational sculptures: a continuously playing and replaying video of a (visibly) decomposing human corpse, freakish human embryos in formaldehyde tanks, and mummified creatures (dogs, sheep, swans, stillborn foals) arranged in mimicry of classic sculptures by Michelangelo, Bernini, Rodin. Within forty-eight hours, Drewe had signed up the Scots sculptor Xenia for the Hildebrand Gallery. Within a week, she'd brought him back in triumph with her to New York City.

Drewe believed that American collectors of avant-garde art and the more adventurous museums would soon compete for Xenia's work.

"Not Hieronymus Bosch but Warhol. Xenia will be the twenty-first century Andy Warhol."

Xenia laughed smugly, scratching at his chest. Beneath the expensive Armani jacket Xenia wore a cheap nylon sports shirt in Day-Glo green. His small moist beady eyes on me slid like grease.

Sure, Warhol was one of his heroes, Xenia conceded. Naturally, you want to eat the hearts of your heroes.

Xenia divided his time between New York City where he lived

as a guest in Drewe's lavish condominium overlooking the East River, and Chateauguay Springs, where Drewe had arranged for him to be a resident artist. (There was some bitterness about the Scots sculptor at Chateauguay Springs since Xenia had not applied for a residency like the others. He boasted of having never heard of the "famous American artists' colony" until Drewe had informed him he'd been granted a six-month renewable residency.)

Drewe had purchased the notorious *Blood Mask I* for her private collection and had it enshrined, on display, in the Hildebrand Gallery. Payment for the sensational artwork was rumored to be in the "high six figures."

"And one day, Marta, we may commission Xenia to do *you*."

Again the adults laughed. A strange excitement in their laughter. I thought *They are fond of me, they won't hurt me.*

Brandishing the key, Drewe locked up the freezer-display case. She and Xenia were awaited at a dinner party. I was to be driven back to Chateauguay Springs by Drewe's chauffeur. Marta wasn't welcome in the East Side apartment where tonight Xenia would share the bedroom of his wealthy patroness.

The long drive back to Chateauguay Springs, north along the Hudson River, in darkness.

The driver Noah Rathke had no reason to speak to me except to ask politely, as such drivers do, if the "air temperature" in the car was all right. I told him yes. I slouched down in the cushioned rear of the limousine to avoid being seen by him in the rearview mirror.

Didn't want anyone to see! My eyes sullen and brimming with tears, my mouth twisted like wire.

Didn't want Noah Rathke to say in his polite startled voice *Excuse me is something wrong?*

My hands smelled. A man's fetid blood. For days I would wash, wash, wash my hands that were already chapped and reddened but the blood-odor would remain.

Trust

There is a kind of peace in it, Marta. Giving yourself up.

Those months at Chateauguay Springs he was living with us, drawing her blood in his syringes. Warm blood to be chilled in pint jars in a refrigeration unit in Xenia's studio. In preparation for the sculpting of *Blood Mask II*.

The blood-drawing required approximately eight weeks. Otherwise, Aunt Drewe would become anemic from blood loss.

If you trust the syringe-bearer. No pain.

From Xenia's studio in a newer wing of the Big Barn they summoned me to assist. CD speakers in the open, cluttered space boomed high-decibel music while Xenia worked: Pavarotti, Callas, heavy-metal rock, "industrial" rock, contemporary rap staccato and relentless as machine-gun fire. Xenia smoked thin brown cigarillos as he worked, for a nicotine hit. To mellow out, Xenia smoked hashish or plain old American high-school pot.

Droplets of Drewe's blood were scattered like tears amid the mess of a sculptor's studio. Not very steadily in his big-knuckled hands Xenia wielded the syringe. His eyes were blood-veined, his stubby teeth shone. Drewe half-lay on a chair, Xenia crouched over her. He was not trained to wield a syringe. Crimson blood from a vein in Drewe's forearm jerked up into the syringe in a gesture of surprise.

"Oh. Oh *oh.*"

Ask why, ask what it meant, wasn't there danger of infection from the needles, wasn't there danger of madness. Now what was rumored of the artists' colony at Chateauguay Springs began to come true.

"Come help, Marta! Tighten this band around my arm so the vein swells . . ."

I was clumsy, I dropped things. Once, a container of warm blood Xenia handed me, my aunt's blood, that fell and splattered onto the floor.

Simultaneously Drewe and the Scots sculptor exclaimed:

"Marta! How could you."

"Clumsy cow."

It was a season of sudden winter storms, pine trees breaking beneath the weight of snow, the wide river clotted with ice. It was a season of loneliness, jealousy. When (almost) I regretted my impulsive decision to quit school and "learn" instead from Aunt Drewe.

I'd vowed to be loyal to her, faithful. In turn, I'd believed that Aunt Drewe had promised to protect me.

"This is my legacy to you, Marta. I hope you will be grateful."

The Scots sculptor was a revolutionary, Drewe had no doubt. As Andy Warhol had changed Drewe's life as a young woman by his mere presence so Xenia might change my life, if I would allow it.

Xenia who never lurched downstairs before 1 P.M. Xenia who

wore designer clothes purchased for him by Drewe—Armani, Issey Miyake—with filthy jeans, Twin Tower T-shirts purchased from sidewalk venders near Ground Zero. Xenia who washed only parts of his hairy body, whose armpits stank of something metallic. Moving among us casting his insolent gaze at us with the swagger of an unshaven god.

Xenia was a perfectionist. Xenia was thrown into a fury by imperfection.

Out of the high-decibel confusion of Xenia's studio a succession of starkly white clay heads was produced by Xenia's hands slowly and it seemed by hit-or-miss and one by one the clay heads were denounced and smashed as "imperfect." In his coked-up trance amid deafening music the sculptor could work for several hours without pause as his model, my aunt Drewe, docile as a chastened child, sat in a straight-backed chair on a draped white sheet in her own trance of oblivion gazing rapturously at the sculptor's eyes, mouth, groping hands. Eventually, over a disjointed period of days, weeks, interruptions and postponements and manic sieges of studio work, Xenia would produce a "head of Drewe" that resembled my aunt in the way that a death mask might resemble a living face, the eyes shuttered, jaws clenched as if in rigor mortis. Seeing the blank-eyed expressionless clay head you could not have said with certainty was it female, male. Nor did Xenia make any attempt to suggest his subject's hair (still short, no longer punk style but brushed back flat), the entire surface of the head was uniformly smooth, white, ghastly. This head, Xenia pronounced "Perfect!"

Drewe stared at the white clay thing with its disproportionately thick neck on the sculptor's worktable. She seemed about to speak, then fell silent. She laughed, wildly and briefly. In a kind of anguish she stroked the sculptor's coarse-haired forearm.

Later saying, "*Is* that me? Or what I will become?"

Next, the "blood-masking."

The blood would naturally thicken, in the pint jars. Xenia would add to it a polymer solution to retard organic decomposition.

Numerous interns vied to work with the Scots sculptor at Chateauguay Springs. I was not one of these.

One of these is your lover, Marta.

   I will choose, for you.

Winter: caravans of vehicles wound through the snow-laden pine woods to my aunt Drewe's "historical" house where, weekends, parties blazed through the sprawling downstairs rooms. These were parties attended by Drewe's and Xenia's ever-shifting and swelling cadre of "friends from New York." To these parties, only a very chosen few of the resident artists were invited, and none of the staff members.

A crowd of strangers who drank and "got high" together through the night, their laughter braying and brittle.

I dreaded Drewe's parties. Drewe pulled me by the hand, to display me.

   Martha, is it?—Marta.

   Drewe's niece, eh? If you say so.

   Not very friendly are you!

My head swam. What I'd been given to drink must have been drugged.

Drewe urged me to "experiment" with men, but only men of her selection. (Men who'd been Drewe's lovers, I understood from the glances between them.) Pressing drinks into my shaky hand, lifting a joint to my lips so that I could inhale the sweet-acrid smoke that left me dazed and coughing.

Clamping her warm hands over my eyes. So close behind me, I felt her heavy breasts against my back. I felt her breath at the nape of my neck. I became strangely passive, unresisting as a wild creature that has been blinded. I could not stagger and fall, there were hands to grip me.

Not to know your first lover's name. Not to know his face.

Don't be frightened, Marta! I will hold you.

There were mouths on mine, a taste of saliva, a pressure of teeth, a prodding tongue. Disembodied hand cupping my breasts, squeezing my thighs, hips. My head swam, spun. I was laughing helplessly. In the high-heeled wedge-soled shoes Drewe had given me I slipped, I lost my balance. The music was deafening. A hot heavy pulse. The room was dimly lighted, I'd been taken to another part of the house. I wasn't frightened any longer, it was soothing to be touched, stroked. The pressure of a stranger's mouth on mine. As if I was a beautiful young woman, a sexually desirable young woman to arouse admiration in others, and in my ever-critical aunt Drewe. Then suddenly my feeling of happiness turned to nausea, I was stricken by a fit of vomiting. Drewe's friends who'd been pressing near quickly leapt back with cries of disgust.

One day I would overhear Drewe say: "Something is abnormal in her. She hasn't matured. She will, though. Soon."

* * *

I began to tramp the woods. Even in freezing weather. Days overcast like gauze, days of snow-blinding sun. Except that I loved my aunt Drewe I might have drifted away into the howling wind.

It was a time of mysterious departures. Artists whose names I had known, whose faces had become familiar to me. Several of the Scots sculptor's assistants. It would be whispered that Drewe Hildebrand "paid them off" but how was this to be believed when so much was said of Drewe Hildebrand that was not to be believed.

Magdalena was upset, such "wild stories"—"nasty lies"—she sometimes overheard in the village, where she shopped. When I asked Magdalena what she'd been hearing she told me never mind, I did not want to know.

Artists formerly favored by Drewe before Xenia's arrival, now slighted by Drewe, seemingly forgotten, their new work of little interest to her, resigned abruptly and vacated their cabins and studios and carried away their wounded egos into the oblivion from which Drewe Hildebrand had plucked them. Even a few staff members quit.

Replacements were hurriedly acquired.

I tramped in the woods and along the rocky trail above the river and always now I was alone, for Aunt Drewe no longer hiked outdoors, it was enough for Drewe to drag herself from bed in the early afternoon and stagger downstairs disheveled and veiny-eyed murmuring *What day is this? What month?*

She was joking. Of course.

"You don't like me, love? Eh?"

Xenia teased, to see me blush like a confused child.

"And why's that? Don't know, do you? Eh?"

The "blood-masking" continued. It seemed to be so, the Scots sculptor was a perfectionist: "A fetishist." Repeatedly he sculpted the blood mask over the clay head, shaping the thickened blood with his fingers, repeatedly he was disappointed with his work, nothing would do but that he must start over again.

Other Xenia-sculptures were being prepared by assistants. Xenia oversaw, but had not time to work on everything that would bear his signature one day to be priceless: *Xenia*. Xenia's American debut was scheduled for mid-April at the Hildebrand Gallery in New York but Drewe had arranged for a preview of the exhibit at Chateauguay Springs a few weeks earlier. So proud was Drewe of her association with the "pre-eminent anatomical-art sculptor" that she'd ordered a large mailing of invitations for the preview, to bring individuals to the arts colony who had never seen Chateauguay Springs before.

Blood Mask II was to be the centerpiece of the preview exhibit in the Big Barn but at least a half-dozen other, equally radical sculptures would be ready to be seen as well. It was Xenia's custom to work on numerous projects simultaneously. His use of assistants was becoming notorious. Yet every enterprising artist from Michelangelo to Jeff Koons has understood that "art" can be executed by anyone with two hands, if the artist oversees and gives his signature to the art.

One day, Xenia intended to "mass-produce" his sculptures. Admittedly, replicating blood masks would be a challenge.

"After me, there will be you. Marta, we must!"

Such pressure Drewe was putting on me, to sit for Xenia, and to submit to a blood mask of my head. I felt an actual pressure like a band around my head.

"*Blood Mask III.* Your youth will be preserved. We can only savor youth a second time, through art."

Xenia's eyes moved on me like grease. He was uninvolved, essentially. He would do what his wealthy patroness wished him to do, so long as he wished to do it. He was bemused by Drewe's feeling for me, he did not share it.

"We can give you something to soothe your nerves. How jumpy you are, like a nervous cat! A calming white powder not 'habit-forming,' I swear."

Drewe had been arguing that, at least, I could sit for the sculptor to mold a clay likeness of my head and if it turned out well, if Xenia was pleased with it, we could advance to the next stage: the blood-drawing.

"It doesn't hurt, really. An initial sting, then it becomes numb. Everything is mental, Marta. We discover life through such adventures. What life 'is,' not merely what 'happens.' "

Drewe had been stroking my hair, my shoulder. The way you would stroke a cat, to calm it. And Drewe's touch did calm me. Except there came Xenia, as if innocently, to take hold of my arm, just a little too tightly, pressing his large thumb into an artery in my forearm even as, again in all innocence, the blunt edge of his hand nudged my breast.

A sensation passed through me, like wildfire.

Xenia was teasing, in a mock-Scots dialect: "Marta, love? Listen to your wise old auntie."

Wise old auntie. This was sly, cruel. It was like Xenia to murmur such remarks to taunt his rich patroness lover.

Drewe said, annoyed, "Marta, stop trembling! It isn't cold in the studio, you're behaving like a child. Here you have the opportunity to pose for a revolutionary artist, it's like having the opportunity to pose for Picasso, and you're resisting. It's an opportunity only my niece would be offered, I hope you realize."

I realized. I was trying to comprehend what the opportunity meant.

More warmly Drewe said, "If you're worried that the needle will hurt, I can take it from you myself. I'm sure I have a natural touch! If you trust the syringe-bearer, as you trust me, you will feel no pain, I promise. There is a kind of peace in it, Marta, giving yourself up to . . ."

I pulled away from them. I backed away. We were alone in Xenia's studio, the three of us. On a platform close by was the ghastly mangled-looking clay head now unevenly covered in coagulated blood, through which my aunt's features could be perceived, dimly. The shuttered eyes had a look of anguish.

Xenia's studio was suffocating, airless. It smelled of indefinable odors: organic rot, chemicals. Xenia hated fresh air, which he called "drafts." He'd ordered assistants to climb on ladders to duct-tape the edges of the skylight overhead, that was set so beautifully in the studio ceiling.

I was walking away, I couldn't breathe in here. Drewe was astonished at my behavior. I heard her call me "ungrateful"—"graceless." I heard her nearly stammering, so outraged, threatening to send me back to Cattaraugus with "your own kind."

I shoved the door open. It was one of the snow-blinding winter days. I heard my aunt's voice as I walked away. "Damn you, Marta: how dare you disobey me?"

* * *

Months later, the man who would become my first lover was to ask why didn't I leave Drewe Hildebrand, why hadn't I run for my life and I told him *How could I, my aunt Drewe was my life.*

Those weeks. February, early March 2003. When Drewe punished me by shutting me out of her life. She and her Scots lover and the "friends from New York" and their frequent trips to New York City to which I was no longer invited telling myself I did not care, I did not even notice, I would continue to work in the Big Barn as a staff member, the most reliable worker of all. Yet thinking *She loves me best. I know this. The way when the sun is hidden by clouds you never doubt it's there. You never doubt it will be returned to you.*

Two Men

That man. Oh!"

Even Magdalena whose temperament seemed to exclude ordinary reasonable complaining had to concede, in all her years of
working at Chateauguay Springs she had never encountered any
"houseguest" so demanding and personally squalid as Xenia.

"He isn't 'Xenia.' His name is 'MacSweeney.' It's a common
Scottish name. I hate him, I wish he would die."

Magdalena was shocked at my words. Sunday mornings she attended a Methodist church in the village of Chateauguay Springs,
on TV she watched religious programs.

I was incensed at Xenia on Magdalena's behalf. The mess he
made of his living quarters, the soiled laundry he expected someone
to take away and clean. The way he called her "Maggie"—"Mag"—
and ordered her around. Wherever Xenia drifted a bluish smoke
haze followed from his thin brown cigarillos, or a sweetish-rancid
odor of marijuana, hashish. He left emptied vodka bottles, emptied
Mountain Dew cans scattered through the house. He talked loudly,
laughed loudly over his cell phone. He had to shout, he claimed, to
be heard "overseas." He did not always flush the toilet after using it,
and Xenia used toilets throughout the house.

Magdalena was most offended, and frightened, that tangled in

Xenia's soiled bedclothes were used syringes. And syringes glistening with blood, underfoot. He was a "mainliner"—injected his veins with a powdery white substance he cooked to liquid, in spoons taken from Magdalena's kitchen. In his bathroom was a store of drugs and drug paraphernalia. His shower, sink, toilet were always so filthy, Magdalena could not bring herself to send in a cleaning woman, the task fell to her.

"I don't want them to be talking about us in town, any more than they are. Somebody could tell the police . . ."

But Magdalena could never bring herself to complain to Drewe. So many times in the past twenty years had Mrs. Hildebrand been kind to her, understanding, extra-generous, Magdalena would not commiserate with me if it implied criticism of her employer.

I said, bitterly, "Wish he'd shoot himself up with an overdose. Heroin, methamphetamine—'coke'—I don't know the names for all the drugs he takes, and Aunt Drewe is paying for it."

Magdalena murmured, "Now, Marta."

"Aunt Drewe doesn't see what he is! When she does, she won't love him anymore."

How like a plaintive child I sounded. Even in my own ears.

Lonely nights when Drewe was away with her lover and the house was quiet, I helped Magdalena with housework, we prepared meals together and ate in the kitchen. Sometimes, if he wasn't working, Noah Rathke ate with us.

I helped Magdalena shop for groceries in the village. Noah Rathke drove us, came into the store with us, loaded the car trunk with care. He was so tall, he had to stoop to place the grocery bags firmly in the rear of the trunk. He was lean and sinewy and alert, with a whippet-look, an expression in his eyes like one wary of being cornered.

Magdalena was fond of Noah Rathke whom she believed to be a natural-born gentleman with "some hurt" in his past. Not that Noah had told her much about himself, he rarely spoke of anything personal. He was moody, given to long brooding silences even at mealtimes while Magdalena chattered and I sat uneasy, thinking *But I am the quiet one. There can't be two of us.*

Drewe was particular about her chauffeur "looking the part" but when Drewe was away Noah wore khakis or jeans, a windbreaker, a soiled baseball cap like most men in rural Chateauguay County. (Though Noah didn't appear to be local, he had no local friends. Somehow I seemed to know that Noah had family in Pennsylvania.) Left to himself, Noah was inclined not to shave every day. His long lean jaws erupted in dark stubble. His hair was sand-colored and stiff as a brush and his eyebrows nearly met over the bridge of his nose. A small wedge of muscle beneath his lower lip gave him a look of stubborn opacity like that of a man who, if you shoved without warning against his chest, you would discover that he'd braced himself for just such a shove, his heels set firm in the earth.

Of her numerous employees, Noah Rathke was the most likely to know where Drewe was at any given time. At least Noah knew where he'd driven her, when he was scheduled to pick her up and bring her home. If Drewe had traveled by plane he knew arrival and departure times, he knew destinations. He kept a chauffeur's log of his employer's travels. Drewe had told me that of the drivers she'd hired at Chateauguay Springs, Noah Rathke was the most reliable as he was the most reticent: "All I require of an employee is that he have no personal life."

Aunt Drewe was joking. Of course.

In fact Noah didn't drive Drewe everywhere, often Drewe preferred to drive herself. She didn't care for the Lincoln, she had two vehicles for her personal use: an elegant cream-colored Mercedes, a handsome steel-colored Jeep. For my sixteenth birthday, in a mood of caring for me, Drewe had taught me to drive the Jeep: "One day you might need such skills, Marta. In a time of cataclysm, a clutch shift and four-wheel drive and a chassis like a tank might just make the difference."

I was too proud to ask Noah Rathke where my aunt was, when she was away. I didn't want to embarrass myself, or Noah.

Into the village of Chateauguay Springs Noah drove Magdalena and me, for grocery shopping. Maybe once a week, up to Newburgh to shop at the mall. (Noah didn't drive the Lincoln at such times but his own car, a nondescript vehicle lightly laced with rust.) Seeing the three of us crossing a parking lot you'd think: older brother, younger sister, mother? grandmother? You'd think rural Chateauguay County.

I was hurrying, my breath panted and steamed. I had made a mistake, a blunder, now I was hurrying to get away. I was bareheaded, I was without a jacket or coat, my feet slipped on the path slick with ice. Behind me Xenia came lurching, laughing. Calling me *darlin'! love!* His eyes blazed, his voice was cajoling. An intermediary had summoned me to the sculptor's studio, and I had gone. And Drewe had not been there. Except the clay head meant to be a likeness of

Drewe's head now nearly covered—"masked"—in her coagulated rich-deep-crimson blood. Xenia was not hurrying after me, Xenia wasn't a man to hurry after any woman or girl. Xenia was possibly teasing, taunting. Whatever blazed in his eyes. Whatever coursed in his ropey veins. I was outside stumbling in snow. My head rang like the clapper of a bell.

Afterward I would wonder if Aunt Drewe knew. If she and the Scots sculptor had talked it over, poor clumsy lovesick Marta summoned to Xenia's studio.

There stood Noah Rathke near the garage. Xenia had not yet seen him.

Noah Rathke in his chauffeur's uniform: dark suit, crisply laundered white shirt, dark cap with a visor. He had just emerged from the garage, a converted stable large enough to contain four vehicles. He was standing very still. In his hand he held car keys, he slipped into a pocket.

Now Xenia sighted Noah Rathke. Who was to him merely the driver, the chauffeur, an anonymous and until now faceless servant to be ordered about.

"Eh, mate? What's with you?"

Between the men there was a snowy distance of about twenty feet.

Between the men I was crossing to the rear door of the house. I was clumsy and frightened but had not fallen on the ice, the cold air had revived me. I heard Xenia's insolent voice, but I heard no reply of Noah's. In another moment I would enter the house, unseen by anyone inside I would run upstairs to my room. A second time I heard Xenia's voice now louder, jeering. In the corner of my eye I saw Noah move swiftly and unerringly as an attack dog. He did not seem to have spoken, very likely his face showed no expression except that of determination. There stood Xenia in his bloodstained work clothes, unshaven, sickly-pale, yet fiery in indignation as a roused god, lifting his fists awkwardly to mid-chest, daring to swing one fist in a blind roundhouse right like a desperate man swinging a tree limb snatched from the ground, but Noah Rathke, younger, leaner, quicker, ducked the punch and struck Xenia a sharp blow to the jaw, and as Xenia staggered and dropped to one knee, struck him a second, harder blow to the side of the head that dropped him farther, onto the ground. Noah stood over the groaning man in the snow as if waiting for him to rise and challenge him and still Noah had not spoken any words that I could hear.

Next time I saw Noah Rathke, a look would pass between us. A look startled and complicit and indefinable. Stricken with emotion I would murmur, "Thank you."

Noah's reply was a mumbled, "Sure."

Next time I saw the Scots sculptor it would be in Aunt Drewe's presence and no look would pass between us at all. Xenia's gaze was opaque as paint, pointedly he ignored me. On his jaw and at his right temple were ugly yellowish-purple bruises and swellings attributed to, as Xenia complained loudly, a fall on a "fucking icy walk" for which someone on Drewe's staff was to be blamed.

The Gift

I love you. Noah Rathke.

 . . . want to love you.

How angry Drewe would be with me, how disgusted. To know that her niece had fallen in love with an employee and not, as she'd seemed to have wanted, her Scots sculptor-lover.

Not that I knew what "love" was. I believed it had to be a ghost-word like "spirit," "soul." A word people used as they wished to use it. A word like a balloon floating overhead. A word to be punctured, dismissed.

You know I love you, Annemarie. And your mother.

My father's whiskey breath, flushed cheeks and edgy eyes. His mind on other matters.

My mother had told me she'd loved me, too. Probably. I think. When I'd been a little girl. That seems likely.

*   *   *

Noah Rathke. I began to wonder who he was.

Suddenly he'd appeared at Chateauguay Springs two years before, hired by my aunt to replace Sammy Ray Lee who'd had to be "dismissed." Drewe had hired Noah quickly, as she often hired employees, trusting her "gut instinct" and not troubling with résumés, letters of recommendation. Her joke that she wanted from employees only that they have no personal life wasn't far from the truth.

Employees at Chateauguay Springs, as at the Hildebrand Gallery, frequently disappointed Aunt Drewe. Her standards were very high, her patience was limited. Often I overheard her speak sharply to staff members and in her wake there was hurt, embarrassment, resentment. As Drewe's niece, I could have no friends on the staff for no one trusted me. Yet if I had not been Drewe's niece, I would not have been on the staff at all.

Sighing, Drewe said she had to concede, any relationship based upon hiring, payment, the authority of one individual over others, is poisoned, doomed from the start.

"Yet, if you have money, you must 'hire' others. If you own a place like Chateauguay Springs, you must hire lots of others. You know that a percentage of these employees resent you, even as they claim to be grateful to you. You know that some of them hate your guts and often you can't blame them."

Alone with me as if alone with herself, Drewe sometimes spoke in this wistful way. With others, like her Scots lover, Drewe tended to speak confidently and even extravagantly, like one made invulnerable by donning a brazen mask.

With others, Drewe was likely to be drinking. This made the mask more brazen.

Once I asked Aunt Drewe if she might be happier without the artists' colony to supervise, so many people, so many distractions and decisions and publicity, and she said, irritably, "Marta, my husband left the property to me, I have a duty to uphold his wishes. *Chateauguay Springs is my life.*"

Drewe laughed, wildly. I smiled uncertainly not knowing what her laughter meant.

Noah Rathke. At supper in the kitchen the night after he'd knocked Xenia into the snow he ate distractedly and in silence. Magdalena chattered. I'd helped Magdalena prepare the meal, when Noah thanked her Magdalena said, "You must thank Marta, too."

Noah's gaze lifted to mine. I hoped that he would smile at me, but he seemed edgy, uneasy. Mumbling, "Thanks, Marta." The word *Marta* was almost inaudible. I thought *I remind him of someone sad.*

I was waiting to hear that Aunt Drewe had fired Noah. That Xenia had complained of him, and Drewe had fired him. But Xenia, for whatever reason, pride, male vanity, chagrin, must not have complained.

Don't like me, love? Eh?

And why's that? Don't know, do you? Eh?

Murmuring, taunting, beneath his breath so that I could only just hear without being certain that I'd heard *Bloody cow.*

* * *

Now when I hiked in the woods and along the rocky trail above the river I had two people to think of: my aunt Drewe, and my friend Noah Rathke. Drewe was angry with me, but would not abandon me, I knew. What Noah felt for me, I could not guess. Except it wasn't what I felt for him. I had to know this.

Bloody cow I was in a man's eyes. Clumsy, "graceless." I knew this. My scalp itched and tingled, the urge to pluck at hairs was very strong. In Cattaraugus, that last year of my father's indictment, trial, conviction I'd begun pulling at my hair when no one could see me. My nerves strung so tight it was the only relief. That quick sharp pain in my scalp and then it's over.

Still my hair was mostly thick, the thinning, coin-sized spot at my hairline could be hidden. Only Magdalena seemed to notice me twining hairs around my fingers half-consciously. Once, Magdalena touched my hand lightly to stop me. As a mother might do, in silent reprimand.

I went away, offended. Leave me alone!

"Neurotic" was a word uttered in contempt by Aunt Drewe who had no patience for weakness physical or mental. It was a frequent complaint of Drewe's that two-thirds of the New Yorkers she knew were neurotic and she was damned tired of shoring them up.

Hiking above the river I broke off branches for a winter bouquet. Shook off snow, scratched my fingers on thorns. I brought back branches of holly leaves that remained glossy-green through the winter, with vivid red berries. There were other berry bushes, with dark red clustered berries, and cream-colored berries hard as pebbles. These I arranged in two bouquets, in clay vases.

I would never be an artist. I dreaded the thought of "art"—it had come to seem a kind of sickness to me, that devoured its victims. But I could arrange beautiful things that had already been created, I could make a new beauty of them, that could hurt no one and was nothing of myself or any human vanity. And maybe someone would see, and say: "Beautiful."

The first of the winter bouquets I gave to Magdalena, who was surprised, and touched. "Marta, thank you! These are beautiful."

The second of the winter bouquets I prepared to give to Noah Rathke. I asked Magdalena if she had a key to his apartment above the garage, if I could use it, to leave a gift for him?

"A gift? For Noah? Why?"

"His birthday."

"Is it Noah's birthday? Today?"

I was feeling giddy, reckless. It was a sensation like drunkenness. I said I didn't know when Noah's birthday was but it had to have been within the past year so I wanted to leave a gift for him, as a surprise.

Magdalena regarded me with alarm. I knew what she was thinking.

Marta is in love! She thinks.

Magdalena hesitated, but provided a key for me, out of her housekeeper's drawer of keys. It would seem like a harmless gesture to her, she had no reason to think that Noah would mind.

"As long as it's you, Marta."

* * *

This I knew: Noah was scheduled to be away for much of the day, with Drewe and Xenia. He had driven them in a minivan to a research laboratory on Long Island where they could purchase "organic materials" needed for several of Xenia's anatomical sculptures. Still, out of caution, I knocked on the door to his apartment.

An outdoor, enclosed stairway led to the second floor of the garage. I had never climbed this stairway before. I would leave a winter bouquet in a clay vase for Noah Rathke, I'd have been too shy to give him in person.

I knocked, there was no reply. Excited, I unlocked the door with Magdalena's key and pushed it open and stepped inside and saw that I was in a room of such ordinary dimensions and furnishings that at first I felt disbelief. Noah Rathke, living here! The room was just slightly larger than my bedroom but it had none of the austere beauty of my bedroom, it had fewer windows, narrow windows, its waterstained ceiling was lower. Of course, Noah Rathke was just an employee at Chateauguay Springs, not even on the managerial staff.

Sammy Ray Lee had been the previous resident here. He'd been fired by my aunt for having been unreliable, "insubordinate." Sammy Ray Lee had spent too much time in Newburgh where he had relatives and friends, but Noah Rathke seemed often to remain at Chateauguay Springs even on his days off.

His bed was plain, lacking a headboard and covered in a coarse gray blanket, the single pillow in its white, much-laundered case exposed. I saw that the bed was neatly, even severely made in the way that I usually made my own bed within minutes of getting up, for I hated the messy look of an unmade bed, all that it implied of messiness in our lives, my mother's unmade bed and the confusion of our

lives that final year I'd lived in Cattaraugus. I could imagine Noah
Rathke frowning as he made up his bed each morning, briskly tucking in sheets, jerking out wrinkles in the coarse gray blanket. On
the back of a chair beside the bed was a shirt I recognized as Noah's,
one of the work-shirts he wore when he wasn't on duty as Drewe's
chauffeur. On a newspaper close beside the door, neatly side by side,
was a pair of scuffed leather boots. I could imagine Noah removing
his boots before he entered the room, shaking off snow out on the
stairway landing.

I felt a wave of emotion, I could not have named. How alone
Noah was! Yet you could not think of him, as you might think of
me, as lonely.

On the raw floorboards was a single remnant-rug that had
grown shabby with use. The grudging-narrow windows had mismatched blinds but no curtains. Now I looked more closely, the
windows were filmed with a thin layer of grime on the outside.
There was a closet with a metal-framed vertical mirror on the outside of the door, which was slightly ajar. A small TV, a radio and CD
player, CDs and books evenly aligned on shelves. The walls were
smudged beige plasterboard, lacking posters or art of any kind. I was
accustomed to my aunt Drewe's world in which walls were designed
to display art, such barrenness struck me as willful, defiant.

I set the vase of dried berries and holly leaves on a chest of drawers beside the bed. Noah would see it immediately when he entered
his room and know that it was a gift from me.

I couldn't leave a note with it. I'd tried to write a few words but
gave up. *Here is something for you, to thank you. Marta.* Or, *I love you
Noah. Your friend Marta.*

So clumsy! "Graceless."

There was nothing else on the top of the chest of drawers, which was made of plain pinewood, except a number of coins, not scattered as if Noah had emptied his pockets, but evenly aligned in ascending order of value. Several pennies, three nickels, a dime, two quarters.

I knew: I should leave. There was no purpose in my remaining longer in Noah Rathke's living quarters.

My attention was drawn to a corner alcove of the room, to a small dingy kitchen. The appliances appeared dwarfed. A cramped counter, a Pullman refrigerator beneath. A stained sink. A hot plate with two burners. A single small cupboard without a door: a few glasses and plates inside, cans of soup, a cereal box or two. Through a small window I could see a corner of my aunt's house, the portentous slate roof, elegant timbering and cream-colored stucco streaked as if with rust. The windows of my room on the other side of the house weren't visible from Noah's windows, mine looked out upon the river and an open expanse of sky.

There was a sudden sound outside: a vehicle pulling up. My heart beat rapidly, though almost immediately I could see that it was just a delivery truck.

I thought *I should leave now! While I have done nothing wrong.*

I would not open any drawers, I would not open the door to the closet or to the bathroom. I would touch nothing. I stood before the closet door, the vertical mirror with its mirror that reflected the startling length of me, staring into it with a look of childish apprehension, anticipation. Usually I avoided mirrors, even washing my face I avoided seeing myself, now I was staring, surprised that, in Noah Rathke's mirror, I didn't look so graceless, clumsy, unattractive as I'd been feeling.

I smiled at myself warily. I couldn't trust this!

Behind me in the mirror was the tall lanky indistinct figure of a man with hair like wood shavings, a blurred and elusive face. It was this man to whom I spoke softly: "I love you."

I knew that I should leave. The delivery truck's arrival and now its departure, a sound of voices at a distance, had made me jumpy. If Noah returned! If someone discovered me! Yet I examined the CDs on Noah's shelves thinking *This would be allowed. These are out in the open.* The CDs were of bands with names like Grass Valley, Done Gone, Cumberland Station, Blue Ridge Junction, Ciderhouse. I had never heard these names before. I would have liked to hear the music.

Books! It surprised me that Noah Rathke had so many books, both hardcover and paperback.

Many of the books had orange stickers on their spines CO-OP USED. They turned out to be textbooks from the Quarrysville State College Co-Op Bookstore: *Principles of General Chemistry, Introduction to Evolutionary Ecology, The Psychology of Moral Behavior.* Individual works, *Great Dialogues of Plato,* Machiavelli's *The Prince, John Stuart Mill: Basic Writings, Selected Poems of Walt Whitman,* Dickens's *Hard Times,* Twain's *Huckleberry Finn.* There were several anthologies, *Great Works of World Literature, Great Writings in Ethics.* On the inside covers was neatly handprinted:

Noah Rathke
53 Stearnes Hall
Quarrysville State College
Quarrysville, PA

Noah had been a college student! He must not have graduated, or he wouldn't be working as a hired driver for my aunt.

Now I knelt on the carpet, I took up books and leafed through them, I was fascinated to see where Noah had underlined and annotated many of the passages. Some of the entries had even been dated, 1996, 1997. I had to suppose that Noah had been a college student then. But I couldn't assume that he'd begun college at the age of eighteen, which would make him only about twenty-five or -six now; he looked older.

He'd been a chemistry major? But *Principles of General Chemistry* was the only chemistry textbook on the shelves. I wondered how many years Noah had been at Quarrysville State College, maybe he'd had to drop out early. I wondered at his life, as a younger man, if he'd been so alone then.

Out of the bulky ethics anthology several items fell.

The first was a surprise: one of the Chateauguay Springs postcards available in the Big Barn, picturing an idyllic grassy scene with the barn in the background, pine woods, paths in the woods, individuals strolling at a distance. The identification was *Chateauguay Springs, The Artists' Colony on the Scenic Hudson River, est. 1964.* The card was addressed to Noah Rathke at a Quarrysville address.

July 15, 1998

Dear Noah,

Sorry I could not get away. My work here is not going so well. Things are complicated right now, I tried to explain. Please don't "drop by" thats not a good idea. Will call soon. Love,

T.

Another postcard, also from Chateauguay Springs, a view of a grassy/rocky bluff overlooking the Hudson River.

April 9, 1998

Dear Noah,

Miss you! But I learning *a lot*. This is for the best, tho' hard work. Sorry "overnight" visitors are not allowed here but will see you on the 20th. Love,

Tania

The other item was a faded Polaroid: a young, smiling, ropey-muscled Noah Rathke in white T-shirt and denim cuffoffs, sitting close beside a striking girl with long straight brown hair parted severely in the center of her head, a girl with an angular face, a small tense smile, eyes fixed upon the camera as if in distrust. Noah's left arm was slung across the girl's slender, somewhat rounded shoulders and the girl's hands were clasped together, tight between her knees. She wore a long skirt, that hid most of her thin, pale legs, and a drooping, drab-colored jersey; while Noah appeared happy, relaxed, or wished to give that impression, the odd upright set of the girl's head and the way she held herself suggested urgency, tension, an arrow poised to fly. I felt a stab of dismay, jealousy. I had never seen Noah Rathke smile in that way. The girl must have been my age, or a little older. The staring eyes, severely parted hair and sharp cheekbones gave her a spare beauty.

On the back was handprinted: *Tania June 1997*.

"Tania Leenaum."

I knew. I knew this. I fumbled to return the postcards and photograph to *Great Writings in Ethics,* replaced the book on the shelf exactly where it had been, arranged the books as evenly as I had found them. Not an edge out of place.

Quickly I went away. I returned the key to Magdalena and I said nothing to anyone of what I had discovered of Noah Rathke. It would be another secret between us, that no one would know not even Noah.

Antichrist

So ashamed."

Swiftly and unexpectedly came the end of the Scots sculptor Xenia at Chateauguay Springs. The end of my aunt Drewe's infatuation with the man. So long I'd been hoping for this, when it happened I was unprepared.

Behold Our Redeemer Cometh, Xenia's preview exhibit of *Blood Mask II* and other newly completed anatomical pieces, was scheduled to open on the first Sunday in March, in the main, vaulted gallery of the Big Barn. This was the premiere event of the artists' colony for the season: more than three hundred invitations had been sent to art collectors and museum curators, supporters of the artists' colony, New York friends, local residents and local media. Drewe had long hoped to establish good relations with her distrustful Chateauguay neighbors by opening her property to the public with art exhibits, crafts fairs, guided tours, slide lectures and receptions. Gaily she said, "Even if they hate 'art' they might like us. Some of us."

At such times Drewe moved among visitors shaking hands and smiling brightly and insincerely, always strikingly dressed, strikingly groomed and regal. Other staff members, responsible for organizing the events, remained in the background.

Anticipation for *Behold Our Redeemer Cometh* was mixed among

the artists' community as well as locally. Lurid rumors had been cir-
culating for weeks of cadavers, fetuses, "dead bodies," desecration.
On the days before the opening the Big Barn office received many
more inquiries than usual, some of them notably unfriendly and
threatening. Marcus Heller insisted upon hiring two security guards
for the event and assigned younger staff workers to direct parking.
As executive director of the arts colony he, not Drewe, was responsible for the opening.

On that Sunday, the first of the protestors appeared in the morning at the front entrance to Chateauguay Springs. They stood at the
edge of the road holding picket signs: RESPECT FOR LIFE! BOY-
COTT BLASPHEMY! BOYCOTT ANTICHRIST ART! They'd
come in minivans, clearly they were organized. They were predominantly men, some of them surprisingly young, most of them neatly
dressed, clean-shaven. They were members of the Chateauguay
Christian Youth, the more militant Christians for Life, members of
local churches. Drewe was upset, angry; Drewe directed Marcus
Heller to call the sheriff's office; but deputies made no arrests, the
picketers were not trespassing on private property, they were "peace-
fully assembled." Drewe said, "Nothing like this has ever happened
at Chateauguay Springs before!" There was a thrill to her voice but
her eyes were frightened.

Drewe Hildebrand wanted publicity for the arts colony, she
wanted controversy and attention, but on her own terms.

Xenia drove Drewe's Jeep out to the highway to observe the protestors and to take videotape "documentation" of the "organized
American resistance" to his art. He told Drewe to arrange for video-
taping through the day: "The reaction of the tribe to revolutionary

art must be recorded, it's part of the art itself. Nothing must be lost."

Blood Mask II was the centerpiece of the exhibit, positioned in the immediate foreground of the gallery space, the first object you saw when you entered. The frozen blood mask of Drewe Hildebrand preserved in a display case on a white pedestal, glaring dark crimson beneath bright lights. A woman's head, a woman's face in sculpted coagulated blood, ghastly and repellent, yet monumental. The effect was as if the outermost layer of skin had been peeled away from a living head. The thick neck gave the head a look of substance and dignity that a neck of merely normal dimensions would have lacked. The first visitors to the exhibit, many of whom were friends and acquaintances of my aunt's, stared at Drewe Hildebrand so transformed: the tight-shut eyes that suggested not sleep or peace but quivering tension, perhaps anger; the tense grip of the jaws; the downward twist of the fleshy lips. There was a grandeur of disdain in the head that was so very like my aunt, I had to concede that the sculptor had captured something of Drewe's essence. What had seemed ugly and messy and obscene in the studio had, through the sculptor's numerous refinements, come to seem "perfect."

I stared at *Blood Mask II* in disbelief, that I could find it so transformed.

"Beautiful! And it's *me*. The sculptor has transformed *me*."

Drewe, in shimmering black, her face gaudily made up and her eyes shining with excitement, grasped my hands in her cold, strong fingers. She seemed to have forgiven me for my disloyalty, or to have forgotten.

Basking in the attention, the stunned silence in the gallery which he chose to interpret as awe, Xenia was answering questions put to him by an arts channel TV interviewer from Albany, in a corner of the room, as a second camera moved over the exhibit and guests, recording their reactions. For the occasion, Xenia wore a sleek Armani jacket like liquid silver, a black T-shirt beneath, designer jeans and ostrich skin boots with a sizable heel. He was fashionably unshaven, with a two-days' growth of beard, but he'd had his head shaved, and his scalp glistened pinkly like the hairless flesh of his cadaver sculptures. He wore ear clamps, something resembling a fishhook glittered in his left eyebrow. His eyes shone with cocaine exuberance and his stained teeth were bared in a feral smile. With the restrained enthusiasm of the practiced self-promoter he was telling the TV interviewer, "My work is 'anatomical' because it is *of,* and literally *is,* the anatomical being. The pieces of *Behold Our Redeemer Cometh* were once organic 'life.' In history, sculpted human figures have always been synthetic representations in stone, marble, clay, wood, but my figures are not mere representations, they are authentic remnants of being. The pulse and warmth of life once moved through them, now you who gaze upon them are the repository of life—temporarily! As in *SuperOvulated* you will see your own mortal face, and it may frighten you." Xenia paused, and continued in a seemingly confiding tone, "Still, I must labor to make my art 'perfect.' Detractors of Xenia say that my art is ready-made but that is far from the truth! Art is not a natural reflex but hard won." Xenia spoke elatedly and yet thoughtfully. The man was arrogant, insolent, outrageous and yet you would almost think that he was a serious artist, and a serious individual.

I could not accept this. I hated him so.

A stream of vehicles was making its way into Chateauguay

Springs, visitors were crowding into the Big Barn. Many of these had never been to Chateauguay Springs before and did not appear to be art patrons. The reception had been scheduled to begin at 6 P.M. and by 6:30 P.M. the Big Barn was becoming uncomfortably crowded. Noah Rathke had volunteered to help with security, and in his somber chauffeur's uniform stood just inside the entrance to the gallery. We watched as newcomers entered the exhibit with wine-glasses and slices of brie and were stopped short by the glaring *Blood Mask II,* whom some could recognize as a demonic likeness of Drewe Hildebrand. The mood of the gathering was subdued, disoriented. As musical accompaniment Xenia had selected an eerie electronic composition by a German composer to be played and replayed, and these sounds intensified the mood of unease. Even supporters of Chateauguay Springs who came frequently to exhibits here of exper-imental art, even Drewe's sophisticated New York art friends, were confounded. No one seemed to know what to make of such willfully ugly art. "Is this real?"—"Is this *real?*"—the question was asked with horror, disgust, disbelief. Middle-aged art patrons squinted through bifocals to read cards attached to the displays cataloging the materials used by the sculptor and in several cases thanking The Tis-sue Engineering and Organ Laboratory of the Nassau Biotech Insti-tute for help with the exhibit.

After *Blood Mask II* the visitor was led to stare at *What Cut Do You Wish Ma'am?*—three humanoid carcasses hanging from meat hooks, bloody inner organs displayed as a life-sized butcher in a blood-smeared white uniform stood with a red plastic cleaver in hand, and an unctuous smile. The butcher, unlike the carcasses, was clearly synthetic, a genial blend of Santa Claus and Uncle Sam; a pa-triarchal elder with reddened cheeks and lips and a twinkle in his icy blue eyes. Next was *Infanta,* an unnervingly realistic Caucasian infant of about six weeks of age, her small body rendered bizarrely transparent except for a dense network of stark red veins and arteries, the result of resins injected into her circulatory system. Next came *TVTIME:* several human fetuses served on frozen TV trays with side orders of French fries, coleslaw, cans of Coke; the fetuses were the size of newborn kittens, with large, misshapen heads. *Patriot* was a life-sized amputee in a wheelchair, head battered and bloody, one eye gouged out and the other, thick-lashed, beautiful, intelligent, fixed on the viewer who stood in front of him. The amputee had no arms or legs, he was swaddled like an infant in a bloody white shroud, his sunken chest bedecked with military medals. (As the attached card indicated, the military medals were authentic, acquired at pawn shops.) *Behold Our Redeemer Cometh,* the most controversial of the anatomical pieces, depicted a plump fetus, or newborn infant, on a plastic cross sprinkled with glitter, spikes through its hands and feet, and a crown of red, white, and blue thorns on its disproportionately large head. *SuperOvulated,* the final piece, was an immense, headless, obese human female allegedly comprised of mucus, blood, tissue, fat (very yellow), and semen from "numerous donors including the sculptor"; this figure, too, was only a torso, with immense sagging breasts spread across her chest and stubs of fatty thighs spread to reveal a patch of wiry pubic hair and, poking through her vagina, a small oval mirror. The unwitting viewer flinched at seeing his or her face captured in such a place and stepped quickly back.

Bright lights as in an operating room illuminated these astonishing pieces that shone like plastic except that they were, in fact, organic flesh treated with a chemical preservative that smelled un-

mistakably of formaldehyde. Air currents moved in a continuous
stream through the gallery, still the fetid odor remained. Visitors set
down their wineglasses and slices of brie. Some were leaving the exhibit quickly, quietly. Some were speaking loudly—"Is this a joke?
Are these *real?*" The security guards, middle-aged men, retirees
from the Newburgh police force, stood at opposite ends of the
gallery, against the walls, with expressions of disbelief and repugnance; Noah Rathke, polite, grim, was positioned closer to Drewe,
who was introducing Xenia to visitors. It was shortly after 7 P.M.
when there came a sudden commotion into the gallery, raised voices,
a sound of breaking glass and a rush in the crowd. Loud, angry
shouts: "Antichrist!"—"Satan's work!"—"God will judge you!" Before anyone could prevent them, several men and women pushed
into the exhibit space and began to knock over the larger anatomical
pieces. By the time the security guards were roused to action, the
crowd began to panic, pushing desperately toward the exits. More
glass was broken, Marcus Heller who'd been trying to intervene was
shoved against the life-sized plastic butcher and the two fell to the
floor in a tangled heap. A furious man with fanatic eyes, later to be
identified as the "spiritual leader" of the militant Christians for Life,
leapt onto a table to exhort the crowd in a preacher's voice: "Blasphemy! Antichrist! Condemned to hell!" He was a man of about
forty, near-bald, with a spade-shaped dark-red goatee, hairs bristling
in his ears, a thickset torso, muscled shoulders and arms; he wore a
rumpled dark suit, a white shirt that appeared to be sweated
through, a narrow tan leather necktie. Xenia and Aunt Drewe were
trapped together between the shoving protestors and a wall, I saw a
look of abject fear come over Xenia's face, as he ducked, shielded his
head with his arms, managed to shove Drewe from him and to flee

behind her, forcing his way, doubled over in panic, or in pain, to an exit. In her high-heeled shoes Drewe stumbled and fell, crying for help. I was close by, stooping over her. I tried to shield both of us with my arms, in terror we'd be trampled. Women were screaming, men were shouting, the militant leader of Christians for Life was denouncing the exhibit, the artist, the "Satan-worshippers" at Chateauguay Springs that ought to be "razed to the ground like the cities of the plain accursed by God."

Noah Rathke was beside Drewe and me, the two of us helped Drewe to her feet. Drewe appeared dazed, bleeding from a cut lip. Noah led us through the struggling crowd to an office, where he shut and locked the door. Drewe sat heavily in a chair. A trickle of blood ran from her upper lip to her chin. "They will burn us down—they will bomb us. 'Christians for Life'—they threatened this. I didn't listen. Now they will kill us." Drewe began to cry softly, I tried to comfort her, soaking up the blood in a tissue as Noah spoke rapidly on a cell phone. Drewe's eyes were dilated, unfocused. Her breath smelled of wine and something acrid and chemical. For the opening, she'd chosen her costume with care: a multi-pleated caftan of some liquid-black fabric that rippled and shimmered as she moved, over matte black trousers; black suede shoes with unusually high heels, and ankle straps. Her eye makeup was elaborate, exotic. Her hair was a lustrous brunette, made thicker and more glamorous with braided extensions. Her face was geisha-pale, only close up could you see a pattern of thin pale tines in her forehead, and bracketing her luscious wide red lips. Now tears had smudged her eye makeup, the trickle of blood had stained the front of the shimmering caftan. Aunt Drewe had been transformed within minutes from a beautiful gracious welcoming hostess to a broken, confused middle-aged woman. I had witnessed Xenia's cowardly, cruel behavior, I'd seen the look in his face as he shoved Drewe from him, but I wasn't sure if Drewe herself comprehended what had happened.

She was murmuring, "Now they will kill us. The wrath of God. So ashamed . . ."

I huddled beside Drewe, I was shivering with fear and excitement. Noah stood by the door, where he'd dragged a chair. Outside, the sounds of breakage and struggle continued. An alarm had gone off, there was a sudden smell of smoke. But by the time sheriff's deputies arrived, the commotion had begun to abate. A small fire had been set in the gallery which volunteer firemen extinguished. All but a few of the protesters had escaped, taking with them, we would learn afterward, the fetuses of *TVTIME* and *Infanta* to be given Christian burials; the spiritual leader of Christians for Life and three of his aides remained behind to publicly surrender to police, their actions captured on film and videotape, to be replicated hundreds, perhaps thousands of times in newspapers and on TV news programs across the country.

More media attention would be given to the protesters than to the art exhibit which was dismissed as "sensationalist trash" and "pseudo-art." Xenia, his name misspelled as "Zenia"—"Zeno"—was dismissed as a "pseudo-artist." Xenia had fled to New York City, in the company of a woman art patron-friend at whose brownstone on East Eighty-seventh Street he would be staying. He would break off all relations with Chateauguay Springs, and with Drewe Hildebrand. He would sue both the Chateauguay Springs Foundation and Drewe Hildebrand for failing to protect his sculptures from the damage which was "irreparable." And Xenia would sue for the nullification of his contract with the Hildebrand Gallery.

Marcus Heller, injured in the scuffle, was hospitalized with a brain concussion and would be on medical disability for a minimum of three months.

"So ashamed."

Elk Lake (I)

You and me, Marta. And no one would ever know."

In the steel-colored Jeep gleaming and sturdy and set high from the ground, Drewe drove us to Elk Lake, in the Shale Mountains, on the following Sunday. For most of the drive she was silent, brooding. She was wearing an old leather jacket, soiled trousers, boots. Her hair had not been shampooed in some time and was brushed back from her forehead like a man's, flat, rather thin, the glamorous extensions removed. She smoked cigarettes down to the butt, as workmen did at Chateauguay Springs, exhaling smoke through flaring nostrils.

Without glancing at me she said, bemused: "Like waking inside a coffin. My life."

Elk Lake. In the Shale Mountains. I had never been taken to Elk Lake before, I had never heard the name.

I was thrilled that Drewe had asked me to accompany her. She might have gone alone, she'd been locked away in her room for much of the week and had not cared to speak with me, only briefly with Magdalena, there was no one with whom my aunt wished to speak except she had wanted my company, she'd told me to get dressed, wear something warm, we'd be going away for a day or two: "To get out of this place."

We were ascending a rocky terrain north and west of the Hudson River, in the Shale River Mountain State Park. This was thirty miles beyond Newburgh. A remote and monotonous landscape of pine trees with infrequent stands of stark white birches looking ethereal, beautiful against the density of straight tall pines. The road was narrow, potholed, ceaselessly winding, hypnotic. Pines crowded close to the roadway, there was little visibility. Dense shadowy woods, miles of woods, snow in crusted heaps, frozen creekbeds beneath rattling plank bridges. The Shale Mountain range was too low to be snowcapped, there was no way to distinguish one wooded peak from another.

Few vehicles passed us on the road. We saw few houses. In Twin Lakes we passed a boarded-up Sunoco station, at Broomtown there was U.S. post office/bait shop, there were scattered wood-frame houses and mobile homes, a church, a volunteer fire company, a high school at Weatherhead. Faded signs pointed toward Mt. Horn, Paris, Grand Gorge, Jewett and East Jewett. This was not tourist terrain in the vicinity of the Hudson River but inland, beyond Chateauguay County into Ulster.

On the day following the protesters' attack, after Xenia's abrupt departure, Drewe had bravely consented to meet with reporters and TV interviewers to answer questions and give public statements in defense of the "freedom of the artist" and her commitment to Chateauguay Springs, in the presence of legal counsel for the Foundation. I was shocked to see so many vehicles parked at the Big Barn. By mid-afternoon, Drewe had become exhausted and disgusted and broke off the interviews, permanently.

Next morning she'd met with lawyers to discuss a lawsuit against the Chateauguay County Sheriff's Department for "failure to protect her person and property" but, abruptly, the plan was dropped. Drewe went away and locked herself in her room.

"Mrs. Hildebrand?"—Magdalena called worriedly, knocking at Drewe's door. But Drewe refused to respond.

Of Xenia who'd behaved so badly to Drewe, she would not speak.

I was elated as if I'd vanquished my aunt's sculptor-lover myself.

He never cared for you. Not as I care for you.

I am the one who loves you.

A light rain had begun to fall, mixed with sleet. Beyond Weatherhead in my aunt's brooding silence I was becoming restless. When I offered to drive for a while Drewe said, with a curious intonation, "No. I am the driver."

I must have fallen asleep, I was wakened by the Jeep bumping through the woods on a lane so rutted and overgrown it had nearly disappeared. Close by, white-tailed deer stared at us, frozen in place.

Drewe was saying, "No one knows about Elk Lake, it's a forgotten property. I haven't been here in years. My husband used to come here to fish but that was a long time ago. We own about a hundred acres—a wilderness. The cabin has no electricity, no indoor toilet. Kerosene lamps. An outdoor privy. We came here together once"— Drewe's voice softened—"a beautiful few days but we left early and never returned."

The lane was becoming impassable, Drewe had to park the Jeep below the cabin and we hiked the rest of the way. The snowy hill was crisscrossed with animal tracks and on all sides was storm damage, fallen tree limbs, debris. The spring thaw was slow to come to the Shale Mountains. The air was fresh and cold and the sky seemed very distant and Chateauguay Springs and shame were distant, my aunt's footsteps quickened with resolve. "My husband was an idealist. But he never took risks. He preferred 'safe' art as he preferred safe investments. I can't be that way. I must have risk, adventure. Even if I've failed, even if my enemies are laughing at me . . ." Drewe's voice trailed off, quivering with indignation.

Quickly I said, "Aunt Drewe, you haven't 'failed.' Think of all the artists you've helped over the years. This was just—him."

The closest I dared to come, alluding to Xenia. Drewe said sadly, "No, Marta. It was me. My judgment. My blindness. But that's behind us now, at Elk Lake. Look."

Drewe was pointing through the trees, at a lake that seemed to have appeared out of nowhere. It was ice-notched at shore, thawing at its center. I could not see the edges of the lake but it seemed to be relatively small. The open water was oddly still, so dark as to appear black. The harsh cries of grackles disturbed the silence but I could see no birds. The lake amid the pine trees was beautiful, the view of mountain peaks beyond was beautiful, yet so lonely, desolate. I felt a sudden stab of panic, my aunt intended to stay in this place overnight.

She'd brought an unwieldy duffel bag. I didn't think that there were groceries in it.

Excitedly she said, "In this place I understand: it's as the Zen Buddhists teach us, the only moment is *now*. The past, history, 'memories'—sorrow, pain, humiliation—where are they? Only in human consciousness, which can be erased. How happy we can be here at Elk Lake, Marta! Our enemies can never follow us here."

The cabin, in an overgrown clearing, was made of rough-hewn logs, smaller than I imagined it would be; I'd grown accustomed to "cabins" and "cottages" in the Catskills owned by Drewe's well-to-do friends. But this was a cabin of ordinary dimensions, with a small front veranda, few windows, a decayed-looking brick chimney. About thirty feet away was an outdoor privy on the verge of collapse.

Drewe fumbled in her pocket for a key to the rusted padlock on the cabin door. I hoped that the key wouldn't fit. Drewe swore, trying to open it, finally handing me the key—"Here, Marta. You try it. My damned hands are trembling."

I took the key and tried to fit it into the padlock as Drewe peered through a cobwebbed window. I was distracted by something close beside the cabin: a tarpaulin loosely draped over an object about the size of a kitchen table. It seemed to me that the tarpaulin had moved. Something dark-furred, the size of a rat, scuttled away into the underbrush.

When I managed to open the padlock, Drewe thanked me, kissed my cheek: "There you are, Marta-girl! Not so clumsy as you pretend."

Inside, the cabin was freezing and airless and depressing. In summer, in sunny warm weather, it might be beautiful in this place, but not in mid-March, still in winter. One large room, with rooms opening to the rear. A wood-burning stove, leather sofa, scattered chairs. A braided carpet, badly faded, on the plank floorboards. A stone fireplace with a few pieces of kindling. Everywhere were cobwebs, underfoot were insect carcasses. *Clumsy* echoed in my ears, *not so clumsy* that was a slap disguised as a caress, or a caress disguised as a slap. Energetically Drewe was opening interior shutters at the windows, a wan wintry light spilled into the cabin through grimy windows. "Look, Marta. So beautiful! 'Beauty' of winter solitude, peace. It's a much clearer view of the lake than in the summer, this is the perfect time for us."

A dank dark smell as of something dead and decayed lifted faintly through the floorboards. Drewe sniffed, crinkling her nose, but said nothing.

I was struggling with the shutters of the remaining windows in the front room. The screens were badly rusted and the sills were layered in the dried husks of insects. Cobwebs caught in my hair, my eyelashes. A living spider scurried across my mouth.

"Ah, candles! I remember."

Drewe located candles in a bureau drawer, forced them into holders and tried to light their damp wicks. She cursed, dropping a match. Wordlessly I took the matches from her and set about lighting candles. I'd found kerosene lamps but there appeared to be no kerosene in the cabin.

"And we'll light a fire. There's a woodpile outside."

Breath steaming in childlike excitement, Drewe strode about investigating the back rooms, the kitchen area, closets. She sat heavily on the leather sofa, dreamily she said, "I could 'disappear' in such a place. Waking in a coffin—back there!—waking to a new life, here! I could be a recluse, a cloistered nun. The sole individual in an order of cloistered nuns. I'd hoped to be a martyr, I think. Stigmata—bleeding palms—an affliction that is a blessing— except: I wasn't Catholic, I didn't believe." Drewe laughed, staring for a moment at the palms of her hands. She seemed to have forgotten what she was saying, her eyes lifted to me as if I had only just materialized before her. "You, Marta, have your role: you will help me. You will help me into my new life, and you will come to see me, sometimes; but not to stay. For I must live alone, I've realized. I was born for aloneness, not for 'love'—the messiness of 'love.' A need for others, a need for men, no more! I have money in accounts no one knows about, Marta, not even my shrewd money managers. I have accounts in the Cayman Islands. Anytime I wish, I can acquire a new 'identity,' a new passport. From Elk Lake I can slip over the border into Canada and from Canada I can travel anywhere I wish, I have friends in Mexico, in Europe . . . My enemies will wonder where I've vanished: but they will never know."

Drewe's mouth twisted in bitterness, "enemies" was uttered like a curse.

I was stunned by what Drewe had said. I stood for a moment fumbling with a candle, that failed to fit upright in one of the holders.

Hesitantly I told Aunt Drewe that she would feel better in a while. It was an upset, what had happened at the exhibit, but it had been only a week ago, she had to give herself more time. The exhibit—

"Marta, don't humor me. I don't happen to feel that 'feeling better' is a particularly noble value. What happened last Sunday opened my eyes: the vanity of my life, the emptiness of 'art.'"

"But, Aunt Drewe, you don't really mean—"

"No. No more. Not a word more."

"Everyone at Chateauguay Springs—"

"I said *no*. Go outside and fetch us some kindling, make yourself useful."

I stumbled outside. My heart was beating against my ribs like a maddened fist. In the freezing air, I'd begun to sweat inside my clothes.

I half-ran, half-slid down to the lake. Down a snowy slope to the lake. There was a badly rotted pier, encrusted with ice like a kind of sculpture. I thought *I will walk on that, it will collapse beneath me,*

Aunt Drewe will be sorry. I hiked along the shore that was strewn with rocks, dense with underbrush. No other cabins or clearings were visible. And at this time of year, no one else was likely to be here. I stumbled on outcroppings of shale, at strange, sharp angles, like a manmade stairway skewed by something violent like an earthquake.

My nose was running. I might have been crying. I wiped my face roughly on my jacket sleeve and headed back to the cabin.

It was a pile of firewood, beneath the rotted tarpaulin. But the pieces of wood were so old, so damp, I doubted that they could be made to burn in the fireplace. And we hadn't brought newspaper, to start the fire with. I thought *It will be too cold even for Drewe, we won't stay this time.*

When I returned to the cabin, Drewe was sprawled on the sofa with a drink in her hand. I was surprised to see a bottle of whiskey on the floor at her feet. Also on the floor was Drewe's compact cell phone, I guessed she'd thrown down, in disgust, when she tried to make a call and hadn't succeeded.

Wordlessly, I picked up the cell phone. Aunt Drewe's extravagant gestures often required me, or another subordinate, to complete them.

"Marta. Have a drink."

I shook my head no thank you! When we drove back to Chauteauguay Springs, I might be driving.

"I said, Marta: have a drink. Sit here with me, and have a drink like a civilized person, not a barbarian from western New York State."

I laughed uneasily, I chose to interpret this as a joke. An affectionate sort of teasing. Between relatives.

Drewe watched me, frowning. She splashed more whiskey into

her glass and drank. She groped for her pack of cigarettes, lit one and tossed the match, still burning, in the direction of the fireplace. It fell short, onto the floor. But the little flame had gone out.

In a casual-seeming voice my aunt Drewe said, "Or, we could disappear together. In the lake, Marta. Or the Shale River. You, and me. And no one would ever know."

III

Damaged

There was a soft knock at the door of my room and I was wakened from a smothering stuporous sleep in mid-afternoon of an unnumbered day and I struggled to become conscious, to speak coherently: "Yes? Magdalena?" and it was Magdalena, opening the door of my room, regarding me with worried eyes for I rarely came downstairs in my aunt's house, I no longer worked in the Big Barn and I no longer answered any ringing telephones, even my own, though phones rang at a distance and there was activity at a distance, reported in the media of which I knew little except that in the mystery of the rich art patroness's abduction and disappearance and possible/probable homicide I was the *abducted niece,* I was identified by police as the *sole witness* yet I was a *damaged witness,* my brain had been injured by crystal meth.

Magdalena was bringing me a potted plant: mums, or a kind of daisy, beautiful white petals and dark-gold centers and the note that accompanied it was printed in a hand immediately recognizable to me.

> for Marta,
> Hope you are getting well & stronger
> Sincerely,
> *Noah Rathke*

I took the flowers from Magdalena's hands but my hands were too shaky so Magdalena took them back to set on a table and seeing that my face was wet with tears she looked away. I asked Magdalena why Noah didn't come to see me, just for a few minutes in all these days I'd been home from the hospital, and Magdalena said quickly, "Oh he wouldn't! Mrs. Hildebrand's driver, she wouldn't want him upstairs in her house."

Interrogation

―――

Marta.' Do you remember me?"

I did. Through April, I'd been awaiting him. But I stared at the card he'd given me as if without recognition.

LUCAS W. ARMSTED
SENIOR DETECTIVE
CHATEAUGUAY CO. SHERIFF'S DEPT.

It was the morning of April 27. Nearly one month since my aunt Drewe had vanished. In those weeks of search and investigation and media attention the predominant note was blunt and unambiguous: *still missing.*

"You are 'Marta,' right? Not 'Annemarie.' So I've learned."

I wasn't sure. If Aunt Drewe was gone, it might be that "Marta" would begin to fade. It might be that "Annemarie Straube" would reemerge.

" 'Marta.' You haven't said if you remember me."

I said, in a voice that cracked and faltered so that the detective had to stoop to hear, "The last time you saw me, Detective, I was crawling under the covers of my hospital bed. I guess that was me."

I laughed in chagrin at such behavior. I'd been crazy but was not crazy now. Wanting Detective Armsted who regarded me with shrewd unsmiling eyes that I was beyond craziness, now.

I had been interviewed by law enforcement officers numerous times and my original statement, given at the Newburgh hospital, had not been substantially altered. For I'd become one of those witnesses who remembers her own statement even to the point of replicating exact words. Still, Armsted wanted to ask me a "few more" questions. And he wanted to "walk through" the abduction in the living room one more time.

I can't. Not again. Not ever.

"You can try, Marta. We'll take it slowly."

During the past several weeks, much of rural Chateauguay County had been searched and many acres of rural Ulster County near the area where I'd been found and the site of Drewe's Jeep submerged in the Shale River. The homes and properties and vehicles of numerous individuals who might have wished to harm Drewe Hildebrand had been searched. Several members of Christians for Life were in police custody in Newburgh. Yet all denied any involvement in the abduction, no one had confessed or implicated anyone else.

Except for the discovery of my aunt's Jeep in the river, nothing else had turned up.

The cabin at Elk Lake had not been searched, so far as I knew.

None of the "forgotten" property at Elk Lake had been searched, evidently.

Armsted, sometimes with his team of detectives, sometimes alone, was the detective who'd come most frequently to Chateauguay Springs. He seemed to have befriended Magdalena and others on the staff, he was an affable good-natured man in suit, white shirt, necktie and sometimes he wore bifocals that gave him the look of a small-town citizen of substance: high school principal, car dealer, realtor. He had spoken with everyone at the artists' colony including each of the resident artists and each of the Big Barn staff that was predominantly young women, he'd spoken with tradesmen in the area, every worker who'd had occasion to set foot on Drewe Hildebrand's property in the past several years, UPS and FedEx delivery men, U.S. postal workers. I knew, from Magdalena, that it was commonly believed in Chateauguay County that the abductors were members of the militant Christians for Life. Magdalena had heard that the abductors had taken me, Drewe's niece, because they hadn't known what to do with me, fearing that I could identify them, but this had been a mistake, they'd wanted only Drewe.

Drewe was "captive" somewhere. Until such time as she "repented."

Magdalena reported such rumors with an air of hope. For Mrs. Hildebrand was still alive, it seemed.

"You don't seem very hopeful, Marta. That your aunt is still alive."

Armsted spoke sympathetically. I thought so. I wanted to explain to him *I am so tired!*

We were in the front, public rooms of the manor house. Which no one on the staff entered except Magdalena or a cleaning woman, to vacuum, dust. I had avoided the living room/gallery since the night of March 29. I was feeling shaky now, approaching it.

So tired it would have been easier to die.

Armsted knew secrets not known to me. He'd flown to western New York State to interview my sullen resentful mother and other relatives of Drewe Hildebrand with plenty to tell him of the wayward ungrateful girl they'd known as Eileen Straube, whose life beyond Cattaraugus they never comprehended nor approved of and whose probable death was what you'd expect, a woman like that. Armsted had traveled to the men's prison at Oriskany to interview my father who would have been a more cooperative witness giving the impression always of speaking sincerely, holding nothing back. I had no doubt that Lucas W. Armsted knew more about Harvey T. Straube and the crimes of embezzlement, fraud, and perjury of which he'd been convicted, than I would ever know. And he would know exactly how much money Harvey Straube's older sister Drewe Hildebrand had "lent" him in the late 1990s.

Badly I wanted to ask Armsted about my father. Oh anything he might tell me!

I would not, though. Never.

Also, Armsted had information on Virgil West who'd been one of a number of suspects eventually cleared by the investigation. He had information on Gregor MacSweeney a.k.a. "Xenia" who had also been cleared. There were ex-protégés of Drewe Hildebrand, some of whom might have been lovers, like the young sculptor Derrick Fell who'd publicly threatened Drewe a few months before her disappearance. How many of these ex-protégés my aunt had accumulated in her art-patroness career, I didn't want to know.

". . . Tania Leenaum? Did you know her?"

As if Armsted had been reading my mind. I stopped dead in my tracks. I'd been asked this question before and had always said no of course not, how could I have known someone who'd died before I had come to Chateauguay Springs and this was what I said now.

"Your aunt never spoke of her, eh?"

Never.

"But others did? In the arts colony?"

Not to me. Not in my presence.

"You know about her, though? How she died, when . . ."

I was vague, I thought so, yes. I knew a few facts.

"And what do you know of your aunt's chauffeur Noah Rathke?"

I saw where this was going. I thought I saw. I stood very still staring at the hardwood floor of the living room/gallery where, a few yards away, beneath a newly purchased rug, an enormous bloodstain from the melted *Blood Mask II* had soaked permanently into the floor.

". . . the most reliable driver she'd ever had, Aunt Drewe said."

Armsted stooped to hear me. I understood then that he was hard of hearing in his right ear. He said, " 'Most reliable driver.' So we've been told. And this is your impression, too, Marta?"

"I think so . . ."

I'd been told that detectives had taken Noah's chauffeur's logbook to examine and that they'd questioned him at length and upset him but I hadn't been told any of this by Noah himself. I'd been dreading to think that the police investigation would surely turn up the link between Tania Leenaum and Noah Rathke and so it was, Armsted was asking if my aunt or anyone on the staff had done a background check on Noah Rathke, and I said I wouldn't know; and Armsted said, in the way of a man springing a surprise on an unsuspecting person, "No one here seems to have known that Noah Rathke had been an intimate friend of Tania Leenaum, not long before she came to Chateauguay Springs, and died. Drewe Hildebrand didn't know, did she?"

I continued to stare at the floor. Blood pounded in my ears. I could not force myself to behave as if I was surprised. I could not lift my eyes to the detective's face.

". . . I'm sure she didn't. I don't think."

"You don't seem very surprised, Marta? That your aunt's driver might have had a motive to get a job here?"

Vaguely I shook my head. Vaguely, I smiled. I was too confused to be surprised. I was too drained of emotion.

Armsted said, an edge of annoyance in his voice, "Would your aunt have hired this man, if she'd known of his involvement with Tania Leenaum?"

I said that I couldn't speak for my aunt Drewe.

"It's possible that she did know . . ."

"And hired the man anyway?" Armsted sounded doubtful.

"Aunt Drewe was not a predictable woman. But she was a generous woman. She . . ."

Was. I had not meant to say *was.* I had to hope that Detective Armsted hadn't heard this.

Of course, he had. He was a detective, trained in questioning subjects who wished to elude him. In my ears blood pounded *was, was, was.*

"Would your aunt have told you, Marta, if she'd known?"

"I don't think so. No."

"Your aunt didn't confide in you?"

"Not about personal matters. No."

"Business matters?"

"No. Never."

"She didn't confide in you about much, then?"

About life. About essential things.

Things you wouldn't understand.

We were in the living room/gallery. On the farther wall, the silk screen of Drewe as a girl, naked, smudged, with stark staring eyes, faced us. I had to wonder if Armsted could have recognized Drewe Hildebrand in that face.

For this interview with the senior detective from the Chateau-guay Springs Sheriff's Department I had wakened early from my night of dreams like riding in a vehicle over a rough, rutted terrain without end and I had taken time to shower, to shampoo my hair and to brush it until it shone, and to plait it as Aunt Drewe had sometimes plaited her hair, to let fall between my shoulder blades. I took care to stand very straight, as Aunt Drewe always stood. I wore fresh clothes, a sweater over a shirt, jeans. My bruised and swollen face had become the face of a normal young woman of my age, I thought. I had made this face up, to a degree. I wore lipstick. I had plucked my eyebrows where they had a tendency to grow together over the bridge of my nose. I thought if the detective saw in me a normal attractive girl he might be more likely to sympathize with me and to like me and badly I wanted to be liked, or I wanted to be perceived as a girl who badly wanted to be liked.

"He has confided in you? Or hasn't?"

I couldn't remember what the subject was. I was distracted by the living room/gallery. I said no.

"Would you describe yourself as a friend of Noah Rathke?"

"I would like to be."

"Mrs. Hildebrand's housekeeper says that you and Noah are friends. She says that you are Noah's 'closest friend' here."

I was surprised to hear this. I felt a wave of tenderness.

I said again, "I would like to be."

"And why is that, Marta?"

"Because . . ."

Because I love him.

"... he's a good person. He's kind, he's ..."

"But you don't really know him well, Marta, do you? You didn't know about his relationship with Tania Leenaum."

"... he might have told me. Sometime. He isn't deceptive. He would never hurt my aunt Drewe. He would never hurt me. He had nothing to do with ..."

"You know this, Marta?"

"I 'know' what I believe. Noah had nothing to do with ..."

"Who did, then? Do you know?"

Those eyes! I thought *He knows me but how can he know me? He can't know me.*

I'd decided that Armsted had nothing to do with my father Harvey Straube who was incarcerated at Oriskany. My father Harvey Straube who was not to be trusted even by those of us who loved him. I had decided that my fears in the hospital had been paranoid and groundless and I must never think such thoughts again, I would be diagnosed by the neurologist at Newburgh as permanently damaged.

I shook my head, no. I continued to stare at the floor stubborn and sullen as my aunt Drewe had often admired in me.

Outside the air was wan, watery. A fine spring rain shading into mist. The recessed lights in the living room/gallery were not on, only this light entered the space. Elegant but not very comfortable black-puckered-leather sofas, chairs with gleaming chrome, oddly designed low tables made mostly of glass. Drewe's favored works of art, paintings, sculpted figures, looked less impressive by ordinary daylight than by the dramatic recessed lighting. I wondered what *Blood Mask II* would have looked like, in the detective's skeptical eyes.

"Try to remember, Marta. Not what you've told us but what actually happened."

Armsted walked me through the abduction scene: beginning on the stairs, ending at the doorway. Like a sleepwalker I moved through it. If I shut my eyes, it was Aunt Drewe who walked me through the steps and I felt a moment's solace, hope: none of this had happened yet, it was only being rehearsed.

"Didn't see their faces, Marta? Not one?"

No.

"Or hear their voices?"

Not clearly enough to identify. No.

"Did one of the men have a beard? No?"

Didn't see. No.

"And where were you, approximately, when the drug was forced into your mouth?"

Crystal meth. I'd forgotten.

One of the men rushing at me, grabbing me and gripping my head in the crook of his arm like a vise, pried open my jaws and forced me to swallow . . .

I pointed at a spot on the floor. I thought it must have been here.

"So near the stairs? Not farther into the room?"

I wasn't sure. In the confusion . . .

Armsted asked if I had seen a crucifix on the fireplace mantel and I said I didn't think that I had, no. In the past I had been asked this question and it didn't seem plausible to me that in the confusion of the moment I could have seen the crucifix on the mantel or anything else on the mantel.

Armsted was saying that a crucifix isn't a Protestant symbol but a Catholic symbol and so it was strange that, if the militant Christians for Life had abducted my aunt, that they would choose to leave a crucifix behind.

I wasn't sure if a question had been asked. My face had gone strangely cold.

"Unless it was a plant. D'you know what a plant is, Marta?"

I thought so, yes probably. I was not a child after all.

Armsted regarded me for a long moment without speaking and I stood very still, my heart beating slowly inside my rib cage. My aunt Drewe had promised *No one will know, no one will ever know* and I thought that might be so. For in my impaired state I could not risk being hypnotized and questioned nor was there any possibility of my taking a polygraph test, the results would be "inconclusive."

Armsted prepared to leave. A middle-aged face that had once been attractive, now losing definition, going soft. A man with shrewd eyes, a slightly flushed skin, a drinker's broken capillaries but a disarming smile. He wore a dark suit, white shirt and nondescript necktie and Magdalena was in a flurry when he spoke with her in a friendly way like one who'd known her years ago when she'd been younger and slimmer and more attractive and Magdalena would give no thought to the fact that this man carried a firearm strapped to his body beneath his clothes, he was not a private citizen but a soldier of the state, with the power to arrest in the name of the law, the power to shoot and to wound and even to kill if necessary. I felt such emotion for this man, I could barely bring myself to look at him.

Deliberately Armsted strolled to the Warhol silk screen looming on the farther wall. I realized that of course he'd recognized Drewe Hildebrand from photographs though he'd never seen her in person. In that wasted-junkie girl smudged and ghostly on the wall he'd seen the object of his search gazing at him with stark haunted eyes. He stooped to read the identification. " 'War-hol'—he's dead now, is he?" Armsted pronounced the name "Ware-hall."

I told him yes, Warhol had been dead a long time.

The Confession (I)

———

Marta! There's news."

Magdalena called to me excitedly. She had reason to believe that Drewe was alive, a man had confessed to having kidnapped her!

It was the morning after Armsted had come to interrogate me. I understood now why he'd come when he had. A man named Arvin Shattuck, forty-two, a resident of Catskill, New York, a founder of Christians for Life who'd participated in the violent protest at Xenia's exhibit, abruptly confessed to police that he'd committed a number of unsolved crimes in the past several years, which he called "victories for God." Shattuck had been previously arrested and questioned in the firebombing of an abortion clinic in Buffalo in 2001, and he'd been a suspect in the sniper wounding of an "abortion doctor" in Erie, Pennsylvania, in 1999, and in police custody at Newburgh having dismissed his attorney Shattuck gave a lengthy statement to police in which he took credit for these crimes and for others, including the abduction of the "Satan-worshipper Hildebrand."

Shattuck talked to police for fifteen hours. His statement was videotaped. Sometimes he spoke calmly and persuasively and some-times he spoke in a rambling and delusional way. Sometimes he provided convincing details, at other times his testimony was vague. He was boastful, righteous. He refused to name others involved in his crimes not even to acknowledge that they were fellow members of Christians for Life. He said that he'd abducted "the Hildebrand woman" from her home and took her to a "safe house" where he and others prayed over her and invited her to pray with them for the salvation of her soul—"Three times I came into the woman's presence that she would repent her sins and her blasphemy against Jesus our savior and three times the woman scorned me." Shattuck told police that the Satan-worshipper was in a place where she would never be found awaiting the deliverance of her soul. Shattuck hinted that this place was not in New York State but hundreds of miles away in a "valley protected by mountain peaks and blessed by God." He'd dismissed his lawyer and had decided to confess to these victories for God in order to speak the truth directly to the American people. He was not an ordained minister but a soldier in Jesus' army and he would make of himself a martyr in the struggle for the soul of America that was being devoured by Satan in these terrible times.

Arvin Shattuck was the squat muscled man with the spade-shaped beard and fanatic eyes who'd leapt on the table at Xenia's exhibit. On TV footage he would appear and re-appear and he would be the subject of many news stories in the local and national press. Of the crimes for which he wished to take credit, the firebombing of the abortion clinic was the one that seemed to authorities most credible for Shattuck had long been a leading suspect in that case. He had less that was convincing to say about the other crimes and nothing at all to say about Drewe Hildebrand's nineteen-year-old niece who'd been abducted at the same time as Drewe Hildebrand, he ignored questions about her. Nor did he seem to know how Drewe Hildebrand's Jeep had come to be driven into the Shale River.

Quoted everywhere in the media was Arvin Shattuck's remark: "The Hildebrand woman will be released when she repents. Pray for her!"

The Confession (II)

―――

I was the one. I killed my aunt Drewe Hildebrand.

If my aunt is dead, I was the one.

Because I loved her, I'd come to that remote place with her. I would never betray her. I would never disobey her. But I would kill her, in a panic to save myself. I think I was the one.

If my aunt is dead, at Elk Lake.

The black plastic crucifix, she'd bought from a sidewalk vendor on Fourteenth Street, New York City. Never handled with her bare hands only with gloves. Laughing/gloating she was so clever! On the mantel the crucifix would be placed.

My enemies. They have humiliated me, now I will humiliate them.

Blood Mask II she'd come to despise would be placed on the hardwood floor.

To bleed out, through the night. By morning when Magdalena discovered it nothing would remain of it but the bloodstained clay bust beneath that would seem to be floating in a pool of dark coagulated blood.

* * *

Magdalena and others on the staff would be provided for, the Foundation would continue to function as always without interruption as it had not been interrupted when Drewe's husband died, who was the founder of the artists' colony. *I am the dispensable one,* Drewe said. *I am the one to be sacrificed.*

Wild nights! After Magdalena retired to the rear of the house, like sisters we conspired.

Drewe was the elder sister. Those nights in March, the wind howled off the river and made our pulses race. No question, I was the younger sister, I adored her.

Though I could not trust her yet I loved her and in fact I would trust her with my life. If she had ceased to love me I could not bear my existence so there was no loss, if I trusted her with my life and that life was taken from me.

There are the small-souled, and there are the large-souled. The small soul can be fitted inside the large soul snug and warm and protected from all harm.

If there's an unsolved mystery, many will wish to solve it.

Once the mystery is solved the story is over but until then the story is not over and many storytellers will wish to tell it and so Drewe Hildebrand will be both a martyr and a legend.

The perfect revenge on my enemies and my false lovers and my so-called friends, who will never forget Drewe Hildebrand.

*   *   *

I drank with my aunt Drewe for she disliked drinking alone in the house and in the days and nights following the Scots sculptor's departure I drank with her but if I drank I became sleepy, I was no use to her. There are other ways, Aunt Drewe said, to sharpen a dull mind.

It was the drugs that frightened me but I wished to surrender to them if that was her wish.

Laughing, biting her lip laughing as she tried on the shiny-black curly wig staring into the mirror.

" 'Hey there baby: I'm Doris Kirchgessner. Goin' my way?' "

I laughed but I felt so lonely then. The black bouffant wig, heavy oval plastic owl-glasses that made my aunt look middle-aged and beige matte makeup that gave her skin a coarse appearance. Shiny red lipstick like plastic lips.

When she planned to leave Elk Lake was Drewe's secret. And where she would be driving. Doris Kirchgessner in polyester pants suit driving a 1993 Honda Civic with Rhode Island plates, where Drewe had acquired this old car was her secret, too. The handsome steel-colored Jeep she would not drive from Elk Lake.

Pleading I said, I could come with you then, Aunt Drewe. I could help you drive.

Drewe who despised weakness, pleading and begging, any sort of manipulation, ignored me. Primping in the mirror as Doris Kirchgessner who was fifty-three, divorced and her children grown and gone. I felt a wave of rage sweep over me, I hated Aunt Drewe then. For she would leave me without a backward glance as she'd left other favorites of hers, I knew.

But in the mirror then our eyes locked. Drewe relented *After I'm settled in the new place. Maybe.*

The Jeep was to be driven to a designated site above the Shale River which Drewe had selected. I would leap from the cab, the Jeep would roll unimpeded down the incline and into the river to be submerged in approximately fifteen feet of fast-moving water. This was crucial to Drewe's plan for the river would be dredged and the surrounding area searched for Drewe Hildebrand's body and in this, my aunt Drewe believed, there would be public/media acknowledgment of the loss of Drewe Hildebrand which would be a kind of martyrdom. For Drewe believed that there would be public outrage at her abduction and death at the hands of religious fanatics, her enemies and former lovers would be stricken with guilt, her friends would mourn her for the remainder of their lives.

If my body is never found, so my story will never end!

The plan would be enacted sometime past midnight of March 29.

Days and nights preceding Drewe entered my room at any time barefoot and partially dressed, hair disheveled and her eyes luminous, I could feel heat lifting from her skin. She spoke rapidly and in bright flashes of words as if thinking aloud yet she seemed to require me, to be her witness. She was planning her escape from the coffin as she called it. Planning her rebirth at Elk Lake.

In her imagination the intruders had entered the house, she had been overcome and thrown to the floor and when I approached to help her the intruders seized me, too; and forced me to ingest a powerful hallucinogenic, carried me away with them and released me in a desolate place yet not so desolate that I would not be found, and returned to bear witness. With each telling Drewe became more incensed, more indignant as if the martyrdom had actually occurred. With each telling the story became more imprinted in my mind, almost it seemed that this had happened, I had only to remember.

On March 29, Drewe's driver Noah Rathke had to be sent away on an errand to the farthest edge of Long Island. That night, Magdalena could be trusted to go to bed at her usual hour and sleep heavily through the night. It wasn't unusual for vehicles to be arriving and departing, Drewe's friends from New York City, no one among the resident artists in their cabins scattered through the woods would observe anything out of the ordinary. We would use the private drive to the River Road. In the Jeep and in the Honda Civic we had brought supplies to the cabin at Elk Lake the previous day, now in these separate vehicles we would depart.

Drewe would not return to Chateauguay Springs. Never!

In the story Drewe was telling, Marta would return.

A bag of pharmaceuticals, as Drewe called them. Emptying out the wide shallow top drawer of a bedroom dresser that glittered incongruously with loose items of jewelry and with Drewe's cache of drugs. For in her wake, strangers would explore the rooms in which she'd lived, this drawer must be disguised, cleaned with disinfectant and paper towels so no trace would be left behind. Drewe's voice gay and giddy with such plans.

Drewe's drugs: some were prescription painkillers, antidepressants, barbiturates, others were of mysterious origins. There were capsules, tablets, small plastic bags of white powder both fine-ground and granular. One of the tablets Drewe insisted was harmless, to be shared with her in a glass of red wine, *Marta this is a calming potion, we must calm your excitable soul,* and in slow dream-shapes such thoughts came to me, that were not my own.

No fingerprints! No trace.

Drewe wore rubber-thin gloves. Drewe helped me to draw on identical gloves. These would be buried in the earth at Elk Lake with other items.

Carefully Drewe removed the blood-masked replica of her own head from the display case in the living room/gallery. Placing it on the floor with a look of revulsion. The shuttered eyes that were eerily lifelike, the strain of the mouth so like her own, the width and heaviness of the head like a Roman bust, she'd come to despise. So passionately she despised the Scots sculptor who'd betrayed her and publicly humiliated her and she despised the weak, ignorant, ridiculous woman who had submitted to such betrayal.

Blood Mask II, commissioned for a very large sum of money, she could not bear to look at, now. With her foot she set it rolling like a decapitated head in a cartoon.

It will melt! My polluted blood! It will be only a puddle by morning.

The black plastic crucifix with its metallic-gleaming crucified Christ she placed carefully on the mantel above the fireplace, upright.

The story was one of invasion, struggle, upset. Drewe would

point to an object, a chair or a lamp, one of the metallic sculptures, carefully I would place it on the floor or overturn it.

Drewe had plaited my hair tight, to prevent it falling into my feverish face.

My daughter if I'd wanted a daughter. Which I don't.

Laughing and kissing me wetly on the mouth and pushing me from her.

Rehearsing Marta's testimony.

Say very little when questioned for you will be questioned many times. Only say what I have instructed you. For all that you will say is naturally confused for your memory has been impaired by the drug forced upon you.

No need to prove anything, Drewe told me. The least probable of stories is likely to be the true story. No one will call you liar. No one will call you accomplice. Your role in the story is to be hurt, wounded and pitied and a witness. And so they will tell and retell my story, they will be captivated by the vanished Drewe Hildebrand as they were not captivated when I was among them and I will summon you to me, it might be to another country, it might be close by. The time of summoning might be next year, or next month. In time when Drewe Hildebrand is declared legally dead you will inherit a certain sum of money, you will inherit certain works of art and other rewards, have faith.

But don't try to find me, Marta: I will not be where you seek me.

* * *

Yet at Elk Lake in the gray dawn in a chill rain turning to sleet there was a change upon my aunt Drewe of a kind I had sometimes seen after periods of giddiness and euphoria and wet-mouth-kisses had run their course. The wonderful heat of her skin turned clammy, her beautiful eyes turned opaque, the words she uttered were cruel and cutting and frightened me.

You! you! you! damn to hell how can I trust you.

Already on the highway driving north into the foothills of the Shale Mountains in our separate vehicles as Drewe had insisted, I tried to follow the Jeep at a safe distance but always Drewe was easing away as if to torment me. On twisting roads the Jeep hurtled forward, taillights winking red in mockery.

And in the cabin where I built a fire, panting and exhausted from the excitement of the past several hours, I squatted on my haunches confused and frightened and Drewe shouted at me, slammed a door behind her and tried to sleep but could not, I heard her gagging and vomiting and pressed my hands over my ears. And waking dry-mouthed and my heart thudding and it was morning, I'd slept in my clothes. And Drewe was outside smoking a cigarette. My aunt Drewe's face strained and sickly pale and her eyes red-rimmed and her nostrils red-rimmed and damp from the fine-grained white powder she'd been inhaling, that made her nostrils bleed. Saying now bitterly *Maybe we should die together, this is such shit.* It was the hour for me to leave to drive the Jeep into the river, approximately nine miles to the site Drewe had selected, I was to wander on foot afterward dazed and confused from the crystal meth but when Drewe pressed it on me at first I pushed away her hands. Yet, I gave in, I swallowed some of the burning powder, Drewe was laughing and angry clutching my head in the crook of her strong arm like a vise and forcing my jaws open and I was frightened thinking *She is poisoning me, she wants me to die with her.* Drewe was saying maybe I should not leave in the Jeep, I should stay with her. We might die together, that would be the purest act Drewe said. I would like that wouldn't I, I would share her martyrdom. I was struggling to break away. The inside of my mouth burned, I was gagging and coughing, the poison burned like lye. I said no Aunt Drewe, no please Aunt Drewe begging though I knew how my aunt despised weakness. Why so abruptly she was angry with me, why she was shoving and slapping me, I didn't know. I would never know. She pulled me to the ground in her arms, she was panting, cursing. *Get up get up can't be here, it must be at the lake god damn you I know you will let me down like the others, I should have strangled you snoring in your sleep.* I was on one knee, I picked up a jagged rock. It must have been shale, a thin rock shaped like a step. Drewe was cursing me, and I was pleading with her, the sounds we uttered lifted upward into silence and were lost. There was no one to hear us, no one to help me. A flame rushed across my brain. I felt my eyes bulge in their sockets. I swung the rock, to drive my aunt Drewe away from me. I struck at her blindly. She laughed, she was scornful of me, she had no fear of me, clumsy Marta. The rock seemed to leap at her, both my hands gripped it, the jeering mouth went slack. I was stooping over my aunt Drewe striking her with the rock again, again, couldn't trust her where she'd fallen, I was panicked this had to be a trick, I must not be fooled. I struck her head until I saw blood, until I felt the skull crack, the hard skull suddenly soft and cracking and blood pouring from the lacerated scalp and abruptly my aunt's shouts had ceased, I crawled away panting and sobbing and must have fainted and then forcing myself awake, crawling to the cabin, on my feet and inside the cabin not knowing what I was doing, my trembling hands I washed with soap, my hands that were sticky with blood, I washed in bottled water awkwardly spilling into the sink, I had to change my bloodied clothes and put on clean clothes and would throw away the bloodied clothes in the woods, then I remembered my aunt Drewe outside where it was cold and the ground damp from last night's sleet and stumbled to her thinking by now she would have recovered, I had to beg her to forgive me, I'd forgotten what I had done but knew that Aunt Drewe was angry with me, still she might forgive me as so often she'd forgiven me but she was lying on the ground with her arms out-flung like a jumper, one of her knees twisted beneath her, I was astonished to see my aunt Drewe on the ground, no one has ever seen Drewe Hildebrand lying on the ground, on her back, covered in blood and unmoving.

Her eyes were part-shuttered as in the blood-masked head but I believed that she was watching me. I could see her chest rising and falling in the down jacket, I was sure. I saw blood glistening on her head, on her face, soaking into the jacket but it wasn't the rich dark coagulated blood of the blood mask but a fresh bright-red blood, terrible to see. I dragged the rotted tarpaulin from the woodpile and covered my aunt Drewe with it, I backed off from her speaking to her, begging her to forgive me, I saw the tarpaulin move, I think I saw the tarpaulin move, and then I turned away, and ran.

I thought that I would conclude the story as Aunt Drewe had directed. I drove the Jeep out of the foothills at Elk Lake and to the Shale River. It was fully morning now, I could see clearly. I could see anything I looked at no matter how minute, the smallest tree limbs, individual pine needles, pinecones, the flash of a bird's wing, my eyes were so strong. My mind worked swiftly, thoughts swift as knives, it was wonderful how I didn't drop a single one of these knives. Unerring I found the site Drewe had designated which was marked by a very tall pine tree that looked to have been struck by lightning. The tree was above the river and beyond the roadway was an incline. I aimed the Jeep in that direction. I leapt from the cab as we'd rehearsed. *Good girl Marta!* my aunt laughed with pleasure. *Not so clumsy as you pretend to be.*

I knew then that Aunt Drewe loved me, I would not mind dying now.

Why they dragged me from beneath the cabin where I'd crawled to die, I don't know. I tried to fight them. I tried to bite them. But once they have hold of your ankles, you are theirs.

Hunger

I don't believe it."

These were Noah's first words. After I'd told him.

Not *I don't believe you* but *I don't believe it.* I had to think there was a distinction.

We were walking on the bluff above the river. Shorebirds and wide-winged hawks circled overhead. A pair of hawks swooped near, emitting sharp aggressive cries. Noah grabbed my arm and pulled me forward, there must have been a hawks' nest hidden in the underside of the bluff.

At the crest of a hill, we stopped. We were breathless and not entirely aware of our surroundings.

"Jesus, Marta! I don't believe it."

Noah spoke in a slow stunned voice. His eyes on me were astonished.

My words, my confession, had seemed to leap from me. I'd intended to tell Noah who was my friend before I told the police, and turned myself in as Drewe Hildebrand's murderer.

Turn myself in. I smiled at this figure of speech.

". . . turn myself inside-out. It's time."

It was the day following Arvin Shattuck's confession to the Newburgh police, that had so astonished everyone. It was a time of media excitement and renewed interest in Drewe Hildebrand and it was a time of confusion and upset at Chateauguay Springs. Magdalena had wept with relief, at the prospect of Drewe being alive, perhaps someday soon to be released.

Poor Magdalena! I hated my aunt Drewe the more, for her cruelty in manipulating this woman.

As Drewe had foretold, many stories would be told of her. Many legends. *If my body is never found.*

When I'd first heard about Arvin Shattuck's confession, I'd been stunned and halfway wondered if what the leader of the Christians for Life had said might somehow be true except—how could it be true? I knew where my aunt Drewe's body was, I had to be the only living person who knew.

What was strange was, until I began telling Noah what had happened, I hadn't remembered much of it. Those feverish days and nights leading to March 29 that Drewe had rehearsed "our story" were confused with what happened afterward, like muddy water swirling in clear water. Until a few minutes ago, I hadn't remembered the hateful black wig, I hadn't remembered the hateful name "Doris Kirchgessner" and the sound of Aunt Drewe's laughter uttering that name. I hadn't remembered the fire I'd built in the cabin that night, exhausted and stumbling and splinters in the palms of both my hands as Drewe shuttered the windows from the inside. I hadn't clearly remembered the muddy, rotted tarpaulin I had dragged over Drewe's limp body in the morning. I hadn't remembered the the weight of the sharp-edged piece of shale I'd gripped and I hadn't remembered the terrible *crack*! of the skull.

Crack! crack! the shock of the blows running up both my arms to the elbows.

Yet Noah Rathke refused to believe. He was shaking his head, adamant. "Marta, no. For Christ's sake. You're imagining it. What you've told me is crazy. I don't believe a word of it. Some weird drug delusion. They gave you crystal meth, that's enough to fry anyone's brain. Have you told anyone else what you've told me?"

No I had not told anyone else but I intended to tell the Newburgh detective Armsted.

"No. You're not telling anyone, yet. We can check out Elk Lake. We can drive out today. It's a terrible thing you've told me, Marta, Keep this to yourself. Christ!"

Like everyone at Chateauguay Springs, Noah wished to believe what Arvin Shattuck had confessed.

We were alone together on the hiking trail above the river because Noah had come to see me to say goodbye. He was leaving Chateauguay Springs. He might have continued as a driver for the Foundation, for the arts colony would continue to function even if Drewe Hildebrand never returned, but he'd given notice, he was leaving. The link between Noah and the deceased Tania Leenaum had recently come to light in the media but Noah had intended to leave in any case.

Also he'd come to tell me that he would miss me. That he hoped he would see me again, soon. That he wanted me to know he'd had nothing to do with what had happened to my aunt.

I told him I knew this. I told him how I knew. I told him that I was the one.

Now Noah said, "I think, why you've told me this, you want me to understand that you don't think that I had anything to do with what happened. That's why you've invented this story."

Unexpectedly, as if exasperated with me, Noah grabbed my hand and squeezed it hard. As if to awaken me, warn me.

The first time he'd touched me like this. I felt a powerful wave of tenderness for this man, glaring at me, disbelieving and yet dreading what he might have to believe, who wished to protect me even now.

"That's why, Marta. See?"

We'd been climbing the trail from Chateauguay Springs only half-conscious of our surroundings. Across the wide river was the dense-wooded Hudson Highlands. It must have been early afternoon. A windy sun-splotched day in spring. We'd gone off together needing to be alone in knowledge that what we had to tell each other would alter our lives irrevocably. Not far from us, above the river, the wide-winged hawks soared and circled high in the air, riding wind currents as they sought prey: smaller birds, fish. Once when we were hiking here together in a happier time my aunt Drewe had identified the hawks as sparrow hawks that nested in rocks on the side of the bluff, there was a colony of them and you had to be careful when they were nesting and fiercely protective of their young. *Such graceful predators* Drewe said *you want to believe in their freedom, not that they are hunters, ceaseless hunters whose lives are dominated by hunger.*

That afternoon, Noah Rathke and I set out for Elk Lake in Noah's car.

Elk Lake (II)

———

Maybe he will love me, anyway. In spite of what we find.

Trying not to think what lay beneath the tarpaulin at Elk Lake after four weeks of rain and warming weather.

It was the first time Noah Rathke and I had been alone together in his car. Always in the past Magdalena had been with us. We were uneasy, excited. No one knew where we were, where we were going. I was to guide Noah since he had no idea where Elk Lake was except somewhere in the Shale Mountains.

On the drive, Noah began to tell me about Tania Leenaum.

I would never tell him what I already knew of the young woman who'd died, scandalously, of a heroin overdose on Drewe Hildebrand's property. I would never tell him how I'd leafed through the books on his shelf, to discover the postcards from Tania Leenaum he'd kept, the fading Polaroid in which Noah had looked so young, and so happy. To confess to a murder was a profound and terrible thing but to confess to an act so petty and ignoble was not possible. Noah confided in me he'd fallen in love with Tania Leenaum thinking he'd known her, but evidently he had not. They'd met at Quarrysville State College in northern Pennsylvania where Noah had gone, as a slightly older student, in the mid-1990s. The halting way he spoke of Tania Leenaum, the pain in his face, I understood that

Noah had loved her very much and had been wounded by her and was baffled and haunted still by the memory of her and I understood that I could never mean to him what Tania Leenaum meant and that I must accept this.

Tania had been an artist, a painter of abstract landscapes and figures, the first person Noah had ever met who'd seemed sure of what she wanted from her life, only not so sure how to get it. Even at nineteen, Tania was ambitious. She had a reputation at Quarrysville. Her models were woman artists who were hardly more than names even to her fellow art students—Alice Neel, Louise Bourgeois, Dorothea Tanning. There were no artists among her relatives nor art-sympathizers. Her parents owned a small-town real estate agency and were considered well-to-do in Honesdale, Pennsylvania. Tania seemed to be estranged from her family and would not discuss them. She was a beautiful young woman and men were attracted to her but after she'd met Noah she ceased to see any other men though she was often distant with Noah, withdrawn, moody. He knew little about art, especially contemporary art, but Noah believed that Tania was very gifted; she took little comfort in his opinions, even the opinions of her art instructors. She hid from friends the medications she took, anti-depressants, barbiturates. In a fever she often painted through the night then become disgusted with what she'd done afterward, threw canvases away and started again. She and Noah lived together at Quarrysville, to a degree. Tania insisted that she loved him but was wary of marriage, he'd had to respect that. She was still an undergraduate when she started applying to art schools and entered competitions and took her portfolio to New York City galleries and when she was rejected, she became devastated. She applied for residencies at MacDowell, Yaddo, Provincetown, Chateauguay

Springs. When she was accepted at Chateauguay Springs for a six-month residency, it was headline news in the Quarrysville papers. Tania was jubilant, euphoric. She quit Quarrysville State College the next day.

Noah said bitterly, "As soon as Tania moved to Chateauguay Springs, into one of the cabins in the woods, she was gone from me. I visited her a few times, I never felt welcome. Even her paintings began to change. Tania was thrilled to be taken up by this woman Drewe Hildebrand who was the patroness of the artists' colony and all her talk was of Drewe, Drewe, Drewe. 'The most brilliant woman'—'the most beautiful woman'—'the most generous woman.' Instead of coming home at Christmas for a few days as she'd planned, at the last minute Tania flew with Drewe Hildebrand 'and a few friends' to Aruba. Instead of seeing me for a weekend, Tania called to ask me not to come, Drewe was taking her to an exhibit opening and party in New York City. 'Drewe Hildebrand is my mother if I'd been born to a mother who knew my soul or cared to know it'— 'Drewe Hildebrand is what a woman can be, if she has the courage.' From her excitement on the phone I had reason to think that Tania was taking drugs, some kind of speed maybe. I had the idea that Drewe Hildebrand and her friends provided Tania with drugs at their parties. She had a way about her of breezy confidence at times but really she was vulnerable, something in her curled up in defeat if she was rejected, hurt. For no reason Tania ever understood, Drewe lost interest in her after a few months. First, Drewe lost interest in Tania's art, then in Tania herself. Tania began to call me, distraught and crying. I was her only friend at Quarrysville but no advice I gave her seemed to make any difference, she seemed scarcely to listen to me. What she wanted to know was why Drewe Hildebrand had dropped her and how she could be restored to Drewe Hildebrand's friendship, nothing else mattered. Tania was terrified of leaving Chateauguay Springs at the end of her residency, she had nowhere to go, nowhere she wanted to go. She told me that Drewe had 'unofficially' promised her that her residency would be extended for another six months but the Foundation director informed her that this wasn't so, she would have to vacate her cabin by September first, and whatever happened after that, about a week later she was dead. By this time Tania hadn't been returning my calls for weeks. One day I was told that she'd been found dead in the woods at Chateauguay Springs of a 'heroin overdose'—she'd been missing for several days, her body was found 'in a state of decomposition.' It was a terrible shock. I guess I've never gotten over it. It was like Tania had just forgotten me, I'd meant nothing to her. Still I keep thinking there was something I might have done, something different, I might have saved her. I dropped out of Quarrysville in my junior year, kind of drifted around for a few years. Fucked up my life."

Noah's voice quivered with hurt, anger. I told him how sorry I was he'd lost someone he loved. I felt that my words were weak, inadequate. I wanted to touch his hand, his fist gripping the steering wheel but I was afraid he might shake me off. I said, "Your friend Tania was like Drewe herself, at that age. Leaving home, being 'estranged' from her family. Maybe that was why—"

"Fuck 'why.' Who gives a shit 'why.'"

I stared through the windshield at the highway. We were turning off onto a smaller road beyond Newburgh. Ascending into the foothills of the Shale Mountain range to the west.

Noah said, "The Newburgh police asked me a dozen times 'why' I'd come to work for Drewe Hildebrand, what my 'motive' was. I told them I didn't know what my motive was. I told them yes maybe I'd intended to accuse her, or hurt her in some way, mostly I wanted to know what the hell had happened to Tania, who was responsible. People were saying that Drewe Hildebrand was this 'evil' woman so I wanted to see if this was so. I wanted to see if she'd learn who I was, and how she would react. If she'd fire me. Or if she felt guilty. It was never clear who provided Tania with heroin, whether it was a dealer out of Newburgh or someone at Chateauguay Springs. There was a lawsuit Tania's family started against Drewe Hildebrand and the Foundation but that was dropped, legally there was no 'probability' of guilt. People blamed Drewe Hildebrand but the fact was, Tania had made her own choices, you had to concede that. It came out that Drewe wasn't even at Chateauguay Springs at the time Tania died. When I first came to work for Drewe, I hated her, but it was hard to hate Drewe when she was so gracious to me, always treated me with respect as her driver. Her personality was sort of overwhelming, as you know: you wanted Drewe Hildebrand to like you. I understood, if Drewe teased me or joked with me, in a kind of familiar way, it had to be one-sided exclusively, I was her driver, I kept everything formal between us. Other guys on the staff, young guys Drewe would sort of flirt with, they'd be flattered at Mrs. Hildebrand's interest wanting to think they were favored by her, but I knew better. That's how you got 'dismissed' with no explanation. Eventually, I came to feel sorry for Drewe. She wasn't 'evil' or a 'Satan-worshipper' only just this rich woman who used people but was used by them—some of them— too. It was like madness in her, how blind she could be. Her own power, she didn't seem to understand. Sure I thought that Drewe should have to pay for what happened to Tania but I had to know more, to be sure. And I never did know. And I never was sure."

Quickly I said, "Aunt Drewe was a generous woman. She didn't mean to hurt only to help." Maybe this was true. I wanted to think that it was true. "She saved my life, Noah. She brought me to live with her when my family broke up. My father was sent to prison at Oriskany, my mother has been in rehab on and off for years. Drewe took me in when I was fifteen. She hardly knew me, only that I was her brother's daughter. Drewe 'lent' money to my father knowing she would never get any of it back. She gave money to relatives in Cattaraugus who were scornful of her and never grateful. She wasn't evil, essentially in her soul she was generous, she was *good*."

And yet: I had killed her.

The evil in her, maybe: that was what I'd killed.

Noah looked over at me, surprised. Of all that I'd said in this rush of words, he seemed to have heard only the part about my father.

"Your father's in prison, Marta? Why?"

My father is falsely imprisoned. My father went to prison for crimes he didn't commit.

"My father was convicted of embezzling forty thousand dollars from a company in Cattaraugus he'd been doing accounts for. The owners were men who were friends of his, men who'd trusted him. For a long time I believed him, the money had been stolen by one of the partners in the company, Daddy was the 'fall guy.' Most of the family believed him. Except my mother, I think in her heart she knew he was lying, she knew he was guilty, he'd needed the money to pay back gambling debts, but she said nothing, it was bottled up inside her like poison." I spoke calmly, even quietly. So this was what had happened! Until now, I hadn't seemed to comprehend.

Noah whistled through his teeth. Immediately he was sympathetic.

This account of a crime, he had no trouble believing.

He asked me how long my father would be in prison and I told him. He asked me if I'd gone to visit him and I said no.

I told him I'd been in eighth grade when it began: my father's "business" problem. Then, it became a "legal" problem. It seemed to go on and on and nobody would explain it to me and finally one day it was a front-page story in the Cattaraugus paper. "I had to come home from school, that first day. It was like my head was inside a bell, a bell being rung, I could barely walk straight. The cruel thing was, at every stage of the investigation and eventually the trial Daddy lied. He promised me that everything would be 'cleared up' and the newspaper would have to print a 'retraction.' I wanted to believe him, I was desperate to believe him. Even now. I've talked to him on the phone and he still says, 'Annemarie, you know that I'm an innocent man, don't you? Annemarie, have faith in me.'" I wiped angrily at my eyes, I hadn't meant to burden Noah Rathke with all this.

He said, "'Annemarie.' That's a beautiful name. That's your real name, not 'Marta'?"

"No. 'Marta' is my name now. 'Marta' is what my aunt Drewe decided to call me."

"Why?"

Why! I couldn't remember.

Noah said, "When I first saw you, and Magdalena told me you were Mrs. Hildebrand's niece who'd come to live with her, I thought 'They can't be related, they look nothing alike.'"

We drove for some time in silence. We were passing through such unincorporated places as Twin Lakes, Broomtown, Weatherhead. Steadily we were ascending on curving dirt roads.

The air quivered with moisture. It had become a warmly sunny day. It seemed strange to me, in this countryside without seeing patches of snow and ice.

Half consciously I sat very still in the passenger's seat beside Noah like one being delivered to her fate. As I'd been delivered to the Newburgh General Hospital, strapped to a stretcher. I sat with my hands clasped tight together and my knees gripping my hands tight. The horror of what awaited us at Elk Lake was overwhelming, beyond my comprehension.

And then I felt a childish stab of hope, maybe nothing had happened at Elk Lake! As Noah believed, I'd imagined it.

He said, as if this was the subject we'd been discussing, "A thing will happen, or won't happen. Like with your father. Like with your aunt Drewe. You think you can change it, or influence it somehow, but when it's people in your family, who have power over you, probably you can't. But you can get free of it."

I didn't believe this. I would never be free of Daddy and most of all I would never be free of Aunt Drewe.

"You'll have to go away from there, Marta. You'll have to leave Chateauguay Springs, like me."

"And go where?"

"Somewhere."

I wondered if, living above the garage at Chateauguay Springs, Noah had looked from his windows in the direction of the woods, where the artists' cabins were hidden. I wondered if he had explored the woods. If he'd learned which cabin had been Tania Leenaum's cabin and if he'd learned where Tania Leenaum's body had been found and if he had gone to see that spot. How many times he'd gone.

I didn't ask him this. I asked him where he'd be going after Chateauguay Springs and he said to another kind of work and back to school to finally get a degree. He'd lost four years of his life at least, he was thirty-two now. I asked what he wanted to study when he returned to school and he said he wasn't sure, except it wouldn't be art.

I said, "You look like you'd be good at engineering, or science."

"Do I?"

"Physics, maybe. Chemistry."

"I have that look, do I?" Noah smiled.

"I'm just guessing."

"I've gotten interest in the law, after Tania. But also, if you want to make a difference in the world, like with the environment, helping people who can't help themselves, you have to know the law, and if you're dealing with lawyers, it would help to be a lawyer."

"Except then you'd be one of them. A lawyer."

"That's one thing that could stop me. There might be others."

We were passing signs for Mt. Horn, Paris. Eleven miles to Grand Gorge. The sun was slanting in the sky, in the west. I was so very frightened. Noah reached over to squeeze my hand. He said, to break the sudden strained silence, "Most of these places are ghost towns now. Folks have moved away."

Adding, a moment later, as if I'd questioned him, though I had not questioned him, and would not have thought of questioning him, "If the places are like little towns in Pennsylvania, in the Poconos Mountains where I'm from."

He's lying, he has been here. With her.

He isn't lying. Noah Rathke is the one person, who isn't lying.

* * *

A few miles south of Elk Lake, I began to lose my way. A kind of static interfered with my thinking. We began to make wrong turns. Noah was patient laboring to turn the car around on narrow roads. I said, "We could go back. You don't have to see this, Noah." We drove on.

By the time we reached the narrow unmarked lane leading into the woods, into my aunt Drewe's hidden property, the sun had slanted considerably in the sky and I'd begun to tremble with cold. Now in late April the way to the cabin had become badly over-grown, newly budded branches slapped against the windshield as the car jolted forward. It had taken much longer for us to reach Elk Lake than we had calculated and there was the question, as Noah urged the car onward, into and out of mud puddles in the lane, whether we'd be able to turn the car around to get back out.

Finally, Noah braked the car to a stop. We'd emerged into a kind of clearing, but storm debris blocked the lane. Panicked thoughts rushed at me like birds with broken wings and I could not believe that I had returned to this terrible place, and had brought another person with me.

"Marta? This is it?"

"Yes."

My hand was on the car door handle but I couldn't seem to open it. I saw, through a haze of dread, the flat-mirror surface of the lake several hundred yards away beyond a stand of pines. I couldn't see the cabin above the lake but I knew that it was there.

"Can you get out, Marta? Is the door blocked?"

Noah came to my side of the car to open the door and help me climb out, my legs were so weak. My fingers were icy in his. I understood that he was frightened, too. Still he smiled at me, tried to smile. Brushing my forehead with his cold lips.

"It will be over in a few minutes, Marta. I'm with you, see?"

Hand in hand like lovers hiking in the woods, above the beautiful hidden lake that looked deserted, we climbed the rest of the way to the cabin. For suddenly there was the cabin. It was smaller than I remembered, and more derelict. The windows were opaque, shuttered from inside. A brick chimney leaned to one side on the verge of collapse. The outdoor privy had in fact collapsed, nearly hidden by weeds and broken tree limbs. But I could see the rotted tarpaulin on the ground where I'd dragged it to cover the dying woman, closer by several feet to the cabin than I remembered. Calmly I pointed: "There it is."

Still there was something wrong here. This setting in warm weather and not cold. I expected to see patches of snow in the shadows. I expected to see my steaming breath.

"Stay here, Marta. I'll look."

Noah approached the tarpaulin, which was partly obscured by a broken tree limb, and pulled it away, slowly. Long I would remember the deliberation with which Noah moved, the grip of his fingers on the filthy tarpaulin, the ease with which he tugged it toward him.

"Marta. There's nothing here."

From where I was standing, I couldn't seem to see. Slow as a convalescent on her first day out of the hospital I approached Noah. My heart was beating so rapidly, I couldn't catch my breath.

By this time Noah had pulled the tarpaulin entirely away, and let it fall on the ground behind him. He squatted to examine the ground that was covered in pine needles, not rock-hard as I recalled but soft from recent rain. He groped with both hands, pushing away debris. "No bloodstains, Marta. No sign of anything. Nothing."

In April there'd been torrential rains. Any sign would have been washed away.

I told him this. It was a simple fact, Noah would himself know. I told him I'd heard the skull crack. My aunt Drewe's skull, I had heard crack. The *crack*! that was a shock running up my arms like an electric current. I told him I'd seen the blood.

"I don't think so, Marta. Not here."

"I washed the blood off my hands. I remember, in the cabin. I had to use a gallon jug of water we'd brought, spring water. It was very clumsy. I tried to spill the water into the sink but—"

"Marta, no. I don't think so."

"Yes. I did. It happened here."

"Where is the body, then? You can see there's nothing anywhere around here."

I came closer. I stared at the ground where my aunt had fallen. Where I'd struck her with the piece of shale, more than once. For a long moment I stood there looking for something that wasn't there, which was my aunt's body, what remained of my aunt's body, and the bloodstained piece of shale shaped like a man-made step, sharp-edged as a knife blade. I could not comprehend how there was only an emptiness here, an absence; ordinary bare ground covered in pine needles, broken tree limbs, not a woman's decomposed body with skeleton arms outflung as if she'd leapt from a great height to her death.

"But—where is she?"

My voice rose, a kind of laughter.

Noah was at the cabin, on the veranda and trying to peer into the windows. There was a badly rusted screen door and the inner door was padlocked. I remembered the screen door now, I'd forgotten it until now. What was strange was the smallness of the cabin, how ordinary a log cabin it was. There was an air of abandonment, dereliction. Noah tried the padlock, which was locked of course. I went to examine it but my eyes were flooded with moisture.

The air quivered with moisture. Soon it would be dusk, birds were calling to one another at the lakeshore.

"Noah, she must be here. She's here somewhere. She might be hiding, watching us."

Noah took my hand and held it for a while. He let me talk, whatever I had to say he allowed me to say. Then he said, "Near as I can figure, Marta, you've hallucinated it. You were drugged. Whatever you think you did, it was the drug."

"No. It was before the drug took effect. I'd just swallowed it, what Drewe forced me to swallow. I felt her skull crack . . ."

I circled the cabin, trying to see inside. The windows were covered in rusted and ripped screens and the panes were very grimy and shuttered from inside. "Hello? Hello? Hello? Hello? Is anybody in there? Aunt Drewe?" I was pounding at the side of the cabin with my fists, Noah caught at me to stop me. I pushed from him and ran into the woods. It was an ordinary pine woods, dense with underbrush and parts of broken trees. I was slipping, stumbling. My knee struck an exposed rock. I ran until I couldn't run farther and I stood panting and staring thinking *She crawled here to die. Her skeleton is here.* Noah called to me, I made my way toward the lakeshore, now stumbling downhill. Half-glimpsed creatures scuttled away in panic. Large clumsy birds shaped like chickens flew up at my approach. There were agitated bird cries overhead. I saw the narrow pebbly beach where fishermen might stand and cast out their lines. I saw the badly rotted wooden pier encrusted with bird droppings white as detergent. I thought *I will walk on that, it will collapse beneath me, that is my punishment.* But as soon as I stepped onto the pier, my foot smashed through a blackened plank into a few inches of mud. Noah was calling: "Marta! Wait."

Noah came to walk with me, to allow me to talk, and to calm me. We walked along the edge of the lake for some time. There seemed to be a path at times. At other times, we walked in the brackish water, a few inches of water. Large ungainly birds with broad tails that might have been grackles shrieked at us and flew in darting swoops overhead. And there were frogs croaking in alarm and leaping into the shallow water at shore in comical splashes, to escape us. Noah was gripping my hand. I had to repeat what I'd already told him because I had no other words. These were the words I had, I had no other words to explain to him what, why. What I had done, why I had done it. A flame passed over my brain, the terrible white poison in my brain, someone had fed me. When I became overly excited, Noah paused to hold me. I'd seen frantic children held in such a way, arms pinioned at their sides until the fit passed. We walked until we saw that the sun was about to set beyond a bank of massed thunderheads that had arisen out of nowhere into the seemingly clear sky. Noah said we'd better turn back, it would be dark in a few minutes. We would be lost in the dark. We wouldn't be able to find the car in the dark. The sun was swollen glaring-red and beautiful as something burst and blinding if you stared directly at it. It was unexpected, how swiftly dusk could come in the mountains. Already trees at the farther shore had begun to emerge into a single darkness. I stood at the edge of the lake in an inch or two of brackish water watching the sun in a kind of fascination for I could see it moving, sinking. I was less anxious now, I knew that something had been decided. *My daughter if I'd wanted a daughter. My body if it's never found.*

"Marta, come on. We've got about ten minutes."

Noah pulled at my arm, we turned back. Except we'd been following the edge of the lake we could not have easily seen where we'd come from.

We ran.